Close Range

Annie Proulx lives in Wyoming. She published her first novel, *Postcards*, in 1991 at the age of 56. Her second novel *The Shipping News* (Fourth Estate, 1993), won the Pulitzer, the National Book Award and the *Irish Times* International Prize. Her third novel, *Accordion Crimes*, was published in 1996. She is the author of an earlier short story collection, *Heart Songs* (Fourth Estate, 1994).

'Like a mystic seeing the transfigured universe, she re-creates the beauty of ordinary things.' *Independent on Sunday*

'These stories astonish . . . thrilling power and humour, crafted with the mastery that one associates with dead greats rather than mere living writers.' *Mail on Sunday*

'The detail is meticulous, the prose poetic and Proulx's fiction teems with life. Above all, her stories engage the heart. Magical.' *Tatler*

'It is her skill at catching a private moment, life's silences and pauses, and the way she slips effortlessly resonant metaphors on to every page which make *Close Range* so shiveringly brilliant.' *Sunday Herald*

'These short stories are the perfect way to appreciate one of America's great storytellers. She tells of people facing the darker side of their psyches, set against the unforgiving landscape of Wyoming.' *Red*

Books of the Year 1999

'The eleven stories in Annie Proulx's *Close Range* – many of them masterpieces – are about Wyoming, the "tough and unforgiving place" where their author lives. The elemental vastness of the region provides a formidable backdrop to tales of ordeal and endurance. Macabre humour and laconic dead-pan wit flicker out from narratives of remarkable emotive power. Despite the tally of deaths and disasters they heap up, Proulx's stories pulse with vitality; characters are brought alive with an immediacy that almost puts them in the room with you.' Peter Kemp, *Sunday Times*

'My favourite short story collection was Annie Proulx's *Close Range: Wyoming Stories*. Sturdy language and strong emotions underpin her austere and beautiful structures.'
Hilary Mantel, *Guardian*

'Annie Proulx's collection of Wyoming stories, *Close Range*, seemed to me magnificent, her fierce grip on and grip by her physical territory combining a wonderfully intense sense of location with the thrill of being constantly on the edge.' Graham Swift, *TLS*

'The stories are the rural equivalent of urban myths – strange narratives of violence and longing told with a precision and elegance that bring mercy to Proulx's themes of hardship and endurance.'
Jane Shilling, *The Times*

'The spare, perceptive and dryly funny prose of Annie Proulx, in her eleven stories of today's Wild West, "Close Range" and especially "Brokeback Mountain" for me blasts the border trilogy of novels by Cormac McCarthy to kingdom come: no one could imagine that the horses in Proulx's West are pretty.'
Christopher Frayling, *Observer*

'Unmissable.' Cressida Connolly, *Observer*

ANNIE PROULX

Close Range

WYOMING STORIES

FOURTH ESTATE • *London*

This paperback edition published in 2000
First published in Great Britain in 1999 by
Fourth Estate Limited
6 Salem Road
London W2 4BU
www.4thestate.co.uk

'Brokeback Mountain', 'The Mud Below', 'The Blood Bay' and
'The Bunchgrass Edge of the World' originally appeared in *The
New Yorker*; 'The Half-Skinned Steer' appeared in *The Atlantic*;
'People in Hell Just Want a Drink of Water' appeared in *GQ*.

1 3 5 7 9 10 8 6 4 2

A catalogue record for this book is available from the
British Library.

ISBN 1-84115-076-2

Typeset in Linotype Bembo by Rowland Phototypesetting Ltd,
Bury St Edmunds, Suffolk.
Printed in Great Britain by Clays Ltd, St Ives plc

These stories are for my children

Muffy

Jon

Gillis

Morgan

Acknowledgements

The encouragement and support of many people saw me through the writing of these stories and I am grateful to them. Special thanks to my editor, Nan Graham, for advice and counsel. Thanks to my agent, Liz Darhansoff, and the staff of Darhansoff and Verrill for every kind of help. I'm grateful to my old friend Tom Watkin for putting up with long discussions of minute facets of characters' lives. My thanks to Elizabeth Guheen, Sharon Dynak, and Keith Troll of Ucross Foundation for a hundred kindnesses, and to John and Barbara Campbell of the Foundation's Big Red Ranch for their generous hospitality, information and gripping plane rides with John over the landscape. It was both a pleasure and an education working with *The New Yorker* fiction editor Bill Buford in adapting several of these stories for publication in that magazine. Thanks to Paul Etchepare for talk about sixties sheep camps, and to musician and songwriter Skip Gorman who persuaded me to go to the Cowboy Poetry Gathering in Elko, Nevada, where I met Texas songwriter and singer Tom Russell. I thank Tom Russell for his kind permission to use as story title part of the title of his powerful song "The Sky Above, the Mud Below." At Elko I also met the painter William Matthews whose extraordinary work accompanies the

American edition of these stories, and to whom I am intensely grateful. Thanks to Buzzy Malli, proprietor of the Arvada Bar, who asked for a story set in that town and got it—"The Blood Bay"—a Wyoming twist on the folktale "The Calf That Ate the Traveler," known in many stock-raising cultures. Another story, "The Half-Skinned Steer," which was first published in *The Atlantic Monthly,* is based on an old Icelandic folktale, "Porgeir's Bull." I am also an aficionado of local histories and for years have collected memoirs and accounts of regional lives and events in many parts of North America. I found I could not forget a few disturbing paragraphs in Helena Thomas Rubottom's 1987 fine regional Wyoming history, *Red Walls and Homesteads* (edited and published by Margaret Brock Hansen) and that real-life anecdote was the takeoff point for the story "People in Hell Just Want a Drink of Water."

The lines of poetry quoted in "The Governors of Wyoming" are by the seventeenth-century poet Edward Taylor from the 1960 Yale University Press *The Poems of Edward Taylor* edited by Donald E. Stanford.

"The Half-Skinned Steer" set this collection in motion when the Nature Conservancy asked me to contribute something to a proposed collection of short fiction (*Off the Beaten Path,* Farrar, Straus & Giroux, 1998). The stories were to be inspired by a visit to one or more Nature Conservancy preserves. I agreed, if I could visit a Wyoming site. That was the 10,000-acre Ten Sleep Preserve on the south slope of the Big Horns where I spent several days. My grateful thanks to Phil Shephard and Anne Humphrey for their time and help. I found working again in the short story form so interesting and challenging (short stories are very difficult for me) that the idea of a collection of short fiction set in Wyoming seized me entirely. I am fortunate in having a publisher who allowed me this side trip.

The epigraph "Reality's never been of much use out here" comes from an anonymous rancher quoted in Jack Hitts's "Where the Deer and the Zillionaires Play," *Outside,* October 1997. The elements of unreality, the fantastic and improbable, color all of these stories as they color real life. In Wyoming not the least fantastic situation is the determination to make a living ranching in this tough and unforgiving place.

Most of all, deepest thanks to my children for putting up with my strangled, work-driven ways.

Contents

"Reality's never been of much use out here."
—Retired Wyoming rancher

Close Range

The Half-Skinned Steer

In the long unfurling of his life, from tight-wound kid hustler in a wool suit riding the train out of Cheyenne to geriatric limper in this spooled-out year, Mero had kicked down thoughts of the place where he began, a so-called ranch on strange ground at the south hinge of the Big Horns. He'd got himself out of there in 1936, had gone to a war and come back, married and married again (and again), made money in boilers and air-duct cleaning and smart investments, retired, got into local politics and out again without scandal, never circled back to see the old man and Rollo bankrupt and ruined because he knew they were.

They called it a ranch and it had been, but one day the old man said it was impossible to run cows in such tough country where they fell off cliffs, disappeared into sink-holes, gave up large numbers of calves to marauding lions, where hay couldn't grow but leafy spurge and Canada thistle throve, and the wind packed enough sand to scour windshields opaque. The old man wangled a job deliver-ing mail, but looked guilty fumbling bills into his neigh-bors' mailboxes.

Mero and Rollo saw the mail route as a defection from the work of the ranch, work that fell on them. The breeding herd was down to eighty-two and a cow wasn't worth more than fifteen dollars, but they kept mending fence, whittling ears and scorching hides, hauling cows out of mudholes and hunting lions in the hope that sooner or later the old man would move to Ten Sleep with his woman and his bottle and they could, as had their grandmother Olive when Jacob Corn disappointed her, pull the place taut. That bird didn't fly and Mero wound up sixty years later as an octogenarian vegetarian widower pumping an Exercycle in the living room of a colonial house in Woolfoot, Massachusetts.

One of those damp mornings the nail-driving telephone voice of a woman said she was Louise, Tick's wife, and summoned him back to Wyoming. He didn't know who she was, who Tick was, until she said, Tick Corn, your brother Rollo's son, and that Rollo had passed on, killed by a waspy emu though prostate cancer was waiting its chance. Yes, she said, you bet Rollo still owned the ranch. Half of it anyway. Me and Tick, she said, we been pretty much running it the last ten years.

An emu? Did he hear right?

Yes, she said. Well, of course you didn't know. You heard of Down Under Wyoming?

He had not. And thought, what kind of name was Tick? He recalled the bloated grey insects pulled off the dogs. This tick probably thought he was going to get the whole damn ranch and bloat up on it. He said, what the hell was this about an emu? Were they all crazy out there?

That's what the ranch was now, she said, Down Under Wyoming. Rollo'd sold the place way back when to the Girl Scouts, but one of the girls was dragged off by a lion and the G.S.A. sold out to the Banner ranch next door who ran cattle on it for a few years, then unloaded it on a rich Australian businessman who started Down Under Wyoming but it was too much long-distance work and he'd had bad luck with his manager, a feller from Idaho with a pawnshop rodeo buckle, so he'd looked up Rollo and offered to swap him a half-interest if he'd run the place. That was back in 1978. The place had done real well. Course we're not open now, she said, it's winter and there's no tourists. Poor Rollo was helping Tick move the emus to another building when one of them turned on a dime and come right for him with its big razor claws. Emus is bad for claws.

I know, he said. He watched the nature programs on television.

She shouted as though the telephone lines were down all across the country, Tick got your number off the computer. Rollo always said he was going to get in touch. He wanted you to see how things turned out. He tried to fight it off with his cane but it laid him open from belly to breakfast.

Maybe, he thought, things hadn't finished turning out. Impatient with this game he said he would be at the funeral. No point talking about flights and meeting him at the airport, he told her, he didn't fly, a bad experience years ago with hail, the plane had looked like a waffle iron when it landed. He intended to drive. Of course he knew how far it was. Had a damn fine car, Cadillac, always drove Cadillacs, Gislaved tires, interstate highways, excellent driver, never had an accident in his life knock on wood, four days, he would be there by Saturday afternoon. He heard the amazement in her voice, knew she was plotting his age, figuring he had to be eighty-three, a year or so older than Rollo, figuring he must be dotting around on a cane too, drooling the tiny days away, she was probably touching her own faded hair. He flexed his muscular arms, bent his knees, thought he could dodge an emu. He would see his brother dropped in a red Wyoming hole. That event could jerk him back; the dazzled rope of lightning against the cloud is not the downward bolt, but the compelled upstroke through the heated ether.

He had pulled away at the sudden point when it seemed the old man's girlfriend—now he couldn't remember her name—had jumped the track, Rollo goggling at her bloody bitten fingers, nails chewed to the quick, neck veins like wires, the outer forearms shaded with hairs, and the cigarette glowing, smoke curling up, making her wink her bulged mustang eyes, a teller of tales of hard deeds and mayhem. The old man's hair was falling out, Mero was twenty-three and Rollo twenty and she played them all like a deck of cards. If you admired horses you'd go for her with her arched neck and horsy buttocks, so high and haunchy you'd want to clap her on the rear. The wind bellowed around the house, driving crystals of snow through the cracks of the warped log door and all of them in the kitchen seemed charged with some intensity of purpose. She'd balanced that broad butt on the edge of the dog food chest, looking at the old man and Rollo, now and then rolling her glossy eyes over at Mero, square teeth nipping a rim of nail, sucking the welling blood, drawing on her cigarette.

The old man drank his Everclear stirred with a peeled

willow stick for the bitter taste. The image of him came
sharp in Mero's mind as he stood at the hall closet con-
templating his hats; should he bring one for the funeral?
The old man had had the damnedest curl to his hat brim,
a tight roll on the right where his doffing or donning hand
gripped it and a wavering downslope on the left like a
shed roof. You could recognize him two miles away. He
wore it at the table listening to the woman's stories about
Tin Head, steadily emptying his glass until he was nine-
times-nine drunk, his gangstery face loosening, the
crushed rodeo nose and scar-crossed eyebrows, the stub
ear dissolving as he drank. Now he must be dead fifty
years or more, buried in the mailman sweater.

The girlfriend started a story, yeah, there was this guy
named Tin Head down around Dubois when my dad was
a kid. Had a little ranch, some horses, cows, kids, a wife.
But there was something funny about him. He had a
metal plate in his head from falling down some cement
steps.

Plenty of guys has them, said Rollo in a challenging
way.

She shook her head. Not like his. His was made out of
galvy and it eat at his brain.

The old man held up the bottle of Everclear, raised his
eyebrows at her: Well, darlin?

She nodded, took the glass from him and knocked it
back in one swallow. Oh, that's not gonna slow *me* down,
she said.

Mero expected her to neigh.

So what then, said Rollo, picking at the horse shit

under his boot heel. What about Tin Head and his galvanized skull-plate?

I heard it this way, she said. She held out her glass for another shot of Everclear and the old man poured it and she went on.

Mero had thrashed all that ancient night, dreamed of horse breeding or hoarse breathing, whether the act of sex or bloody, cut-throat gasps he didn't know. The next morning he woke up drenched in stinking sweat, looked at the ceiling and said aloud, it could go on like this for some time. He meant cows and weather as much as anything, and what might be his chances two or three states over in any direction. In Woolfoot, riding the Exercycle, he thought the truth was somewhat different: he'd wanted a woman of his own without scrounging the old man's leftovers.

What he wanted to know now, tires spanking the tar-filled road cracks and potholes, funeral homburg sliding on the backseat, was if Rollo had got the girlfriend away from the old man, thrown a saddle on her and ridden off into the sunset?

The interstate, crippled by orange pylons, forced traffic into single lanes, broke his expectation of making good time. His Cadillac, boxed between semis with hissing air brakes, snuffled huge rear tires, framed a looming Peterbilt in the back window. His thoughts clogged as if a comb working through his mind had stuck against a snarl. When the traffic eased and he tried to cover some ground the highway patrol pulled him over. The cop, a pimpled, mustached specimen with mismatched eyes, asked his name, where he was going. For the minute he couldn't think what he was doing there. The cop's tongue dapped at the scraggy mustache while he scribbled.

Funeral, he said suddenly. Going to my brother's funeral.

Well you take it easy, Gramps, or they'll be doing one for you.

You're a little polecat, aren't you, he said, staring at the ticket, at the pathetic handwriting, but the mustache was a mile gone, peeling through the traffic as Mero had peeled out of the ranch road that long time ago, squinting through the abraded windshield. He might have made a more graceful exit but urgency had struck him as a blow on the humerus sends a ringing jolt up the arm. He believed it was the horse-haunched woman leaning against the chest and Rollo fixed on her, the old man swilling Everclear and not noticing or, if noticing, not caring, that had worked in him like a key in an ignition. She had long grey-streaked braids, Rollo could use them for reins.

Yah, she said, in her low and convincing liar's voice. I'll tell you, on Tin Head's ranch things went wrong. Chickens changed color overnight, calves was born with three legs, his kids was piebald and his wife always crying for blue dishes. Tin Head never finished nothing he started, quit halfway through a job every time. Even his pants was half-buttoned so his wienie hung out. He was a mess with the galvy plate eating at his brain and his ranch

25

and his family was a mess. But, she said. They had to eat, didn't they, just like anybody else?

I hope they eat pies better than the ones you make, said Rollo, who didn't like the mouthful of pits that came with the chokecherries.

His interest in women began a few days after the old man had said, take this guy up and show him them Indan drawrings, jerking his head at the stranger. Mero had been eleven or twelve at the time, no older. They rode along the creek and put up a pair of mallards who flew downstream and then suddenly reappeared, pursued by a goshawk who struck the drake with a sound like a handclap. The duck tumbled through the trees and into deadfall trash and the hawk shot as swiftly away as it had come.

They climbed through the stony landscape, limestone beds eroded by wind into fantastic furniture, stale gnawed breadcrusts, tumbled bones, stacks of dirty folded blankets, bleached crab claws and dog teeth. He tethered the horses in the shade of a stand of limber pine and led the anthropologist up through the stiff-branched mountain mahogany to the overhang. Above them reared corroded cliffs brilliant with orange lichen, pitted with holes and ledges darkened by millennia of raptor feces.

The anthropologist moved back and forth scrutinizing the stone gallery of red and black drawings: bison skulls, a line of mountain sheep, warriors carrying lances, a turkey stepping into a snare, a stick man upside-down dead and falling, red ochre hands, violent figures with rakes on their heads that he said were feather headdresses, a great red bear dancing forward on its hind legs, concentric circles and crosses and latticework. He copied the drawings in his notebook, saying rubba-dubba a few times.

That's the sun, said the anthropologist who resembled an unfinished drawing himself, pointing at an archery target, ramming his pencil into the air as though tapping gnats. That's an atlatl and that's a dragonfly. There we go. You know what this is; and he touched a cloven oval, rubbing the cleft with his dusty fingers. He got down on his hands and knees, pointed out more, a few dozen.

A horseshoe?

A horseshoe! The anthropologist laughed. No boy, it's a vulva. That's what all of these are. You don't know what that is, do you? You go to school on Monday and look it up in the dictionary.

It's a symbol, he said. You know what a symbol is?

Yes, said Mero, who had seen them clapped together in the high school marching band. The anthropologist laughed and told him he had a great future, gave him a dollar for showing him the place. Listen, kid, the Indians did it just like anybody else, he said.

He had looked the word up in the school dictionary, slammed the book closed in embarrassment, but the image was fixed for him (with the brassy background sound of a military march), blunt ochre tracing on stone, and no fleshy examples ever conquered his belief in the subterranean stony structure of female genitalia, the pubic bone a proof, except for the old man's girlfriend whom he imagined down on all fours, entered from behind and whinnying like a mare, a thing not of geology but flesh.

★

27

Thursday night, balked by detours and construction, he was on the outskirts of Des Moines and no farther. In the cinderblock motel room he set the alarm but his own stertorous breathing woke him before it rang. He was up at five-fifteen, eyes aflame, peering through the vinyl drapes at his snow-hazed car flashing blue under the motel sign SLEEP SLEEP. In the bathroom he mixed the packet of instant motel coffee and drank it black without ersatz sugar or chemical cream. He wanted the caffeine. The roots of his mind felt withered and punky.

A cold morning, light snow slanting down: he unlocked the Cadillac, started it and curved into the vein of traffic, all semis, double- and triple-trailers. In the headlights' red glare he missed the westbound ramp and got into torn-up muddy streets, swung right and right again, using the motel's SLEEP sign as a landmark, but he was on the wrong side of the interstate and the sign belonged to a different motel.

Another mudholed lane took him into a traffic circle of commuters sucking coffee from insulated cups, pastries sliding on dashboards. Halfway around the hoop he spied the interstate entrance ramp, veered for it, collided with a panel truck emblazoned STOP SMOKING! HYPNOSIS THAT WORKS!, was rammed from behind by a stretch limo, the limo in its turn rear-ended by a yawning hydroblast operator in a company pickup.

He saw little of this, pressed into his seat by the air bag, his mouth full of a rubbery, dusty taste, eyeglasses cutting into his nose. His first thought was to blame Iowa and those who lived in it. There were a few round spots of blood on his shirt cuff.

A star-spangled Band-Aid over his nose, he watched his

crumpled car, pouring dark fluids onto the highway, towed away behind a wrecker. A taxi took him, his suitcase, the homburg funeral hat, in the other direction to Posse Motors where lax salesmen drifted like disorbited satellites and where he bought a secondhand Cadillac, black like the wreck, but three years older and the upholstery not cream leather but sun-faded velour. He had the good tires from the wreck brought over and mounted. He could do that if he liked, buy cars like packs of cigarettes and smoke them up. He didn't care for the way it handled out on the highway, throwing itself abruptly aside when he twitched the wheel and he guessed it might have a bent frame. Damn, he'd buy another for the return trip. He could do what he wanted.

He was half an hour past Kearney, Nebraska, when the full moon rose, an absurd visage balanced in his rearview mirror, above it a curled wig of a cloud, filamented edges like platinum hairs. He felt his swollen nose, palped his chin, tender from the stun of the air bag. Before he slept that night he swallowed a glass of hot tap water enlivened with whiskey, crawled into the damp bed. He had eaten nothing all day yet his stomach coiled at the thought of road food.

He dreamed that he was in the ranch house but all the furniture had been removed from the rooms and in the yard troops in dirty white uniforms fought. The concussive reports of huge guns were breaking the window glass and forcing the floorboards apart so that he had to walk on the joists and below the disintegrating floors he saw galvanized tubs filled with dark, coagulated fluid.

On Saturday morning, with four hundred miles in

front of him, he swallowed a few bites of scorched eggs, potatoes painted with canned *salsa verde,* a cup of yellow coffee, left no tip, got on the road. The food was not what he wanted. His breakfast habit was two glasses of mineral water, six cloves of garlic, a pear. The sky to the west hulked sullen, behind him smears of tinselly orange shot through with blinding streaks. The thick rim of sun bulged against the horizon.

He crossed the state line, hit Cheyenne for the second time in sixty years. There was neon, traffic and concrete, but he knew the place, a railroad town that had been up and down. That other time he had been painfully hungry, had gone into the restaurant in the Union Pacific station although he was not used to restaurants and ordered a steak, but when the woman brought it and he cut into the meat the blood spread across the white plate and he couldn't help it, he saw the beast, mouth agape in mute bawling, saw the comic aspects of his revulsion as well, a cattleman gone wrong.

Now he parked in front of a phone booth, locked the car although he stood only seven feet away, and telephoned the number Tick's wife had given him. The ruined car had had a phone. Her voice roared out of the earpiece.

We didn't hear so we wondered if you changed your mind.

No, he said, I'll be there late this afternoon. I'm in Cheyenne now.

The wind's blowing pretty hard. They're saying it could maybe snow. In the mountains. Her voice sounded doubtful.

I'll keep an eye on it, he said.

He was out of town and running north in a few minutes.

The country poured open on each side, reduced the Cadillac to a finger-snap. Nothing had changed, not a goddamn thing, the empty pale place and its roaring wind, the distant antelope as tiny as mice, landforms shaped true to the past. He felt himself slip back, the calm of eighty-three years sheeted off him like water, replaced by a young man's scalding anger at a fool world and the fools in it. What a damn hard time it had been to hit the road. You don't know what it was like, he told his ex-wives until they said they did know, he'd pounded it into their ears two hundred times, the poor youth on the street holding up a sign asking for work, and the job with the furnace man, *yatata yatata ya.* Thirty miles out of Cheyenne he saw the first billboard, DOWN UNDER WYOMING, *Western Fun the Western Way,* over a blown-up photograph of kangaroos hopping through the sagebrush and a blond child grinning in a manic imitation of pleasure. A diagonal banner warned, *Open May 31.*

So what, Rollo had said to the old man's girlfriend, what about that Mr. Tin Head? Looking at her, not just her face, but up and down, eyes moving over her like an iron over a shirt and the old man in his mailman's sweater and lopsided hat tasting his Everclear and not noticing or not caring, getting up every now and then to lurch onto the porch and water the weeds. When he left the room the tension ebbed and they were only ordinary people to whom nothing happened. Rollo looked away from the woman, leaned down to scratch the dog's ears, saying,

Snarleyow Snapper, and the woman brought a dish to the sink and ran water on it, yawning. When the old man came back to his chair, the Everclear like sweet oil in his glass, glances resharpened and inflections of voice again carried complex messages.

Well well, she said, tossing her braids back, every year Tin Head butchers one of his steers, and that's what they'd eat all winter long, boiled, fried, smoked, fricasseed, burned and raw. So one time he's out there by the barn and he hits the steer a good one with the axe and it drops stun down. He ties up the back legs, hoists it up and sticks it, shoves the tub under to catch the blood. When it's bled out pretty good he lets it down and starts skinning it, starts with the head, cuts back of the poll down past the eye to the nose, peels the hide back. He don't cut the head off but keeps on skinning, dewclaws to hock up the inside of the thigh and then to the cod and down the middle of the belly to brisket to tail. Now he's ready to start siding, working that tough old skin off. But siding is hard work— (the old man nodded)—and he gets the hide off about halfway and starts thinking about dinner. So he leaves the steer half-skinned there on the ground and he goes into the kitchen, but first he cuts out the tongue which is his favorite dish all cooked up and eat cold with Mrs. Tin Head's mustard in a forget-me-not teacup. Sets it on the ground and goes in to dinner. Dinner is chicken and dumplins, one of them changed-color chickens started out white and ended up blue, yessir, blue as your old daddy's eyes.

She was a total liar. The old man's eyes were murk brown.

★

Onto the high plains sifted the fine snow, delicately clouding the air, a rare dust, beautiful, he thought, silk gauze, but there was muscle in the wind rocking the heavy car, a great pulsing artery of the jet stream swooping down from the sky to touch the earth. Plumes of smoke rose hundreds of feet into the air, elegant fountains and twisting snow devils, shapes of veiled Arab women and ghost riders dissolving in white fume. The snow snakes writhing across the asphalt straightened into rods. He was driving in a rushing river of cold whiteout foam. He could see nothing, trod on the brake, the wind buffeting the car, a bitter, hard-flung dust hissing over metal and glass. The car shuddered. And as suddenly as it had risen the wind dropped and the road was clear; he could see a long, empty mile.

How do you know when there's enough of anything? What trips the lever that snaps up the STOP sign? What electrical currents fizz and crackle in the brain to shape the decision to quit a place? He had listened to her damn story and the dice had rolled. For years he believed he had left without hard reason and suffered for it. But he'd learned from television nature programs that it had been time for him to find his own territory and his own woman. How many women were out there! He had married three or four of them and sampled plenty.

With the lapping subtlety of incoming tide the shape of the ranch began to gather in his mind; he could recall the intimate fences he'd made, taut wire and perfect corners,

the draws and rock outcrops, the watercourse valley steep-
ening, cliffs like bones with shreds of meat on them rising
and rising, and the stream plunging suddenly under-
ground, disappearing into subterranean darkness of blind
fish, shooting out of the mountain ten miles west on a
neighbor's place, but leaving their ranch some badland red
country as dry as a cracker, steep canyons with high caves
suited to lions. He and Rollo had shot two early in that
winter close to the overhang with the painted vulvas.
There were good caves up there from a lion's point of
view.

He traveled against curdled sky. In the last sixty miles the
snow began again. He climbed out of Buffalo. Pallid flakes
as distant from each other as galaxies flew past, then more
and in ten minutes he was crawling at twenty miles an
hour, the windshield wipers thumping like a stick dragged
down the stairs.

The light was falling out of the day when he reached
the pass, the blunt mountains lost in snow, the greasy hair-
pin turns ahead. He drove slowly and steadily in a low
gear; he had not forgotten how to drive a winter mountain. But the wind was up again, rocking and slapping the
car, blotting out all but whipping snow and he was sweat-
ing with the anxiety of keeping to the road, dizzy with the
altitude. Twelve more miles, sliding and buffeted, before
he reached Ten Sleep where streetlights glowed in revolv-
ing circles like Van Gogh's sun. There had not been electricity when he left the place. In those days there were
seventeen black, lightless miles between the town and the
ranch, and now the long arch of years compressed into

that distance. His headlights picked up a sign: 20 MILES TO DOWN UNDER WYOMING. Emus and bison leered above the letters.

He turned onto the snowy road marked with a single set of tracks, faint but still discernible, the heater fan whirring, the radio silent, all beyond the headlights blurred. Yet everything was as it had been, the shape of the road achingly familiar, sentinel rocks looming as they had in his youth. There was an eerie dream quality in seeing the deserted Farrier place leaning east as it had leaned sixty years ago, the Banner ranch gate, where the companionable tracks he had been following turned off, the gate ghostly in the snow but still flying its wrought iron flag, unmarked by the injuries of weather, and the taut five-strand fences and dim shifting forms of cattle. Next would come the road to their ranch, a left-hand turn just over the crest of a rise. He was running now on the unmarked road through great darkness.

Winking at Rollo the girlfriend said, yes, she had said, yes sir, Tin Head eats half his dinner and then he has to take a little nap. After a while he wakes up again and goes outside stretching his arms and yawning, says, guess I'll finish skinning out that steer. But the steer ain't there. It's gone. Only the tongue, laying on the ground all covered with dirt and straw, and the tub of blood and the dog licking at it.

It was her voice that drew you in, that low, twangy voice, wouldn't matter if she was saying the alphabet, what you heard was the rustle of hay. She could make you smell the smoke from an unlit fire.

How could he not recognize the turnoff to the ranch? It was so clear and sharp in his mind: the dusty crimp of the corner, the low section where the snow drifted, the run where willows slapped the side of the truck. He went a mile, watching for it, but the turn didn't come up, then watched for the Bob Kitchen place two miles beyond, but the distance unrolled and there was nothing. He made a three-point turn and backtracked. Rollo must have given up the old entrance road, for it wasn't there. The Kitchen place was gone to fire or wind. If he didn't find the turn it was no great loss; back to Ten Sleep and scout a motel. But he hated to quit when he was close enough to spit, hated to retrace black miles on a bad night when he was maybe twenty minutes away from the ranch.

He drove very slowly, following his tracks, and the ranch entrance appeared on the right although the gate was gone and the sign down. That was why he'd missed it, that and a clump of sagebrush that obscured the gap.

He turned in, feeling a little triumph. But the road under the snow was rough and got rougher until he was bucking along over boulders and slanted rock and knew wherever he was it was not right.

He couldn't turn around on the narrow track and began backing gingerly, the window down, craning his stiff neck, staring into the redness cast by the taillights. The car's right rear tire rolled up over a boulder, slid and sank into a quaggy hole. The tires spun in the snow, but he got no purchase.

I'll sit here, he said aloud. I'll sit here until it's light and then walk down to the Banner place and ask for a cup of coffee. I'll be cold but I won't freeze to death. It played like a joke the way he imagined it with Bob Banner opening the door and saying, why, it's Mero, come on in and have some java and a hot biscuit, before he remembered that Bob Banner would have to be 120 years old to play that role. He was maybe three miles from Banner's gate, and the Banner ranch house was another seven miles beyond the gate. Say a ten-mile hike at altitude in a snowstorm. On the other hand he had half a tank of gas. He could run the car for a while, then turn it off, start it again all through the night. It was bad luck, but that's all. The trick was patience.

He dozed half an hour in the wind-rocked car, woke shivering and cramped. He wanted to lie down. He thought perhaps he could put a flat rock under the goddamn tire. Never say die, he said, feeling around the passenger-side floor for the flashlight in his emergency bag, then remembering the wrecked car towed away, the flares and car phone and AAA card and flashlight and matches and candle and Power Bars and bottle of water still in it, and probably now in the damn tow-driver's damn wife's car. He might get a good enough look anyway in the snow-reflected light. He put on his gloves and the heavy overcoat, got out and locked the car, sidled around to the rear, bent down. The taillights lit the snow beneath the rear of the car like a fresh bloodstain. There was a cradle-sized depression eaten out by the spinning tire. Two or three flat ones might get him out, or small round ones, he was not going to insist on the perfect stone. The wind tore at him, the snow was certainly drifting up. He began to shuffle on the road, feeling with his feet for rocks he could move, the car's even throbbing promising motion and escape. The wind was sharp and his ears ached. His wool cap was in the damn emergency bag.

My lord, she continued, Tin Head is just startled to pieces when he don't see that steer. He thinks somebody, some neighbor don't like him, plenty of them, come and stole it. He looks around for tire marks or footprints but there's nothing except old cow tracks. He puts his hand up to his eyes and stares away. Nothing in the north, the south, the east, but way over there in the west on the side of the mountain he sees something moving stiff and slow, stumbling along. It looks raw and it's got something bunchy and wet hanging down over its hindquarters. Yah, it was the steer, never making no sound. And just then it stops and it looks back. And all that distance Tin Head can see the raw meat of the head and the shoulder muscles and the empty mouth without no tongue open wide and its red eyes glaring at him, pure teetotal hate like arrows coming at him, and he knows he is done for and all of his kids and their kids is done for, and that his wife is done for and that every one of her blue dishes has got to break, and the dog that licked the blood is done for, and the house where they lived has to blow away or burn up and every fly or mouse in it.

There was a silence and she added, that's it. And it all went against him, too.

That's it? said Rollo. That's all there is to it?

Yet he knew he was on the ranch, he felt it and he knew this road, too. It was not the main ranch road but some lower entrance he could not quite recollect that cut in below the river. Now he remembered that the main entrance gate was on a side road that branched off well before the Banner place. He found a good stone, another, wondering which track this could be; the map of the ranch in his memory was not as bright now, but scuffed and obliterated as though trodden. The remembered gates collapsed, fences wavered, while the badland features swelled into massive prominence. The cliffs bulged into the sky, lions snarled, the river corkscrewed through a stone hole at a tremendous rate and boulders cascaded from the heights. Beyond the barbwire something moved.

He grasped the car door handle. It was locked. Inside, by the dashboard glow, he could see the gleam of the keys in the ignition where he'd left them to keep the car running. It was almost funny. He picked up a big two-handed rock and smashed it on the driver's-side window, slipped his arm in through the hole, into the delicious warmth of the car, a contortionist's reach, twisting behind the steering wheel and down, and had he not kept limber with exercise and nut cutlets and green leafy vegetables he never could have reached the keys. His fingers grazed and then grasped the keys and he had them. This is how they sort the men out from the boys, he said aloud. As his fingers closed on the keys he glanced at the passenger door. The lock button stood high. And even had it been locked as well, why had he strained to reach the keys when he had only to lift the lock button on the driver's side? Cursing, he pulled out the rubber floor mats and arranged them over the stones, stumbled around the car once more. He was dizzy, tremendously thirsty and hungry, opened his mouth to snowflakes. He had eaten nothing for two days but the burned eggs that morning. He could eat a dozen burned eggs now.

The snow roared through the broken window. He put the car in reverse and slowly trod the gas. The car lurched and steadied in the track and once more he was twisting his neck, backing in the red glare, twenty feet, thirty, but slipping and spinning; there was too much snow. He was backing up an incline that had seemed level on the way in but showed itself now as a remorselessly long hill studded with rocks and deep in snow. His incoming tracks twisted like rope. He forced out another twenty feet spinning the tires until they smoked, and the rear wheels slewed sideways off the track and into a two-foot ditch, the engine died and that was it. It was almost a relief to have reached this point where the celestial fingernails were poised to nip his thread. He dismissed the ten-mile distance to the Banner place: it might not be that far, or maybe they had pulled the ranch closer to the main road. A truck might come by. Shoes slipping, coat buttoned awry, he might find the mythical Grand Hotel in the sagebrush.

On the main road his tire tracks showed as a faint pattern in the pearly apricot light from the risen moon, winking behind roiling clouds of snow. His blurred shadow strengthened whenever the wind eased. Then the violent country showed itself, the cliffs rearing at the moon, the snow smoking off the prairie like steam, the white flank of the ranch slashed with fence cuts, the sagebrush glittering and along the creek black tangles of willow bunched like dead hair. There were cattle in the field beside the road, their plumed breaths catching the moony glow like comic strip dialogue balloons.

He walked against the wind, his shoes filled with snow, feeling as easy to tear as a man cut from paper. As he walked he noticed one from the herd inside the fence was keeping pace with him. He walked more slowly and the animal lagged. He stopped and turned. It stopped as well, huffing vapor, regarding him, a strip of snow on its back like a linen runner. It tossed its head and in the howling, wintry light he saw he'd been wrong again, that the half-skinned steer's red eye had been watching for him all this time.

The Mud Below

RODEO NIGHT IN A HOT LITTLE OKIE TOWN AND Diamond Felts was inside a metal chute a long way from the scratch on Wyoming dirt he named as home, sitting on the back of bull 82N, a loose-skinned brindle Brahma-cross identified in the program as Little Kisses. There was a sultry feeling of weather. He kept his butt cocked to one side, his feet up on the chute rails so the bull couldn't grind his leg, brad him up, so that if it thrashed he could get over the top in a hurry. The time came closer and he slapped his face forcefully, bringing the adrenaline roses up on his cheeks, glanced down at his pullers and said, "I guess." Rito, neck gleaming with sweat, caught the free end of the bull-rope with a metal hook, brought it delicately to his hand from under the bull's belly, climbed up the rails and pulled it taut.

"Aw, this's a sumbuck," he said. "Give you the sample card."

Diamond took the end, made his wrap, brought the rope around the back of his hand and over the palm a second time, wove it between his third and fourth fingers, pounded the rosined glove fingers down over it and into his palm. He laid the tail of the rope across the bull's back and looped the excess, but it wasn't right—everything had gone

45

a little slack. He undid the wrap and started over, making the loop smaller, waiting while they pulled again and in the arena a clown fired a pink cannon, the fizzing discharge diminished by a deep stir of thunder from the south, Texas T-storm on the roll.

Night perfs had their own hot charge, the glare, the stiff-legged parade of cowboy dolls in sparkle-fringed chaps into the arena, the spotlight that bucked over the squinting contestants and the half-roostered crowd. They were at the end of the night now, into the bullriding, with one in front of him. The bull beneath him breathed, shifted roughly. A hand, fingers outstretched, came across his right shoulder and against his chest, steadying him. He did not know why a bracing hand eased his chronic anxiety. But, in the way these things go, that was when he needed twist, to auger him through the ride.

In the first go-round he'd drawn a bull he knew and got a good scald on him. He'd been in a slump for weeks, wire stretched tight, but things were turning back his way. He'd come off that animal in a flying dismount, sparked a little clapping that quickly died; the watchers knew as well as he that if he burst into flames and sang an operatic aria after the whistle it would make no damn difference.

He drew o.k. bulls and rode them in the next rounds, scores in the high seventies, fixed his eyes on the outside shoulder of the welly bull that tried to drop him, then at the short-go draw he pulled Kisses, rank and salty, big as a boxcar of coal. On that one all you could do was your best and hope for a little sweet luck; if you got the luck he was money.

The announcer's galvanized voice rattled in the speakers above the enclosed arena. "Now folks, it ain't the

Constitution or the Bill a Rights that made this a great country. It was *God* who created the mountains and plains and the evenin sunset and put us here and let us look at them. Amen and God bless the Markin flag. And right now we got a bullrider from Redsled, Wyomin, twenty-three-year-old Diamond Felts, who might be wonderin if he'll ever see that beautiful scenery again. Folks, Diamond Felts weighs one hundred and thirty pounds. Little Kisses weighs two thousand ten pounds, he is a big, big bull and he is thirty-eight and one, last year's Dodge City Bullriders' choice. Only one man has stayed on this big bad bull's back for eight seconds and that was Marty Casebolt at Reno, and you better believe that man got all the money. *Will* he be rode tonight? Folks, we're goin a find out in just a minute, soon as our cowboy's ready. And listen at that rain, folks, let's give thanks we're in a enclosed arena or it would be deep mud below."

Diamond glanced back at the flank man, moved up on his rope, nodded, jerking his head up and down rapidly. "Let's go, let's go."

The chute door swung open and the bull squatted, leaped into the waiting silence and a paroxysm of twists, belly-rolls and spins, skipping, bucking and whirling, powerful drop, gave him the whole menu.

Diamond Felts, a constellation of moles on his left cheek, dark hair cropped to the skull, was more than good-looking when cleaned up and combed, in fresh shirt and his neckerchief printed with blue stars, but for most of his life he had not known it. Five-foot three, rapping, tapping, nail-biting, he radiated unease. A virgin at eighteen—not many of either sex in his senior class in that condition—his tries at changing the situation went wrong and as far as his despairing thought carried him, always would go wrong in the forest of tall girls. There were small women out there, but it was the six-footers he mounted in the privacy of his head.

All his life he had heard himself called Half-Pint, Baby Boy, Shorty, Kid, Tiny, Little Guy, Sawed-Off. His mother never let up, always had the needle ready, even the time when she had come into the upstairs hall and caught him stepping naked from the bathroom; she had said, "Well, at least you didn't get shortchanged that way, did you?"

In the spring of his final year of school he drummed his fingers on Wallace Winter's pickup listening to its swan-necked owner pump up a story, trying for the laugh, when a knothead they knew only as Leecil—god save the one who said Lucille—walked up and said, "Either one a you want a work this weekend? The old man's fixin a brand and he's short-handet. Nobody wants to, though." He winked his dime-size eyes. His blunt face was corrugated with plum-colored acne and among the angry swellings grew a few blond whiskers. Diamond couldn't see how he shaved without bleeding to death. The smell of livestock was strong.

"He sure picked the wrong weekend," said Wallace. "Basketball game, parties, fucking, drinking, drugs, car wrecks, cops, food poisoning, fights, hysterical parents. Didn't you tell him?"

"He didn't ast me. Tolt me get some guys. Anyway it's good weather now. Stormt the weekend for a month." Leecil spit.

Wallace pretended serious consideration. "Scratch the weekend I guess we get paid." He winked at Diamond who grimaced to tell him that Leecil was not one to be teased.

"Yeah, six per, you guys. Me and my brothers got a work for nothin, for the ranch. Anyway, we give-or-take quit at suppertime, so you can still do your stuff. Party, whatever." He wasn't going to any town blowout.

"I never did ranch work," Diamond said. "My momma grew up on a ranch and hated it. Only took us up there once and I bet we didn't stay an hour," remembering an expanse of hoof-churned mud, his grandfather turning away, a muscular, sweaty Uncle John in chaps and a filthy hat swatting him on the butt and saying something to his mother that made her mad.

"Don't matter. It's just work. Git the calves into the chute, brand em, fix em, vaccinate em, git em out."

"Fix em," said Diamond.

Leecil made an eloquent gesture at his crotch.

"It could be very weirdly interesting," said Wallace. "I got something that will make it weirdly interesting."

"You don't want a git ironed out too much, have to lay down in the mud," said Leecil severely.

"No," said Wallace. "I fucking don't want to do that. O.k., I'm in. What the hell."

Diamond nodded.

Leecil cracked his mouthful of perfect teeth. "Know where our place is at? There's a bunch a different turnoffs. Here's how you go," and he drew a complicated map on the back of a returned quiz red-marked F. That solved one puzzle; Leecil's last name was Bewd. Wallace looked at Diamond. The Bewd tribe, scattered from Pahaska to

Pine Bluffs, filled a double-X space in the local pantheon of troublemakers.

"Seven a.m.," said Leecil.

Diamond turned the map over and looked at the quiz. Cattle brands fine-drawn with a sharp pencil filled the answer spaces; they gave the sheet of paper a kind of narrow-minded authority.

The good weather washed out. The weekend was a windy, overcast cacophony of bawling, manure-caked animals, mud, dirt, lifting, punching the needle, the stink of burning hair that he thought would never get out of his nose. Two crotchscratchers from school showed up; Diamond had seen them around, but he did not know them and thought of them as losers for no reason but that they were inarticulate and lived out on dirt road ranches; friends of Leecil. Como Bewd, a grizzled man wearing a kidney belt, pointed this way and that as Leecil and his brothers worked the calves from pasture to corral to holding pen to branding chute and the yellow-hot electric iron, to cutting table where ranch hand Lovis bent forward with his knife and with the other hand pulled the skin of the scrotum tight over one testicle and made a long, outside cut through skin and membrane, yanked out the hot balls, dropped them into a bucket and waited for the next calf. The dogs sniffed around, the omnipresent flies razzed and turmoiled, three saddled horses shifted from leg to leg under a tree and occasionally nickered.

Diamond glanced again and again at Como Bewd. The man's forehead showed a fence of zigzag scars like white barbwire. He caught the stare and winked.

"Lookin at my decorations? My brother run over me with his truck when I was your age. Took the skin off from ear to here. I was all clawed up. I was scalloped."

They finished late Sunday afternoon and Como Bewd counted out their pay carefully and slowly, added an extra five to each pile, said they'd done a pretty fair job, then, to Leecil, said, "How about it?"

"You want a have some fun?" said Leecil Bewd to Diamond and Wallace. The others were already walking to a small corral some distance away.

"Like what," said Wallace.

Diamond had a flash that there was a woman in the corral.

"Bullridin. Dad's got some good buckin bulls. Our rodeo class come out last month and rode em. Couldn't hardly stay on one of em."

"I'll watch," said Wallace, in his ironic side-of-the-mouth voice.

Diamond considered rodeo classes the last resort of concrete-heads who couldn't figure out how to hold a basketball. He'd taken martial arts and wrestling all the way through until they spiked both courses as frills. "Oh man," he said. "Bulls. I don't guess so."

Leecil Bewd ran ahead to the corral. There was a side pen and in it were three bulls, two of them pawing dirt. At the front of the pen a side-door chute opened into the corral. One of the crotchscratchers was in the arena, jumping around, ready to play bullfighter and toll a bull away from a tossed rider.

To Diamond the bulls looked murderous and wild, but even the ranch hands had a futile go at riding them, Lovis scraped off on the fence; Leecil's father, bounced down in

51

three seconds, hit the ground on his behind, the kidney belt riding up his chest.

"Try it," said Leecil, mouth bloody from a face slam, spitting.

"Aw, not me," said Wallace. "I got a life in front of me."

"Yeah," said Diamond. "Yeah, I guess I'll give it a go."

"Atta boy, atta boy," said Como Bewd, and handed him a rosined left glove. "Ever been on a bull?"

"No sir," said Diamond, no boots, no spurs, no chaps, T-shirted and hatless. Leecil's old man told him to hold his free hand up, not to touch the bull or himself with it, keep his shoulders forward and his chin down, hold on with his feet and legs and left hand, above all not to think, and when he got bucked off, no matter what was broke, get up quick and run like hell for the fence. He helped him make the wrap, ease down on the animal, said, shake your face and git out there, and grinning, blood-speckled Lovis opened the chute door, waiting to see the town kid dumped and dive-bombed.

But he stayed on until someone counting eight hit the rail with the length of pipe to signal time. He flew off, landed on his feet, stumbling headlong but not falling, in a run for the rails. He hauled himself up, panting from the exertion and the intense nervy rush. He'd been shot out of the cannon. The shock of the violent motion, the lightning shifts of balance, the feeling of power as though he were the bull and not the rider, even the fright, fulfilled some greedy physical hunger in him he hadn't known was there. The experience had been exhilarating and unbearably personal.

"You know what," said Como Bewd. "You might make a bullrider."

Redsled, on the west slope of the divide, was fissured with thermal springs which attracted tourists, snowmobilers, skiers, hot and dusty ranch hands, banker bikers dropping fifty-dollar tips. It was the good thing about Redsled, the sulfurous, hellish smell and the wet heat buzzing him until he could not stand it, got out and ran to the river, falling into its dark current with banging heart.

"Let's hit the springs," he said on the way back, still on the adrenaline wave, needing something more.

"No," said Wallace, his first word in an hour. "I got something to do."

"Drop me off and go on home then," he said.

In the violent water, leaning against the slippery rocks, he replayed the ride, the feeling his life had doubled in size. His pale legs wavered under the water, pinprick air beads strung along each hair. Euphoria ran through him like blood, he laughed, remembered he had been on a bull before. He was five years old and they took a trip some-where, he and his mother and, in those lost days, his father who was still his father, brought him in the afternoons to a county fair with a merry-go-round. He was crazy about the merry-go-round, not for the broad spin which made him throw up, nor for the rear view of the fiberglass horses with their swelled buttocks and the sinister holes where the ends of the nylon tails had been secured before vandals jerked them out, but for the glossy little black bull, the only bull among the ruined horses, tail intact, red saddle and smiling eyes, the eye shine depicted by a painted wedge of white. His father had lifted him on and stood with his hand reaching across Diamond's shoulder, steadying him as the bull went up and down and the galloping music played.

Monday morning on the schoolbus he went for Leecil sitting in the back with one of the crotchscratchers. Leecil touched thumb and forefinger in a circle, winked.

"I need to talk to you. I want to know how to get into it. The bullriding. Rodeo."

"Don't think so," said the crotchscratcher. "First time you git stacked up you'll yip for mama."

"He won't," said Leecil, and to Diamond, "You bet it ain't no picnic. Don't look for a picnic—you are goin a git tore up."

It turned out that it was a picnic and he did get tore up.

His mother, Kaylee Felts, managed a tourist store, one of a chain headquartered in Denver: HIGH WEST—*Vintage Cowboy Gear, Western Antiques, Spurs, Collectibles.* Diamond had helped open boxes, dust showcases, wire-brush crusty spurs since he was twelve and she told him there was probably a place in the business for him after college, one of the other stores if he wanted to see the world. He thought it was his choice but when he told her he was going to bullriding school in California she blew up.

"No. You can't. You're going to college. What is this, some kid thing you kept to yourself all this time? I worked like a fool to bring you boys up in town, get you out of the mud, give you a chance to make something out of yourselves. You're just going to throw everything away to be a rodeo bum? My god, whatever I try to do for you, you kick me right in the face."

"Well, I'm going to rodeo," he answered. "I'm going to ride bulls."

"You little devil," she said. "You're doing this to spite me and I know it. You are just hateful. You're not going to get any cheerleading from me on this one."

"That's all right," he said. "I don't need it."

"Oh, you need it," she said. "You need it, all right. Don't you get it, rodeo's for ranch boys who don't have the good opportunities you do? The stupidest ones are the bullriders. We get them in the shop every week trying to sell us those pot-metal buckles or their dirty chaps."

"Doing it," he said. It could not be explained.

"I can't stop a train," she said. "You're a royal pain, Shorty, and you always were. Grief from day one. You make this bed you'll lie in it. I mean it. You've got the stubbornness in you," she said, "like him. You're just like him, and that's no compliment."

Shut the fuck up, he thought, but didn't say it. He wanted to tell her she could give that set of lies a rest. He was nothing like him, and could not ever be.

"Don't call me Shorty," he said.

At the California bullriding school he rode forty animals in a week, invested in a case of sports tape, watched videos until he fell asleep sitting up. The instructor's tireless nasal voice called, push on it, you can't never think you're goin a lose, don't look into the well, find your balance point, once you're tapped, get right back into the pocket, don't never quit.

Back in Wyoming he found a room in Cheyenne, a junk job, bought his permit and started running the Mountain Circuit. He made his PRCA ticket in a month, thought he was in sweet clover. Somebody told him it was beginner's luck. He ran into Leecil Bewd at almost every rodeo, got drunk with him twice, and, after a time of red-eye solo driving, always broke, too much month and not enough money, they hooked up and traveled together, riding the jumps, covering bulls from one little rodeo to another, eating road dust. He had chosen this rough, bruising life with its confused philosophies of striving to win and apologizing for it when he did, but when he got on there was the dark lightning in his gut, a feeling of blazing real existence.

Leecil drove a thirty-year-old Chevrolet pickup with a bent frame, scabbed and bondo'd, rewired, re-engined, remuffled, a vehicle with a strong head that pulled fiercely to the right. It broke down at mean and crucial times. Once, jamming for Colorado Springs, it quit forty miles short. They leaned under the hood.

"Shoot, I hate pawin around in these goddamn greasy guts, all of a whatness to me. How come you don't know nothin about cars neither?"

"Just lucky."

A truck pulled up behind them, calf roper Sweets Musgrove riding shotgun and his pigtailed wife Neve driving. Sweets got out. He was holding a baby in pink rompers.

"Trouble?"

"Can't tell if it's trouble. Both so ignorant it might be good news and we wouldn't know it."

"I do this for a paycheck," said Musgrove getting under

the hood with his baby and pulling at the truck's intestinal wires. "Had to live on rodeo we couldn't make the riffle, could we, baby?" Neve sauntered over, scratched a match on her boot sole and lit a cigarette, leaned on Musgrove.

"You want a knife?" said Leecil. "Cut the sumbuck?"

"You're getting your baby dirty," said Diamond, wishing Neve would take it.

"I rather have a greasy little girl than a lonesome baby, mhhmhhmhh?" he said into the baby's fat neck. "Try startin it now." It didn't go and there wasn't any time to waste fooling with it.

"You can't both squeeze in with us and my mare don't like sharin her trailer. But that don't mean pig pee because there's a bunch a guys comin on. Somebody'll pick you up. You'll get there." He jammed a mouthguard—pink, orange and purple—over his teeth and grinned at his charmed baby.

Four bullriders with two buckle bunnies in a convertible gathered them up and one of the girls pressed against Diamond from shoulder to ankle the whole way. He got to the arena in a visible mood to ride but not bulls.

It worked pretty well for a year and then Leecil quit. It had been a scorching, dirty afternoon at a Colorado fairgrounds, the showers dead and dry. Leecil squirted water from a gas station hose over his head and neck, drove with the window cranked down, the dry wind sucking up the moisture immediately. The venomous blue sky threw heat.

"Two big jumps, wrecked in time to git stepped on. Man, he ate me. Out a the money again. I sure wasn't packin enough in my shorts today to ride that trash. Say what, the juice ain't worth the squeeze. Made up my mind while I was rollin in the dirt. I used a think I wanted a rodeo more than anything," said Leecil, "but shoot, I got a say I hate it, the travelin, traffic and stinkin motels, the rest of it. Tired a bein sored up all the time. I don't got that thing you got, the style, the fuck-it-all-I-love-it thing. I miss the ranch bad. The old man's on my mind. He got some medical problem, can't hardly make his water good, told my brother there's blood in his bull stuff. They're doin tests. And there's Renata. What I'm tryin a say is, I'm cuttin out on you. Anyway, guess what, goin a get married." The flaring shadow of the truck sped along a bank cut.

"What do you mean? You knock Renata up?" It was all going at speed.

"Aw, yeah. It's o.k."

"Well shit, Leecil. Won't be much fun now." He was surprised that it was true. He knew he had little talent for friendship or affection, stood armored against love, though when it did come down on him later it came like an axe and he was slaughtered by it. "I never had a girl stick with me more than two hours. I don't know how you get past that two hours," he said.

Leecil looked at him.

He mailed a postcard of a big yellow bull on the charging run, ropes of saliva slung out from his muzzle, to his younger brother Pearl, but did not telephone. After Leecil quit he moved to Texas where there was a rodeo every night for a fast driver red-eyed from staring at pin headlights miles distant alternately dark and burning as the road swelled and fell away.

The second year he was getting some notice and making money until a day or so before the big Fourth of July weekend. He came off a great ride and landed hard on his feet with his right knee sharply flexed, tore the ligaments and damaged cartilage. He was a fast healer but it put him out for the summer. When he was off the crutches, bored and limping around on a cane, he thought about Redsled. The doctor said the hot springs might be a good idea. He picked up a night ride with Tee Dove, a Texas bullrider, the big car slingshot at the black hump of range, dazzle of morning an hour behind the rim, not a dozen words exchanged.

"It's a bone game," Tee Dove said and Diamond thought he meant injuries, nodded.

For the first time in two years he sat at his mother's table. She said, "Bless this food, amen, oh boy, I knew you'd be back one of these days. And look at you. Just take a look at you. Like you climbed out of a ditch. Look at your hands," she said. "They're a mess. I suppose you're broke." She was dolled up, her hair long and streaked blond, crimped like Chinese noodles, her eyelids iridescent blue.

Diamond extended his fingers, turned his carefully scrubbed hands palm up, palm down, muscular hands with cut knuckles and small scars, two nails purple-black and lifting off at the base.

"They're clean. And I'm not broke. Didn't ask you for money, did I?"

"Oh, eat some salad," she said. They ate in silence, forks clicking among the pieces of cucumber and tomato. He disliked cucumber. She got up, clattered small plates with gold rims onto the table, brought out a supermarket lemon meringue pie, began to cut it with the silver pie server.

"All right," said Diamond, "calf-slobber pie."

Pearl, his ten-year-old brother, let out a bark.

She stopped cutting and fixed him with a stare. "You can talk ugly when you're with your rodeo bums, but when you are home keep your tongue decent."

He looked at her, seeing the cold blame. "I'll pass on that pie."

"I think all of us will after that unforgettable image. You'll want a cup of coffee." She had forbidden it when he lived at home, saying it would stunt his growth. Now it was this powdered stuff in the jar.

"Yeah." There wasn't much point in getting into it his first night home but he wanted a cup of real blackjack, wanted to throw the fucking pie at the ceiling.

She went out then, some kind of western junk meeting at the Redsled Inn, sticking him with the dishes. It was as if he'd never left.

He came down late the next morning. Pearl was sitting at the kitchen table reading a comic book. He was wearing the T-shirt Diamond had sent. It read, *Give Blood, Ride Bulls*. It was too small.

"Momma's gone to the shop. She said you should eat cereal, not eggs. Eggs have cholesterol. I saw you on t.v. once. I saw you get bucked off."

Diamond fried two eggs in butter and ate them out of the pan, fried two more. He looked for coffee but there was only the jar of instant dust.

"I'm going to get a buckle like yours when I'm eighteen," Pearl said. "And I'm not going to get bucked off because I'll hold on with the grip of death. Like this." And he made a white-knuckled fist.

"This ain't a terrific buckle. I hope you get a good one."

"I'm going to tell Momma you said 'ain't.'"

"For Christ sake, that's how everybody talks. Except for one old booger steer roper. I could curl your hair. And I *ain't* foolin. You want an egg?"

"I hate eggs. They aren't good for you. Ain't good for you. How does the old booger talk? Does he say 'calf-slobber pie'?"

"Why do you think she buys eggs if nobody's supposed to eat them? The old booger's religious. Lot of prayers and stuff. Always reading pamphlets about Jesus. Actually he's not old. He's no older than me. He's younger than me. He don't never say 'ain't.' He don't say 'shit' or 'fuck' or 'cunt' or 'prick' or 'goddamn.' He says 'good lord' when he's pissed off or gets slammed up the side of his head."

Pearl laughed immoderately, excited by the forbidden words and low-down grammar spoken in their mother's kitchen. He expected to see the floor tiles curl and smoke.

"Rodeo's full of Jesus freaks. And double and triple sets of brothers. All kinds of Texas cousins. There's some fucking strange guys in it. It's like a magic show some-times, all kinds of prayers and jujus and crosses and amulets and superstitions. Anybody does anything good, makes a good ride, it's not them, it's their mystical power connection helping them out. Guys from all over, Brazil, Canada, Australia dipping and bending, bowing heads, making signs." He yawned, began to rub the bad knee, thinking about the sulfur water deep to his chin and blue sky overhead. "So, you're going to hold on tight and not get bucked off?"

"Yeah. Really tight."

"I'll have to remember to try that," said Diamond.

He called the Bewd ranch to give Leecil a hello but the number had been disconnected. Information gave him a Gillette number. He thought it strange but called throughout the day. There was no answer. He tried again late that night and got Leecil's yawning croak.

"Hey, how come you're not out at the ranch? How come the ranch number's disconnected?" He heard the bad stuff coming before Leecil said anything.

"Aw, I'll tell you what, that didn't work out so good. When Dad died they valued the ranch, said we had a pay two million dollars in estate taxes. Two million dollars? That took the rag off the bush. We never had a pot to piss in, where was we supposed a get that kind a money for our own place that wasn't nothin when Dad took it over? You know what beef is bringin? Fifty-five cents a pound. We went round and round on it. Come down to it we had to sell. Sick about it, hell, I'm red-assed. I'm up here workin in the mines. Tell you, there's somethin wrong with this country."

"That's a dirty ride."

"Yeah. It is. It's been a dirty ride sinct I come back. Fuckin government."

"But you must have got a bunch of money for the place."

"Give my share to my brothers. They went up B.C. lookin for a ranch. It's goin a take all the money buy it, stock it. Guess I'm thinkin about goin up there with em. Wyomin's sure pulled out from under us. Hey, you're doin good with the bulls. Once in a while I think I might git back in it, but I git over that idea quick."

"I was doing o.k. until I messed up my knee. So what about your kid, was it a girl or a boy? I never heard. You didn't pass out cigars."

"You sure do ast the sore questions. That didn't turn out too good neither and I don't want to git into it just now. Done some things I regret. So, anyway, that's what I been doin, goin a funerals, hospitals, divorce court and real estate closins. You make it up here this weekend, get drunk? My birthday. Goin a be twenty-four and I feel like I got mileage on for fifty."

"Man, I can't. My knee's messed up enough I can't drive. I'll call you, I will call you."

It could be the worst kind of luck to go near Leecil.

On Thursday night, sliding the chicken breasts into the microwave, she prodded Pearl to get the silverware. She whipped the dehydrated potatoes with hot water, put the food on the table and sat down, looked at Diamond.

"I smell sulfur," she said. "Didn't you take a shower after the springs?"

"Not this time," he said.

"You reek." She shook open her napkin.

"All rodeo cowboys got a little tang to em."

"Cowboy? You're no more a cowboy than you are a little leather-winged bat. My grandfather was a rancher and he *hired* cowboys or what passed for them. My father gave that up for cattle sales and he hired ranch hands. My brother was never anything but a son-of-a-bee. None of them were cowboys but all of them were more cowboy than a rodeo bullrider ever will be. After supper," she said to Diamond, pushing the dish of pallid chicken breasts at him, "after supper I've got something I want you to see. We'll just take us a little ride."

"Can I come?" said Pearl.

"No. This is something I want your brother to see. Watch t.v. We'll be back in an hour."

"What is it," said Diamond, remembering the dark smear on the street she had brought him to years before. She had pointed, said, he didn't look both ways. He knew it would be something like that. The chicken breast lay on his plate like an inflated water wing. He should not have come back.

She drove through marginal streets, past the scrap-metal pile and the bentonite plant and, at the edge of town, crossed the railroad tracks where the road turned into rough dirt cutting through prairie. To the right, under a yellow sunset, stood several low metal buildings. The windows reflected the bright honey-colored west.

"Nobody here," said Diamond, "wherever we are," a kid again sitting in the passenger seat while his mother drove him around.

"Bar J stables. Don't worry, there's somebody here," said his mother. Gold light poured over her hands on the steering wheel, her arms, splashed the edges of her crimped hair. Her face, in shadow, was private and severe. He saw the withering skin of her throat. She said, "Hondo Gunsch? You know that name?"

"No." But he had heard it somewhere.

"Here," she said, pulling up in front of the largest building. Thousands of insects barely larger than dust motes floated in the luteous air. She walked quickly, he followed, dotting along.

"Hello," she called into the dark hallway. A light snapped on. A man in a white shirt, the pocket stiffened with a piece of plastic to hold his ballpoint pens, came through a door. Under his black hat, brim bent like the wings of a crow, was a face crowded with freckles, spectacles, beard and mustache.

"Hey there, Kaylee." The man looked at her as though she were hot buttered toast.

"This is Shorty, wants to be a rodeo star. Shorty, this is Kerry Moore."

Diamond shook the man's hot hand. It was an exchange of hostilities.

"Hondo's out in the tack room," said the man, looking at her. He laughed. "Always in the tack room. He'd sleep there if we let him. Come on out here."

He opened a door into a large, square room at the end of the stables. The last metaled light fell through high windows, gilding bridles and reins hanging on the wall. Along another wall a row of saddle racks projected, folded blankets resting on the shining saddles. A small refrigerator hummed behind the desk, and on the wall above it Diamond saw a framed magazine cover, *Boots 'N Bronks*, August 1960, showing a saddle bronc rider straight, square and tucked on a high-twisted horse, spurs raked all the way up to the cantle, his outflung arm in front of him. His hat was gone and his mouth open in a crazy smile. A banner read: *Gunsch Takes Cheyenne SB Crown*. The horse's back was humped, his nose pointed down, hind legs straight in a powerful jump and five feet of daylight between the descending front hooves and ground.

In the middle of the room an elderly man worked leather cream into a saddle; he wore a straw hat with the brim rolled high on the sides in a way that emphasized his long head shape. There was something wrong in the set of the shoulders, the forward slope of his torso from the hips. The room smelled of apples and Diamond saw a basket of them on the floor.

"Hondo, we got visitors." The man looked past them at nothing, showing the flat bulb of crushed nose, a dished cheekbone, the great dent above the left eye which seemed sightless. His mouth was still pursed with concentration. There was a pack of cigarettes in his shirt pocket. Emanating from him was a kind of carved-wood quietude common to those who have been a long time without sex, out of the traffic of the world.

"This here's Kaylee Felts and Shorty, stopped by to say howdy. Shorty's into rodeo. Guess *you* know something about rodeo, don't you, Hondo?" He spoke loudly as though the man was deaf.

The bronc rider said nothing, his blue, sweet gaze returning to the saddle, the right hand holding a piece of lambswool beginning again to move back and forth over the leather.

"He don't say much," said Moore. "He has a lot of difficulty but he keeps tryin. He's got plenty of try, haven't you, Hondo?"

The man was silent, working the leather. How many years since he had spurred a horse's shoulders, toes pointed east and west?

"Hondo, looks like you ought a change them sorry old floppy stirrup leathers one day," said Moore in a commanding tone. The bronc rider gave no sign he had heard.

"Well," said Diamond's mother after a long minute of watching the sinewy hands, "it was wonderful to meet you, Hondo. Good luck." She glanced at Moore, and Diamond could see a message fly but did not know their language.

They walked outside, the man and woman together, Diamond following, so deeply angry he staggered.

"Yeah. He's kind a deaf, old Hondo. He was a hot saddle bronc rider on his way to the top. Took the money two years runnin at Cheyenne. Then, some dinky little rodeo up around Meeteetse, his horse threw a fit in the chute, went over backwards, Hondo went down, got his head stepped on. Oh, 1961, and he been cleanin saddles for the Bar J since then. Thirty-seven years. That's a long, long time. He was twenty-six when it happened. Smart as anybody. Well, you rodeo, you're a rooster on Tuesday, feather duster on Wednesday. But like I say, he's still got all the try in the world. We sure think a lot a Hondo."

They stood silently watching Diamond get into the car.

"I'll call you," said the man and she nodded.

Diamond glared out the car window at the plain, the railroad tracks, the pawnshop, the Safeway, the Broken Arrow bar, Custom Cowboy, the vacuum cleaner shop. The topaz light reddened, played out. The sun was down and a velvety dusk coated the street, the bar neons spelling good times.

As she turned onto the river road she said, "I would take you to see a corpse to get you out of rodeo."

"You won't take me to see anything again."

The glassy black river flowed between dim willows. She drove very slowly.

"My god," she shouted suddenly, "what you've cost me!"

"*What!* What have I cost you?" The words shot out like flame from the mouth of a fire-eater.

The low beams of cars coming toward them in the dusk lit the wet run of her tears. There was no answer until she turned into the last street, then, in a guttural, adult woman's voice, raw and deep, as he had never heard it, she said, "You hard little man—*everything.*"

He was out of the car before it stopped, limping up the stairs, stuffing clothes in his duffel bag, not answering Pearl.

"Diamond, you can't go yet. You were going to stay for two weeks. You only been here four days. We were going to put up a bucking barrel. We didn't talk about Dad. Not one time."

He had told Pearl many lies beginning "Dad and me and you, when you were a baby"—that was the stuff the kid wanted to hear. He never told him what he knew and if he never found out that was a win.

"I'll come back pretty soon," he lied, "and we'll get her done." He was sorry for the kid but the sooner he learned it was a tough go the better. But maybe there was nothing for Pearl to know. Maybe the bad news was all his.

"Momma likes me better than you," shouted Pearl,

saving something from the wreck. He stripped off the T-shirt and threw it at Diamond.

"This I know." He called a taxi to take him to the crackerbox airport where he sat for five hours until a flight with connections to Calgary left.

In his cocky first year he had adopted a wide-legged walk as though there was swinging weight between his thighs. He felt the bull in himself, hadn't yet discerned the line of inimical difference between roughstock and rider. He dived headlong into the easy girls, making up for the years of nothing. He wanted the tall ones. In that bullish condition he tangled legs with the wife of Myron Sasser, his second traveling partner. They were in Cheyenne in Myron's truck and she was with them, sitting in the backseat of the club cab. All of them were hungry. Myron pulled into the Burger Bar. He left the truck running, the radio loud, a dark Texas voice entangled in static.

"How many you want, Diamond, two or three? Londa, you want onions with yours?"

They had picked her up at Myron's parents' house in Pueblo the day before. She was five-eleven, long brown curls like Buffalo Bill, had looked at Diamond and said to Myron, "You didn't say he was hardly fryin size. Hey there, chip," she said.

"That's me," he said, "smaller than the little end of nothing whittled to a point," smiled through murder.

She showed them an old heart-shaped waffle iron she had bought at a yard sale. It was not electric, a gadget from the days of the wood-burning range. The handles were of twisted wire. She promised Myron a Valentine breakfast.

"I'll git this," said Myron and went into the Burger Bar.

Diamond waited with her in the truck, aroused by her orchidaceous female smell. Through the glass window they could see Myron standing near the end of a long line. He thought of what she'd said, moved out of the front seat and into the back with her and pinned her, wrestled her 36-inseam jeans down to her ankles and got it in, like fucking sandpaper, and his stomach growling with hunger the whole time. She was not willing. She bucked and shoved and struggled and cursed him, she was dry, but he wasn't going to stop then. Something fell off the seat with a hard sound.

"My waffle iron," she said and nearly derailed him—he finished in five or six crashing strokes and it was done. He was back in the front seat before Myron reached the head of the line.

"I heard it called a lot of things," he said, "but never a waffle iron," and laughed until he choked. He felt fine.

She cried angrily in the seat behind him, pulling at her clothes.

"Hey," he said. "Hush up. It didn't hurt you. I'm too damn small to hurt a big girl like you, right? I'm the one should be crying—could have burred it off." He couldn't believe it when she opened the door and jumped down, ran into the Burger Bar, threw herself at Myron. He saw Myron putting his head over to listen to her, glancing out at the parking lot where he could see nothing, wiping the tears from her face with a paper napkin he took from the counter, and then charging toward the door with squared, snarling mouth. Diamond got out of the truck. Might as well meet it head-on.

"What a you done to Londa."

"Same thing you did to that wormy Texas buckle

bunny the other night." He didn't have anything against Myron Sasser except that he was a humorless fascist who picked his nose and left pliant knobs of snot on the steering wheel, but he wanted the big girl to get it clear and loud.

"You little pissant shit," said Myron and came windmilling at him. Diamond had him flat on the macadam, face in a spilled milk shake, but in seconds more lay beside him knocked colder than a wedge by the waffle iron. He heard later that Myron had sloped off to Hawaii without his amazon wife and was doing island rodeo. Let them both break their necks. The girl had too much mustard and she'd find it out if she came his way again.

That old day the bottom dropped had been a Sunday, the day they usually had pancakes and black cherry syrup, but she had not made the pancakes, told him to fix himself a bowl of cereal, feed Pearl his baby pears. He was thirteen, excited about the elk hunt coming up in three weekends. Pearl stank and squirmed in full diapers but by then they were seriously fighting. Diamond, sick of hearing the baby roar, had cleaned him up, dropped the dirty diaper in the stinking plastic pail.

They fought all day, his mother's voice low and vicious, his father shouting questions that were not answered but turned back at him with vindictive silences as powerful as a swinging bat. Diamond watched television, the sound loud enough to damp the accusations and furious abuse cracking back and forth upstairs. There were rushing footsteps overhead as though they were playing basketball, cries and shouts. It had nothing to do with him. He felt sorry for Pearl who bawled every time he heard their mother's anguished sobbing in the room above. One or two long silences held but they could not be mistaken for peace. In the late afternoon Pearl fell asleep on the living room couch with his fist knotted in his blanket. Diamond went out in the yard, kicked around, cleaned the car windshield for something to do. It was cold and windy, a cigar cloud poised over the mountain range forty miles west. He picked up rocks and threw them at the cloud pretending they were bullets fired at an elk. He could hear them inside, still at it.

The door slammed and his father came across the porch carrying the brown suitcase with a tiny red trademark horse in the corner, strode toward the car as if he were late.

"Dad," said Diamond. "The elk hunt—"

His father stared at him. In that twitching face his pupils were black and huge, eating up the hazel color to the rim.

"Don't never call me that again. Not your father and never was. Now get the fuck out of the way, you little bastard," the words high-pitched and tumbling.

After the breakup with Myron Sasser he bought a third-hand truck, an old Texas hoopy not much better than Leecil's wreck, traveled alone for a few months, needing the solitary distances, blowing past mesas and red buttes piled like meat, humped and horned, and on the highway chunks of mule deer, hair the buckskin color of winter grass, flesh like rough breaks in red country, playas of dried blood. He almost always had a girl in the motel bed with him when he could afford a motel, a half-hour painkiller but without the rush and thrill he got from a bullride. There was no sweet time when it was over. He wanted them to get gone. The in-and-out girls wasped it around that he was quick on the trigger, an arrogant little prick and the hell with his star-spangled bandanna.

"Hit the delete button on you, buddy," flipping the whorish blond hair.

What they said didn't matter because there was an endless supply of them and because he knew he was getting down the page and into the fine print of this way of living. There was nobody in his life to slow him down with love. Sometimes riding the bull was the least part of it, but only the turbulent ride gave him the indescribable rush, shot him mainline with crazy-ass elation. In the arena everything was real because none of it was real except the chance to get dead. The charged bolt came, he thought, because he wasn't. All around him wild things were falling to the earth.

One night in Cody, running out to the parking lot to beat the traffic, Pake Bitts, a big Jesus-loving steer roper, yelled out to him, "You goin a Roswell?"

"Yeah." Bitts was running parallel with him, the big stout guy with white-blond hair and high color. A sticker, *Praise God,* was peeling loose from his gear bag.

"Can I git a ride? My dee truck quit on me up in Livinston. Had to rent a puny car, thing couldn't hardly haul my trailer. Burned out the transmission. Tee Dove said he thought you was headed for Roswell?"

"You bet. Let's go. If you're ready." They hitched up Bitts's horse trailer, left the rental car standing.

"Fog it, brother, we're short on time," said the roper, jumping in. Diamond had the wheels spattering gravel before he closed the door.

He thought it would be bad, a lot of roadside prayers and upcast eyes, but Pake Bitts was steady, watched the gas gauge, took care of business and didn't preach.

Big and little they went on together to Mollala, to Tuska, to Roswell, Guthrie, Kaycee, to Baker and Bend. After a few weeks Pake said that if Diamond wanted a permanent traveling partner he was up for it. Diamond said yeah, although only a few states still allowed steer roping and Pake had to cover long, empty ground, his main territory in the livestock country of Oklahoma, Wyoming, Oregon and New Mexico. Their schedules did not fit into the same box without patient adjustment. But Pake knew a hundred dirt road shortcuts, steering them through scabland and slope country, in and out of the tiger shits, over the tawny plain still grooved with pilgrim wagon ruts, into early darkness and the first storm laying down black ice, hard orange dawn, the world smoking, snaking dust devils on bare dirt, heat boiling out of the sun until the paint on the truck hood curled, ragged webs of dry rain that never hit the ground, through small-town traffic and stock on the road, band of horses in morning fog, two redheaded cowboys moving a house that filled the roadway and Pake busting around and into the ditch to get past, leaving junkyards and Mexican cafés behind, turning into midnight motel entrances with RING OFFICE BELL signs or steering onto the black prairie for a stunned hour of sleep.

★

Bitts came from Rawlins and always he wanted to get to the next rodeo and grab at the money, was interested in no woman but his big-leg, pregnant wife Nancy, a heavy Christian girl, studying, said Bitts, for her degree in geology. "You wont a have a good talk," he said, "have one with Nancy. Good lord, she can tell you all about rock formations."

"How can a geologist believe that the earth was created in seven days?"

"Shoot, she's a Christian geologist. Nothin is impossible for God and he could do it all in seven days, fossils, the whole nine. Life is full a wonders." He laid a chew of long-cut into his cheek for even he had his vices.

"How did you get into it," asked Diamond. "Grow up on a ranch?"

"What, rodeo? Done it since I was a kid. Never lived on a ranch. Never wont to. Grew up in Huntsville, Texas. You know what's there?"

"Big prison."

"Right. My dad's a guard at the pen in Rawlins, but before that he was down at Huntsville. Huntsville had a real good prison rodeo program for years. And my dad took me to all them rodeos. He got me started in the Little Britches program. And here's somethin, my granddad Bitts did most of his ropin at Huntsville. Twist the nose off of a dentist. That bad old cowhand had a tattoo of a rope around his neck and piggin strings around his wrists. He seen the light after a few years and took Jesus into his heart, and that passed on down to my dad and to me. And I try to live a Christian life and help others."

They drove in silence for half an hour, light overcast

dulling the basin grass to the shades of dirty pennies, then Pake started in again.

"Bringin me to somethin I wont a say to you. About your bullridin. About rodeo? See, the bull is not supposed a be your role model, he is your opponent and you have to get the best a him, same as the steer is my opponent and I have to pump up and git everthing right to catch and thow em or I *won't* thow em."

"Hey, I know that." He'd known too that there would be a damn sermon sooner or later.

"No, you don't. Because if you did you wouldn't be playin the bull night after night, you wouldn't get in it with your buddies' wives, what I'd call forcible entry what you done, you would be a man lookin for someone to marry and raise up a family with. You'd take Jesus for a role model, not a dee ornery bull. Which you can't deny you done. You got a quit off playin the bull."

"I didn't think Jesus was a married man."

"Maybe not a married man, but he was a cowboy, the original rodeo cowboy. It says it right in the Bible. It's in Matthew, Mark, Luke *and* John." He adopted a sanctimonious tone: " 'Go into the village in which, at your enterin, ye shall find a colt tied, on which yet never no man sat; loose him and bring him here. The Lord hath need a him. And they brought him to Jesus, and they cast their garments upon the colt and they set Jesus on it.' Now, if that ain't a description a bareback ridin I don't know what is."

"I ride a bull, the bull's my partner, and if bulls could drive you can bet there'd be one sitting behind the wheel right now. I don't know how you figure all this stuff about me."

"Easy. Myron Sasser's my half-brother." He rolled down the window and spit. "Dad had a little bull in him, too. But he got over it."

Pake started in again a day or two later. Diamond was sick of hearing about Jesus and family values. Pake had said, "You got a kid brother, that right? How come he ain't never at none a these rodeos lookin at his big brother? And your daddy and mama?"

"Pull over a minute."

Bitts eased the truck over on the hard prairie verge, threw it into park, mis-guessing that Diamond wanted to piss, got out himself, unzipping.

"Wait," said Diamond standing where the light fell hard on him. "I want you to take a good look at me. You see me?" He turned sideways and back, faced Bitts. "That's all there is. What you see. Now do your business and let's get down the road."

"Aw, what I mean is," said Bitts, "you don't get how it is for nobody but your own dee self. You don't get it that you can't have a fence with only one post."

Late August and hot as billy hell, getting on out of Miles City Pake's head of maps failed and they ended on rimrock south of the Wyo line, tremendous roll of rough country in front of them, a hundred-mile sightline with bands of antelope and cattle like tiny ink flecks that flew from hard-worked nib pens on old promissory notes. They backtracked and sidetracked and a few miles outside Greybull Diamond pointed at the trucks drawn up in front of a slouched ranch house that had been converted into a bar, the squared logs weathered almost black.

"On the end, that's Sweets Musgrove's horse trailer, right? And Nachtigal's rig. Goddamn calf ropers, talk about their horses like they're women. You hear Nachtigal last night? 'She's honest, she's good, she never cheated on me.' Talking about his horse."

"How I feel about my horse."

"Pull in. I am going to drink a beer without taking a breath."

"Lucky if we git out alive goin where them guys are. Nachtigal's crazy. Rest of em don't talk about nothin but their trailers."

"I don't give a shit, Pake. You have your coffee, but I need a couple beers."

Above the door a slab of pine hung, the name of the place, Saddle Rack, scorched deep. Diamond pushed open the plank door, pocked with bullet holes in a range of calibers. It was one of the good places, dark, the log walls burned with hundreds of cattle brands, dim photographs of long-dead bronc busters high in the clouds and roundup crews in sweaters and woolly chaps. At the back of the room stood the oldest jukebox in the world, a crusty, dented machine with the neon gone dead and a flashlight on a string for patrons fussy enough to want to make a choice. The high gliding 1935 voice of Milton Brown was drifting, "*oh bree-yee-yee-yeeze*" over the zinc bar and four tables.

The bartender was a hardheaded old baldy with a beak and a cleft chin. Bottles, spigots, and a dirty mirror—the bartender's territory was not complex. He looked at them and Pake said ginger ale after gauging the tarry liquid on the hot plate. Diamond recognized he was going to get seriously drunk here. Sweets Musgrove and Nachtigal, Ike

78

Soot, Jim Jack Jett, hats off, receding hairlines in full view, sat at one of the tables, Jim Jack drinking red beer, the others whiskey and they were sliding deep down, cigars in honor of Nachtigal's daughter's first barrel race win, the cigars half-puffed and dead in the ashtray.

"What the hell you doin here?"

"Shit, you don't go past Saddle Rack without you stop and git irrigated."

"Looks like it."

Nachtigal gestured at the jukebox, "Ain't you got no Clint Black? No Dwight Yoakam?"

"Shut up and like what you get," said the bartender. "You're hearin early pedal steel. You're hearin priceless stuff. You rodeo boys don't know nothin about country music."

"Horseshit." Ike Soot took a pair of dice from his pocket.

"Roll the bones, see who's goin a pay."

"You buyin, Nachtigal," said Jim Jack. "I'm cleaned out. What little I won, lost it to that Indan sumbitch, Black Vest, works for one a the stock contractors. All or nothin, not a little bit but the whole damn everthing. One throw. He got a pair a bone dice, only one spot between the two, shakes em, throws em down. It's quick."

"I played that with him. Want some advice?"

"No."

It was come and go with the drinks and in a while Jim Jack said something about babies and wives and the pleasures of home which started Pake off on one of his family-hearth lectures, and with the next round Ike Soot cried a little and said the happiest day of his life was when he put that gold buckle in his daddy's hand and said, I done it for you. Musgrove topped them all by confessing that he had split the $8,200 he picked up at the Finals between his grandmother and a home for blind orphans. With five whiskeys and four beers sloshing, Diamond took a turn, addressing them all, even the two dusty, sweat-runneled ranch hands who'd come in off the baler to press their faces against the cold pitcher of beer Ranny stood between them.

"You all make a big noise about family, what I hear, wife and kids, ma and pa, sis and bub, but none of you spend much time at home and you never wanted to or you wouldn't be in rodeo. Rodeo's the family. Ones back at the ranch don't count for shit."

One of the hands at the bar slapped his palm down and Nachtigal marked him with his eye.

Diamond held up the whiskey glass.

"Here's to it. Nobody sends you out to do chores, treats you like a fool. Take your picture, you're on t.v., ask your wild-hair opinion, get your autograph. You're somebody, right? Here's to it. Rodeo. They say we're dumb but they don't say we're cowards. Here's to big money for short rides, here's to busted spines and pulled groins, empty pockets, damn all-night driving, chance to buck out—if you got good medicine, happens to somebody else. Know what I think? I think—" But he didn't know what he thought except that Ike Soot was swinging at him, but it was only a motion to catch him before he smashed into the cigar butts. That was the night he lost his star-spangled bandanna and went into the slump.

"Last time I seen that wipe somebody was moppin puke off the floor with it," said Bitts. "And it weren't me."

In the sixth second the bull stopped dead, then shifted everything the other way and immediately back again and he was lost, flying to the left into his hand and over the animal's shoulder, his eye catching the wet glare of the bull, but his hand turned upside down and jammed. He was hung up and good. Stay on your feet, he said aloud, jump, amen. The bull was crazy to get rid of him and the clanging bell. Diamond was jerked high off the ground with every lunge, snapped like a towel. The rope was in a half-twist, binding his folded fingers against the bull's back and he could not turn his hand over and open the fingers. Everything in him strained to touch the ground with his feet but the bull was too big and he was too small. The animal spun so rapidly its shape seemed to the watchers like mottled streaks of paint, the rider a paint rag. The bullfighters darted like terriers. The bull whipped him from the Arctic Circle to the Mexico border with every plunge. There was bull hair in his mouth. His arm was being pulled from its socket. It went on and on. This time he was going to die in front of shouting strangers. The bull's drop lifted him high and the bullfighter, waiting for the chance, thrust his hand up under Diamond's arm, rammed the tail of the rope through and jerked. The fingers of his glove opened and he fell cartwheeling away from hooves. The next moment the bull was on him, hooking. He curled, got his good arm over his head.

"Oh man, get up, this's a mean one," someone far away called and he was running on all fours, rump in the air, to the metal rails, a clown there, the bull already gone. The audience suddenly laughed and out of the corner of his eye he saw the other clown mocking his stagger. He pressed against the rails, back to the audience, dazed, unable to move. They were waiting for him to get out of the arena. Beyond the beating rain sirens sounded faint and sad.

A hand patted him twice on the right shoulder, someone said, "Can you walk?" Trembling, he tried to nod his head and could not. His left arm hung limp. He profoundly believed death had marked him out, then had ridden him almost to the buzzer, but had somehow wrecked. The man got in under his right arm, someone else grasped him around the waist, half-carried him to a room where a local sawbones sat swinging one foot and smoking a cigarette. No sports medicine team here. He thought dully that he did not want to be looked at by a doctor who smoked. From the arena the announcer's voice echoed as though in a culvert, "What a ride, folks, far as it went, but all for nothin, a zero for Diamond Felts, but you got a be proud a what this young man stands for, don't let him go away without a big hand, he's goin a be all right, and now here's Dunny Scotus from Whipup, Texas—"

He could smell the doctor's clouded breath, his own rank stench. He was slippery with sweat and the roaring pain.

"Can you move your arm? Are your fingers numb? Can you feel this? O.k., let's get this shirt off." He set the jaws of his scissors at the cuff and began to cut up the sleeve.

"This's a fifty-dollar shirt," whispered Diamond. It was a new one with a design of red feathers and black arrows across the sleeves and breast.

"Believe me, you wouldn't appreciate it if I tried to pull your arm out of the sleeve." The scissors worked across the front yoke and the ruined shirt fell away. The air felt cold on his wet skin. He shook and shook. It was a bad luck shirt now anyway.

"There you go," said the doctor. "Dislocated shoulder. Humerus displaced forward from the shoulder socket. All right, I'm going to try to reposition the humerus." The doctor's chin was against the back of his shoulder, his hands taking the useless arm, powerful smell of tobacco. "This will hurt for a minute. I'm going to manipulate this—"

"Jesus *CHRIST!*" The pain was excruciating and violent. The tears rolled down his hot face and he couldn't help it.

"Cowboy up," said the doctor sardonically.

Pake Bitts walked in, looked at him with interest.

"Got hung up, hah? I didn't see it but they said you got hung up pretty good. Twenty-eight seconds. They'll put you on the videos. Thunderstorm out there." He was damp from the shower, last week's scab still riding his upper lip and a fresh raw scrape on the side of his jaw. He spoke to the doctor. "Thow his shoulder out? Can he drive? It's his turn a drive. We got a be in south Texas two o'clock tomorrow afternoon."

The doctor finished wrapping the cast, lit another cigarette. "*I* wouldn't want to do it—right hand's all he's got. Dislocated shoulder, it's not just a question of pop it back in and away you go. He could need surgery. There's injured ligaments, internal bleeding, swelling, pain, could be some nerve or blood vessel damage. He's hurting. He's going to be eating aspirin by the handful. He's going to be in the cast for a month. If he's going to drive, one-handed or with his teeth, I can't give him codeine and you'd better not let him take any either. Call your insurance company, make sure you're covered for injury-impaired driving."

"What insurance?" said Pake, then, "You ought a quit off smokin," and to Diamond, "Well, the Good Lord spared you. When can we get out a here? Hey, you see how they spelled my name? Good Lord." He yawned hugely, had driven all the last night coming down from Idaho.

"Give me ten. Let me get in the shower, steady up. You get my rope and war bag. I'll be o.k. to drive. I just need ten."

The doctor said, "On your way, pal."

Someone else was coming in, a deep cut over his left eyebrow, finger pressed below the cut to keep the blood out of his rapidly swelling eyes and he was saying, just tape it up, tape the fuckin eyes open, I'm gettin on one.

He undressed one-handed in the grimy concrete shower room having trouble with the four-buckle chaps and his bootstraps. The pain came in long ocean rollers. He couldn't get on the other side of it. There was someone in one of the shower stalls, leaning his forehead against the concrete, hands flat against the wall and taking hot water on the back of his neck.

Diamond saw himself in the spotted mirror, two black eyes, bloody nostrils, his abraded right cheek, his hair dark with sweat, bull hairs stuck to his dirty, tear-streaked face, a bruise from armpit to buttocks. He was dizzy with the pain and a huge weariness overtook him. The euphoric charge had never kicked in this time. If he were dead this might be hell—smoking doctors and rank bulls, eight hundred miles of night road ahead, hurting all the way.

The cascade of water stopped and Tee Dove came out of the shower, hair plastered flat. He was ancient, Diamond knew, thirty-six, an old man for bullriding but still doing it. His sallow-cheeked face was a map of surgical repair and he carried enough body scars to open a store. A few months earlier Diamond had seen him, broken nose draining dark blood, take two yellow pencils and push one into each nostril, maneuvering them until the smashed cartilage and nasal bones were forced back into position.

Dove rubbed his scarred torso with his ragged but lucky towel, showed his fox teeth to Diamond, said, "Ain't it a bone game, bro."

Outside the rain had stopped, the truck gleamed wet, gutters flooded with runoff. Pake Bitts was in the passenger seat, already asleep and snoring gently. He woke when Diamond, bare-chested, barefooted, pulled the seat forward, threw in the cut shirt, fumbled one-handed in his duffel bag for an oversize sweatshirt he could get over the cast, jammed into his old athletic shoes, got in and started the engine.

"You o.k. to drive? You hold out two, three hours while I get some sleep, I'll take it the rest a the way. You drive the whole road is not a necessity by no means."

"It's o.k. How did they spell your name?"

"C–A–K–E. Cake Bitts. Nance'll laugh her head off over that one. Burn a rag, brother, we're runnin late." And he was asleep again, calloused hand resting on his thigh palm up and a little open as though to receive something in it.

Just over the Texas border he pulled into an all-night truck stop and filled the tank, bought two high-caffeine colas and drank them, washing down his keep-awakes and pain-stoppers. He walked past the cash registers and aisles of junk food to the telephones, fumbled the phone card from his wallet and dialed. It would be two-thirty in Redsled.

She answered on the first ring. Her voice was clear. She was awake.

"It's me," he said. "Diamond."

"Shorty?" she said. "What?"

"Listen, there's no way I can put this that's gentle or polite. Who was my father?"

"What do you mean? Shirley Custer Felts. You know that."

"No," he said. "I don't know that." He told her what Shirley Custer Felts had said getting into his car ten years earlier.

"That dirty man," she said. "He set you up like a time bomb. He knew the kind of kid you were, that you'd brood and sull over it and then blow up."

"I'm not blowing up. I'm asking you; who was he?"

"I told you." As she spoke he heard a deep smothered cough over the wire.

"I don't believe you. Third time, who was my father?"
He waited.

"Who you got there, Momma? The big slob with the black hat?"

"Nobody," she said and hung up. He didn't know which question she'd answered.

He was still standing there when Pake Bitts came in, shuffling and yawning.

"You wont me a drive now?" He pounded the heel of his hand on his forehead.

"No, get you some sleep."

"Aw, yeah. Piss on the fire, boy, and let's go."

He was o.k. to drive. He would drive all the way. He could do it now, this time, many more times to come. Yet it was as though some bearing had seized up inside him and burned out. It had not been the phone call but the flat minute pressed against the rail, when he could not walk out of the arena.

He pulled back onto the empty road. There were a few ranch lights miles away, the black sky against the black terrain drawing them into the hem of the starry curtain. As he drove toward the clangor and flash of the noon arena he considered the old saddle bronc rider rubbing leather for thirty-seven years, Leecil riding off into the mosquito-clouded Canadian sunset, the ranch hand bent over a calf, slitting the scrotal sac. The course of life's events seemed slower than the knife but not less thorough.

There was more to it than that, he supposed, and heard again her hoarse, charged voice saying "*Everything*." It was all a hard, fast ride that ended in the mud. He passed a coal train in the dark, the dense rectangles that were the cars gliding against indigo night, another, and another, and another. Very slowly, as slowly as light comes on a clouded morning, the euphoric heat flushed through him, or maybe just the memory of it.

Job History

LEELAND LEE IS BORN AT HOME IN CORA, Wyoming, November 17, 1947, the youngest of six. In the 1950s his parents move to Unique when his mother inherits a small dog-bone ranch. The ranch lies a few miles outside town. They raise sheep, a few chickens and some hogs. The father is irascible and, as soon as they can, the older children disperse. Leeland can sing "That Doggie in the Window" all the way through. His father strikes him with a flyswatter and tells him to shut up. There is no news on the radio. A blizzard has knocked out the power.

Leeland's face shows heavy bone from his mother's side. His neck is thick and his red-gold hair plastered down in bangs. Even as a child his eyes are as pouchy as those of a middle-aged alcoholic, the brows rod-straight above wandering, out-of-line eyes. His nose lies broad and close to his face, his mouth seems to have been cut with a single chisel blow into easy flesh. In the fifth grade, horsing around with friends, he falls off the school's fire escape and breaks his pelvis. He is in a body cast for three months. On the news an announcer says that the average American eats 8.6 pounds of margarine a year but only 8.3 pounds of butter. He never forgets this statistic.

When Leeland is seventeen he marries Lori Bovee. They quit school. Lori is pregnant and Leeland is proud of this. His pelvis gives him no trouble. She is a year younger than he, with an undistinguished, oval face, hair of medium length. She is a little stout but looks a confection in pastel sweater sets. Leeland and his mother fight over this marriage and Leeland leaves the ranch. He takes a job pumping gas at Egge's Service Station. Ed Egge says, "You may fire when ready, Gridley," and laughs. The station stands at the junction of highway 16 and a county road. Highway 16 is the main tourist road to Yellowstone. Leeland buys Lori's father's old truck for fifty dollars and Ed rebuilds the engine. Vietnam and Selma, Alabama, are on the news.

The federal highway program puts through the new four-lane interstate forty miles south of highway 16 and parallel with it. Overnight the tourist business in Unique falls flat. One day a hundred cars stop for gas and oil, hamburgers, cold soda. The next day only two cars pull in, both driven by locals asking how business is. In a few months there is a FOR SALE sign on the inside window of the service station. Ed Egge gets drunk and, driving at speed, hits two steers on the county road.

Leeland joins the army, puts in for the motor pool. He is stationed in Germany for six years and never learns a word of the language. He comes back to Wyoming heavier, moodier. He works with a snow-fence crew during spring and summer, then moves Lori and the children—the boy and a new baby girl—to Casper where he drives oil trucks. They live in a house trailer on Poison Spider Road, jammed between two rioting neighbors. On the news they hear that an enormous diamond has been discovered somewhere. The second girl is born. Leeland can't seem to get along with the oil company dispatcher. After a year they move back to Unique. Leeland and his mother make up their differences.

Lori is good at saving money and she has put aside a small nest egg. They set up in business for themselves. Leeland believes people will be glad to trade at a local ranch supply store that saves a long drive into town. He rents the service station from Mrs. Egge who has not been able to sell it after Ed's death. They spruce it up, Leeland doing all the carpenter work, Lori painting the interior and exterior. On the side Leeland raises hogs with his father. His father was born and raised in Iowa and knows hogs.

It becomes clear that people relish the long drive to a bigger town where they can see something different, buy fancy groceries, clothing, bakery goods as well as ranch supplies. One intensely cold winter when everything freezes from God to gizzard, Leeland and his father lose 112 hogs. They sell out. Eighteen months later the ranch supply business goes under. The new color television set goes back to the store.

After the bankruptcy proceedings Leeland finds work on a road construction crew. He is always out of town, it seems, but back often enough for what he calls "a good ride" and so makes Lori pregnant again. Before the baby is born he quits the road crew. He can't seem to get along with the foreman. No one can, and turnover is high. On his truck radio he hears that hundreds of religious cult members have swallowed Kool-Aid and cyanide.

Leeland takes a job at Tongue River Meat Locker and Processing. Old Man Brose owns the business. Leeland is the only employee. He has an aptitude for sizing up and cutting large animals. He likes wrapping the tidy packages, the smell of damp bone and chill. He can throw his cleaver unerringly and when mice run along the wall they do not run far if Leeland is there. After months of discussion with Old Man Brose, Leeland and Lori sign a ten-year lease on the meat locker operation. Their oldest boy graduates from high school, the first in the family to do so, and joins the army. He signs up for six years. There is something on the news about school lunches and ketchup is classed as a vegetable. Old Man Brose moves to Albuquerque.

The economy takes a dive. The news is full of talk about recession and unemployment. Thrifty owners of small ranches go back to doing their own butchering, cutting and freezing. The meat locker lease payments are high and electricity jumps up. Leeland and Lori have to give up the business. Old man Brose returns from Albuquerque. There are bad feelings. It didn't work out, Leeland says, and that's the truth of it.

It seems like a good time to try another place. The family moves to Thermopolis where Leeland finds a temporary job at a local meat locker during hunting season. A hunter from Des Moines, not far from where Leeland's father was born, tips him $100 when he loads packages of frozen elk and the elk's head onto the man's single-engine plane. The man has been drinking. The plane goes down in the Medicine Bow range to the southeast.

During this long winter Leeland is out of work and stays home with the baby. Lori works in the school cafeteria. The baby is a real crier and Leeland quiets him down with spoonsful of beer.

In the spring they move back to Unique and Leeland tries truck driving again, this time in long-distance rigs on coast-to-coast journeys that take him away two and three months at a time. He travels all over the continent, to Texas, Alaska, Montreal and Corpus Christi. He says every place is the same. Lori works now in the kitchen of the Hi-Lo Café in Unique. The ownership of the café changes three times in two years. West Klinker, an elderly rancher, eats three meals a day at the Hi-Lo. He is sweet on Lori. He reads her an article from the newspaper—a strange hole has appeared in the ozone layer. He confuses ozone with oxygen.

One night while Leeland is somewhere on the east coast the baby goes into convulsions following a week's illness of fever and cough. Lori makes a frightening drive over icy roads to the distant hospital. The baby survives but he is slow. Lori starts a medical emergency response group in Unique. Three women and two men sign up to take the first aid course. They drive a hundred miles to the first aid classes. Only two of them pass the test on the first try. Lori is one of the two. The other is Stuttering Bob, an old bachelor. One of the failed students says Stuttering Bob has nothing to do but study the first aid manual as he enjoys the leisured life that goes with a monthly social security check.

Leeland quits driving trucks and again tries raising hogs with his father on the old ranch. He becomes a volunteer fireman and is at the bad February fire that kills two children. It takes the fire truck three hours to get in to the ranch through the wind-drifted snow. The family is related to Lori. When something inside explodes, Leeland tells, an object flies out of the house and strikes the fire engine hood. It is a Nintendo player and not even charred.

Stuttering Bob has cousins in Muncie, Indiana. One of the cousins works at the Muncie Medical Center. The cousin arranges for the Medical Center to donate an old ambulance to the Unique Rescue Squad although they had intended to give it to a group in Mississippi. Bob's cousin, who has been to Unique, persuades them. Bob is afraid to drive through congested cities so Leeland and Lori take a series of buses to Muncie to pick up the vehicle. It is their first vacation. They take the youngest boy with them. On the return trip Lori leaves her purse on a chair in a restaurant. The gas money for the return trip is in the purse. They go back to the restaurant, wild with anxiety. The purse has been turned in and nothing is missing. Lori and Leeland talk about the goodness of people, even strangers. In their absence Stuttering Bob is elected president of the rescue squad.

A husband and wife from California move to Unique and open a taxidermy business. They say they are artists and arrange the animals in unusual poses. Lori gets work cleaning their workshop. The locals make jokes about the coyote in their window, posed lifting a leg against sage-brush where a trap is set. The taxidermists hold out for almost two years, then move to Oregon. Leeland's and Lori's oldest son telephones from overseas. He is making a career of the service.

Leeland's father dies and they discover the hog business is deeply in debt, the ranch twice-mortgaged. The ranch is sold to pay off debts. Leeland's mother moves in with them. Leeland continues long-distance truck driving. His mother watches television all day. Sometimes she sits in

Lori's kitchen, saying almost nothing, picking small stones from dried beans.

The youngest daughter baby-sits. One night, on the way home, her employer feels her small breasts and asks her to squeeze his penis, because, he says, she ate the piece of chocolate cake he was saving. She does it but runs crying into the house and tells Lori who advises her to keep quiet and stay home from now on. The man is Leeland's friend; they hunt elk and antelope together.

Leeland quits truck driving. Lori has saved a little money. Once more they decide to go into business for themselves. They lease the old gas station where Leeland had his first job and where they tried the ranch supply store. Now it is a gas station again, but also a convenience store. They try surefire gimmicks: plastic come-on banners that pop and tear in the wind, free ice cream cones with every fill-up, prize drawings. Leeland has been thinking of the glory days when a hundred cars stopped. Now highway 16 seems the emptiest road in the country. They hold on for a year, then Leeland admits that it hasn't worked out and he is right. He is depressed for days when San Francisco beats Denver in the Super Bowl.

Their oldest boy is discharged from the service and will not say why but Leeland knows it is chemical substances, drugs. Leeland is driving long-distance trucks again despite his back pain. The oldest son is home, working as a ranch hand in Pie. Leeland studies him, looking for signs of addiction. The son's eyes are always red and streaming.

The worst year comes. Leeland's mother dies, Leeland hurts his back, and, in the same week, Lori learns that she has breast cancer and is pregnant again. She is forty-six. Lori's doctor advises an abortion. Lori refuses.

The oldest son is discovered to have an allergy to horses and quits the ranch job. He tells Leeland he wants to try raising hogs. Pork prices are high. For a few days Leeland is excited. He can see it clearly: Leeland Lee & Son, Livestock. But the son changes his mind when a friend he knew in the service comes by on a motorcycle. The next morning both of them leave for Phoenix.

Lori spontaneously aborts in the fifth month of the pregnancy and then the cancer burns her up. Leeland is at the hospital with her every day. Lori dies. The daughters, both married now, curse Leeland. No one knows how to reach the oldest son and he misses the funeral. The youngest boy cries inconsolably. They decide he will live in Billings, Montana, with the oldest sister who is expecting her first child.

Two springs after Lori's death a middle-aged woman from Ohio buys the café, paints it orange, renames it Unique Eats and hires Leeland to cook. He is good with meat, knows how to choose the best cuts and grill or do them chicken-fried style to perfection. He has never cooked anything at home and everyone is surprised at this long-hidden skill. The oldest son comes back and next year they plan to lease the old gas station and convert it to a motorcycle repair shop and steak house. Nobody has time to listen to the news.

The Blood Bay

For Buzzy Malli

THE WINTER OF 1886–87 WAS TERRIBLE. EVERY goddamn history of the high plains says so. There were great stocks of cattle on overgrazed land during the droughty summer. Early wet snow froze hard so the cattle could not break through the crust to the grass. Blizzards and freeze-eye cold followed, the gaunt bodies of cattle piling up in draws and coulees.

A young Montana cowboy, somewhat vain, had skimped on coat and mittens and put all his wages into a fine pair of handmade boots. He crossed into Wyoming Territory thinking it would be warmer, for it was south of where he was. That night he froze to death on Powder River's bitter west bank, that stream of famous dimensions and direction—an inch deep, a mile wide and she flows uphill from Texas.

The next afternoon three cowpunchers from the Box Spring outfit near Suggs rode past his corpse, blue as a whetstone and half-buried in snow. They were savvy and salty. They wore blanket coats, woolly chaps, grease-wool scarves tied over their hats and under their bristled chins, sheepskin mitts and two of them were fortunate enough to park their feet in good boots and heavy socks. The third, Dirt Sheets, a cross-eyed drinker of hair-oil, was all right on top but his luck was running muddy near the bottom, no socks and curl-toe boots cracked and holed.

"That can a corn beef's wearin my size boots," Sheets said and got off his horse for the first time that day. He pulled at the Montana cowboy's left boot but it was frozen on. The right one didn't come off any easier.

"Son of a sick steer in a snowbank," he said, "I'll cut em off and thaw em after supper." Sheets pulled out a Bowie knife and sawed through Montana's shins just above the boot tops, put the booted feet in his saddlebags, admiring the tooled leather and topstitched hearts and clubs. They rode on down the river looking for strays, found a dozen bogged in deep drifts and lost most of the daylight getting them out.

"Too late to try for the bunkhouse. Old man Grice's shack is somewheres up along. He's bound a have dried prunes or other dainties or at least a hot stove." The temperature was dropping, so cold that spit crackled in the air and a man didn't dare to piss for fear he'd be rooted fast until spring. They agreed it must be forty below and more, the wind scything up a nice Wyoming howler.

They found the shack four miles north. Old man Grice opened the door a crack.

"Come on in, puncher or rustler, I don't care."

"We'll put our horses up. Where's the barn."

"Barn. Never had one. There's a lean-to out there behind the woodpile should keep em from blowin away or maybe freezin. I got my two horses in here beside the dish cupboard. I pamper them babies somethin terrible. Sleep where you can find a space, but I'm tellin you don't bother that blood bay none, he will mull you up and spit you out. He's a spirited steed. Pull up a chair and have some a this son-of-a-bitch stew. And I got plenty conversation juice a wash it down. Hot biscuits just comin out a the oven."

It was a fine evening, eating, drinking and playing cards, swapping lies, the stove kicking out heat, old man Grice's spoiled horses sighing in comfort. The only disagreeable tone to the evening from the waddies' point of view was the fact that their host cleaned them out, took them for three dollars and four bits. Around midnight Grice blew out the lamp and got in his bunk and the three punchers stretched out on the floor. Sheets set his trophies behind the stove, laid his head on his saddle and went to sleep.

He woke half an hour before daylight, recalled it was his mother's birthday and if he wanted to telegraph a filial sentiment to her he would have to ride faster than chain lightning with the links snapped, for the Overland office closed at noon. He checked his grisly trophies, found them thawed and pulled the boots and socks off the originals, drew them onto his own pedal extremities. He threw the bare Montana feet and his old boots in the corner near the dish cupboard, slipped out like a falling feather, saddled his horse and rode away. The wind was low and the fine cold air refreshed him.

Old man Grice was up with the sun grinding coffee beans and frying bacon. He glanced down at his rolled-up guests and said, "Coffee's ready." The blood bay stamped and kicked at something that looked like a man's foot. Old man Grice took a closer look.

"There's a bad start to the day," he said, "it is a man's foot and there's the other." He counted the sleeping guests. There were only two of them.

"Wake up, survivors, for god's sake wake up and get up."

The two punchers rolled out, stared wild-eyed at the old man who was fairly frothing, pointing at the feet on the floor behind the blood bay.

"He's ate Sheets. Ah, I knew he was a hard horse, but to eat a man whole. You savage bugger," he screamed at the blood bay and drove him out into the scorching cold. "You'll never eat human meat again. You'll sleep out with the blizzards and wolves, you hell-bound fiend." Secretly he was pleased to own a horse with the sand to eat a raw cowboy.

The leftover Box Spring riders were up and drinking coffee. They squinted at old man Grice, hitched at their gun belts.

"Ah, boys, for god's sake, it was a terrible accident. I didn't know what a brute of a animal was that blood bay. Let's keep this to ourselves. Sheets was no prize and I've got forty gold dollars says so and the three and four bits I took off a you last night. Eat your bacon, don't make no trouble. There's enough trouble in the world without no more."

No, they wouldn't make trouble and they put the heavy money in their saddlebags, drank a last cup of hot coffee, saddled up and rode out into the grinning morning.

When they saw Sheets that night at the bunkhouse they nodded, congratulated him on his mother's birthday but said nothing about blood bays or forty-three dollars and four bits. The arithmetic stood comfortable.

People in Hell
Just Want a Drink of Water

YOU STAND THERE, BRACED. CLOUD SHADOWS race over the buff rock stacks as a projected film, casting a queasy, mottled ground rash. The air hisses and it is no local breeze but the great harsh sweep of wind from the turning of the earth. The wild country—indigo jags of mountain, grassy plain everlasting, tumbled stones like fallen cities, the flaring roll of sky—provokes a spiritual shudder. It is like a deep note that cannot be heard but is felt, it is like a claw in the gut.

Dangerous and indifferent ground: against its fixed mass the tragedies of people count for nothing although the signs of misadventure are everywhere. No past slaughter nor cruelty, no accident nor murder that occurs on the little ranches or at the isolate crossroads with their bare populations of three or seventeen, or in the reckless trailer courts of mining towns delays the flood of morning light. Fences, cattle, roads, refineries, mines, gravel pits, traffic lights, graffiti'd celebration of athletic victory on bridge overpass, crust of blood on the Wal-Mart loading dock, the sun-faded wreaths of plastic flowers marking death on the highway are ephemeral. Other cultures have camped here a while and disappeared. Only earth and sky matter. Only the endlessly repeated flood of morning light. You begin to see that God does not owe us much beyond that.

In 1908, on the run from Texas drought and dusters, Isaac "Ice" Dunmire arrived in Laramie, Wyoming, at three-thirty in the dark February morning. It was thirty-four degrees below zero, the wind shrieking along the tracks.

"It sure can't get more worse than this," he said. He didn't know anything about it.

Although he had a wife, Naomi, and five sons back in Burnet County, for the sake of a job punching cows he swore to the manager of the Six Pigpen Ranch that he was single. The big spread was owned by two Scots brothers who had never seen the #6 and never wished to, any more than the owner of a slave ship wanted to look over the cargo.

At the end of a year, because he never went into town, saved his forty-dollar-a-month wages and was an indefatigable killer of bounty wolves, because he won at Red Dog more often than he lost, Ice Dunmire had four hundred dollars in a blue tin box painted with the image of a pigtailed sailor cutting a curl of tobacco from a golden plug. It wasn't enough. The second spring in the country he quit the #6 and went into the Tetons to kill wapiti elk for their big canine teeth, bought for big money by members of the B.P.O.E. who dangled the ivory from their watch chains.

Now he staked a homestead claim on the Laramie plain south of the Big Hollow, a long, wind-gouged depression below the Snowy Range of the Medicine Bows, put up a sod shanty, registered the Rocking Box brand. The boundary didn't signify—what he saw was the beautiful, deep land and he saw it his, aimed to get as much of it as he could. He bought and stole half a hundred cows, and with pride in this three-up outfit, declared himself a rancher. He sent for the wife and kids, filed on an adjoining quarter section in Naomi's name. His sudden passage from bachelor to family man with five little hen-wranglers, from broke cowpuncher to property-owning rancher, earned him the nickname of "Tricker" which some uneasily misheard as "Trigger."

What the wife thought when she saw the sod hut, ten by fourteen, roofed with planks and more dirt thrown on top, one window and a warped door, can be guessed at but not known. There were two pole beds with belly wool mattresses. The five boys slept in one and in the other Ice quickly begot on Naomi another and another kid as fast as the woman could stand to make them. Jaxon's most vivid memory of her was watching her pour boiling water on the rattlesnakes he and his brothers caught with loops of barbwire, smiling to see them writhe. By 1913, ridden hard and put away dirty, looking for relief, she went off with a cook-pan tinker and left Ice the nine boys—Jaxon, the twins Ideal and Pet, Kemmy, Marion, Byron, Varn, Ritter and Bliss. They all lived except Byron who was bitten by a mosquito and died of encephalitis. Boys were money in the bank in that country and Ice brought them up to fill his labor needs. They got ropes for Christmas, a handshake each birthday and damn a cake.

What they learned was livestock and ranchwork. When they were still young buttons they could sleep out alone on the plain, knees raftered up in the rain, tarp drawn over their heads listening to the water trickle past their ears. In the autumn, after fall roundup, they went up on Jelm Mountain and hunted, not for sport but for meat. They grew into bone-seasoned, tireless workers accustomed to discomfort, took their pleasure in drink, cigarettes, getting work done. They were brass-nutted boys, sinewy and tall, nothing they liked better than to kick the frost out of a horse in early morning.

"Sink them shittin spurs into his lungs, boy!" screamed Ice at a kid on a snorty bronc. "Be a man."

Their endurance of pain was legendary. When a section of narrow mountain trail broke away under Marion's horse, the horse falling with him onto rocks below, the animal's back broken and Marion's left leg, he shot the horse, splinted his own leg with some yucca stalks and his wild rag, whittled a crutch from the limb he shot off a scrub cedar, and in three days hopped twenty miles to the Shiverses' place, asked for a drink of water, swallowed it, pivoted on the cedar crutch, and began to hop toward the home ranch, another seven miles east, before George Shivers cajoled him into a wagon. Shivers saw then what he missed before—Marion had carried his heavy stock saddle the distance.

Jaxon, the oldest, was a top bronc buster but torn up so badly inside by the age of twenty-eight his underwear were often stained with blood; he had to switch to easy horses broke by other men. After a loose-end time he took over the daily operations of the Rocking Box and kept the books, stud records, but in summers turned all that back to his father while he ran as a salesman for Morning Glory windmills, bumping over the country in a Ford truck to ranches, fairs and rodeos. There was a hard need for cash. The Rocking Box had a hard need for cash.

The jolting was enough that he said he might as well be riding broncs. He bought himself a plaid suit, then a roadster, hitched a rubber-tired trailer to the rear bumper. In the trailer bed he bolted a sample-sized Morning Glory windmill supplied by the company. The blades turned showily as he drove. He carried sidelines of pump rod springs, regulators and an assortment of Cowboy's Pal DeLuxe Calendars which featured campfires and saccharine verses or candy-tinted girlies kneeling on Indian blankets. The Morning Glory was a steel-tower, back-geared pumping mill. The blades were painted bright blue and a scallop-tailed vane sheet carried the message NEVER SORRY—MORNING GLORY.

"I got a advantage over those bums got nothin but the pictures and the catalogs. I show em the real thing—that main shaft goin through the roller bearins to the double-pinion gear. You can't show that in a picture, how them teeth mesh in with the big crank gears. The roller bearins are what makes it bite the biscuit. Then some old guy don't want a windmill he'll sure want a couple calendars. Small but it adds up."

He kept his say in ranch affairs—he'd earned the right.

Pet and Kemmy married and set up off the Rocking Box but the others stayed at home and single, finding ceaseless work and an occasional group visit to a Laramie whorehouse enough. Jaxon did not go on these excursions, claiming he found plenty of what he needed on his travels to remote ranches.

"Some a them women can't hardly wait until I get out a the truck," he said. "They'll put their hand right on you soon's you open the door. Like our ma, I guess," he sneered.

111

By the droughty depression of the 1930s the Dunmires were in everything that happened, their opinions based on deep experience. They had seen it all: prairie fire, flood, blizzard, dust storm, injury, sliding beef prices, grasshopper and Mormon cricket plagues, rustlers, scours, bad horses. They ran off hobos and gypsies, and if Jaxon whistled "Shuffle Off to Buffalo," in a month everybody was whistling that tune. The country, its horses and cattle, suited them and if they loved anything that was it, and they ran that country because there were eight of them and Ice and they were of one mind. But there builds up in men who work livestock in big territory a kind of contempt for those who do not. The Dunmires measured beauty and religion by what they rode through every day, and this encouraged their disdain for art and intellect. There was a somber arrogance about them, a rigidity of attitude that said theirs was the only way.

The Tinsleys were a different kind. Horm Tinsley had come up from St. Louis with the expectation of quick success. He often said that anything could happen, but the truth of that was bitter. He was lanky and inattentive, early on bitten by a rattlesnake while setting fence posts, and two months later bitten again at the same chore. On the rich Laramie plain he ended up with a patch of poor land just east of the rain, dry and sandy range with sparse grass, and he could not seem to get ahead, trying horses, cattle, sheep in succession. Every change of season took him by surprise. Although he could tell snow from sunshine he wasn't much at reading weather. He took an interest in his spread but it was skewed to a taste for a noble rock or other trifling scenic vantage.

His failure as a stockman was recognized, yet he was tolerated and even liked for his kindly manner and skill playing the banjo and the fiddle, though most regarded him with contemptuous pity for his loose control of home affairs and his coddling of a crazy wife after her impetuous crime.

Mrs. Tinsley, intensely modest, sensitive and abhorring marital nakedness, suffered from nerves; she was distracted and fretted by shrill sounds as the screech of a chair leg scraping the floor or the pulling of a nail. As a girl in Missouri she had written a poem that began with the line "*Our life is a beautiful Fairy Land.*" Now she was mother to three. When the youngest girl, Mabel, was a few months old they made a journey into Laramie, the infant howling intolerably, the wagon bungling along, stones sliding beneath the wheels. As they crossed the Little Laramie Mrs. Tinsley stood up and hurled the crying infant into the water. The child's white dress filled with air and it floated a few yards in the swift current, then disappeared beneath a bower of willows at the bend. The woman shrieked and made to leap after the child but Horm Tinsley held her back. They galloped across the bridge and to the river's edge below the bend. Gone and gone.

As if to make up for her fit of destruction Mrs. Tinsley developed an intense anxiety for the safety of the surviving children, tying them to chairs in the kitchen lest they wander outside and come to harm, sending them to bed while the sun was still high for twilight was a dangerous time, warning them away from haystacks threaded with vipers, from trampling horses and biting dogs, the yellow

Wyandottes who pecked, from the sound of thunder and the sight of lightning. In the night she came to their beds many times to learn if they had smothered.

By the time he was twelve the boy, Rasmussen, potato-nosed, with coarse brown hair and yellow eyes, displayed a kind of awkward zaniness. He was smart with numbers, read books. He asked complicated questions no one could answer—the distance to the sun, why did not humans have snouts, could a traveler reach China by setting out in any direction and holding steady to it? Trains were his particular interest and he knew about rail connections from study of the timetables, pestered travelers at the station to hear something of distant cities. He was indifferent to stock except for his flea-bitten grey, Bucky, and he threw the weight of his mind in random directions as if the practical problems of life were not to be resolved but teased as a kitten is by a broom straw.

When he was fifteen his interest turned to the distant sea and he yearned for books about ships, books with pictures, and there were none. On paper he invented boats like inverted roofs, imagined the ocean a constant smooth and glassy medium until Mrs. Hepple of Laramie spoke at an evening about her trip abroad, describing the voyage as a purgatory of monstrous waves and terrible winds. Another time a man worked for them five or six months. He had been in San Francisco and told about lively streets, Chinese tong wars, sailors and woodsmen blowing their wages in a single puking night. He described Chicago, a smoking mass shrugging out of the plains, fouling the air a hundred miles east. He said Lake Superior licked the wild shore of Canada.

★

There was no holding Ras. At sixteen this rank gangler left home, headed for San Francisco, Seattle, Toronto, Boston, Cincinnati. What his expectations and experiences were no one knew. He neither returned nor wrote.

The daughter, neglected as daughters are, married a cowboy with bad habits and moved with him to Baggs. Horm Tinsley gave up on sheep and started a truck garden and honey operation, specializing in canning tomatoes, in Moon and Stars watermelons. After a year or so he sold Ras's horse to the Klickas on the neighboring ranch.

In 1933 the son had been gone more than five years and not a word.

The mother begged of the curtains, "Why don't he write?" and saw again the infant in the water, silent, the swollen dress buoying it around the dark bend. Who would write to such a mother?—and she was up in the night and to the kitchen to scrub the ceiling, the table legs, the soles of her husband's boots, rubbing the old meat grinder with a banana skin to bring up the silvery bloom. A murderer she might be but no one could say her house wasn't clean.

Jaxon Dunmire was ready to get back on the road with his Morning Glory pitch and bluster. They'd finished building a new round corral, branding was over, what there was to brand, forget haying—in the scorched fields the hay hadn't made. What in another place might have been a froth of white flowers here was alkali dust blooming in the wind, and a dark horizon not rain but another

115

choking storm of dust or rising cloud of grasshoppers. Ice said he could feel there was worse to come. To save the ranchers the government was buying up cattle for nickels and dimes.

Jaxon lounged against a stall watching shaggy-headed Bliss who bent over a brood mare's hoof, examining a sand crack.

"Last year down by Lingle I seen Mormon crickets eat a live prairie dog," Jaxon said. "In about ten minutes."

"God," said Bliss, who had not tasted candy until he was fourteen and then spat it out, saying, too much taste. He enjoyed Jaxon's stories, thought he might like to be a windmill man himself sometime, or at least travel around a few weeks with Jaxon. "Got a little crack startin here."

"Catch it now, save the horse. We still got half a jar a that hoof dressin. Yeah, see and hear a lot a strange things. Clayt Blay told me that around twenty years ago he run into these two fellers in Laramie. They told him they found a diamond mine up in the Sierra Madres, and then, says Clayt, both a them come down with the whoopin pox and died. Found their bodies in the fall, rotted into the cabin floor. But a *course* they'd told Clayt where their dig was before they croaked."

"You didn't fall for it." Bliss began to cut a pattern into the hoof above the crack to contain it.

"Naw, not likely anything Clayt Blay says would cause me to fire up." He rolled a cigarette but did not light it.

Bliss shot a glance into the yard. "What the hell is that stuff on your skunk wagon?"

"Aw, somebody's threwn flour or plaster on it in Rock Springs. Bastards. Ever time I go into Rock Springs they do me some mess. People's in a bad mood—and nobody got money for a goddamn windmill. You ought a see the homemade rigs they're bangin together. This one guy builds somethin from part of a old pump, balin wire, a corn sheller and some tie-rods. Cost him two dollars. And the son of a bitch worked great. How can I make it against that?"

"Oh lord," said Bliss, finishing with the mare. "I'm done here, I'll warsh that stuff off a your rig."

As he straightened up Jaxon tossed him the sack of tobacco. "There you go, brother boy. And I find the good shears I'll cut your lousy hair. Then I got a go."

A letter came to the Tinsleys from Schenectady, New York. The man who wrote it, a Methodist minister, said that a young man severely injured a year earlier in an auto wreck, mute and damaged since that time, had somewhat regained the power of communication and identified himself as their son, Rasmussen Tinsley.

No one expected him to live, wrote the minister, *and it is a testament to God's goodness that he has survived. I am assured that the conductor will help him make the train change in Chicago. His fare has been paid by a church collection. He will arrive in Laramie on the afternoon train March 17.*

The afternoon light was the sour color of lemon juice. Mrs. Tinsley, her head a wonderful frozen confection of curls, stood on the platform watching the passengers get down. The father wore a clean, starched shirt. Their son emerged, leaning on a cane. The conductor handed down a valise. They knew it was Ras but how could they know him? He was a monster. The left side of his face and head had been damaged and torn, had healed in a mass of crimson scars. There was a whistling hole in his throat and a scarred left eye socket. His jaw was deformed. Multiple breaks of one leg had healed badly and he lurched and dragged. Both hands seemed maimed, frozen joints and lopped fingers. He could not speak beyond a raw choke only the devil could understand.

Mrs. Tinsley looked away. Her fault through the osmosis of guilt.

The father stepped forward tentatively. The injured man lowered his head. Mrs. Tinsley was already climbing back into the Ford. She opened and closed the door twice, catching sudden sunlight. Half a mile away on a stony slope small rain had fallen and the wet boulders glinted like tin pie pans.

"Ras." The father put out his hand and touched the thin arm of his son. Ras pulled back.

"Come on, Ras. We'll take you home and build you up. Mother's made fried chicken," but looked at the warped mouth, sunken from lost teeth, and wondered if Ras could chew anything.

He could. He ate constantly, the teeth on the good side of his mouth gnashing through meats and relishes and cakes. In cooking, Mrs. Tinsley found some relief. Ras no longer tried to say anything after the failure at the train station but sometimes wrote a badly spelled note and handed it to his father.

I NED GIT OTE A WILE

And Horm would take him for a short ride in the truck. The tires weren't good. He never went far. Horm talked steadily during the drives, grasshoppers glancing off the windshield. Ras was silent. There was no way to tell how much he understood. There had been damage, that was clear enough. But when the father signaled for the turn that would take them back home Ras pulled at his sleeve, made a guttural negative. He was getting his strength back. His shoulders were heavier. And he could lift with the crooked arms. But what did he think now of distant cities and ships at sea, he bound to the kitchen and the porch?

He couldn't keep dropping everything to take Ras for a ride. Every day now the boy was writing the same message: I NED GIT OTE A WILE. It was spring, hot, tangled with bobolink and meadowlark song. Ras was not yet twenty-five.

"Well, son, I need a get some work done today. I got plants a set out. Weedin. Can't go truckin around." He wondered if Ras was strong enough to ride. He thought of old Bucky, fourteen years old now but still in good shape. He had seen him in Klicka's pasture the month gone. He thought the boy could ride. It would do him good to ride the plain. It would do them all good.

Late in the morning he stopped at Klicka's place.

"You know Ras come back in pretty bad shape in March. He's gainin but he needs to get out some and I can't be takin him twice a day. Wonder if you'd give some thought to selling old Bucky back to me again. At least the boy could get out on his own. It's a horse I'd trust him with."

He tied the horse to the bumper and led it home. Ras was on the porch bench drinking cloudy water. He stood up when he saw the horse.

"Ucka," he said forcefully.

"That's right. It's Bucky. Good old Bucky." He talked to Ras as though he was a young child. Who could tell how much he understood? When he sat silent and unmoving was he thinking of the dark breath under the trees or the car bucking off the road, metal screaming and the world tipped over? Or was there only a grainy field of dim images? "Think you can ride him?"

He could manage. It was a godsend. Horm had to saddle the horse for him, but Ras was up and out after breakfast, rode for hours. They could see him on the prairie against the sharp green, a distant sullen cloud dispensing lean bolts. But dread swelled in Mrs. Tinsley, the fear that she must now see a riderless horse, saddled, reins slack.

The second week after the horse's return Ras was out the entire day, came in dirty and exhausted.

"Where did you go, son?" asked Horm, but Ras gobbled potato and shot sly glances at them from the good eye.

So Horm knew he had been up to something.

Within a month Ras was out all day and all night, then away for two or three days, god knows where, elusive, slipping behind rocks, galloping long miles on the dry, dusty grass, sleeping in willows and nests of weeds, a half-wild man with no talk and who knew what thoughts.

The Tinsleys began to hear a few things. Ras had appeared on the Hanson place. Hanson's girls were out hanging clothes and suddenly Ras was there on the grey horse, his hat pulled low, saying garbled things, and then as quickly gone.

The party line rang four short times, their ring, and when Mrs. Tinsley answered a man's voice said, keep that goddamn idiot to home. But Ras was gone six days and before he returned the sheriff came by in a new black Chevrolet with a star painted white on the side and said Ras had showed himself to a rancher's wife way the hell down in Tie Siding, forty miles away.

"He didn't have nothin she hadn't see before, but she didn't preciate the show and neither did her old man. Unless you want your boy locked up or hurt you better get him hobbled. He's got a awful face on him, ain't it?"

When Ras came home the next noon, gaunt and starving, Horm took the saddle and put it up in the parents' bedroom.

"I'm sorry, Ras, but you can't go around like you're doin. No more."

The next morning the horse was gone and so was Ras.

"He's rid him bareback." There was no keeping him at home. His circle was smaller but he was on the rove again.

In the Dunmires' noon kitchen a greasy leather sofa, worn as an old saddle, stood against the wall and on it lay Ice Dunmire, white hair ruffed, his mouth open in sleep. The plank table, twelve feet long and flanked by pants-polished benches, held a dough tray filled with forks and spoons. The iron sink tilted, a mildew smell rose from the wooden counter. The dish cupboard stood with the doors off, shelves stacked with heavy rim-nicked plates. The beehive radio on a wall shelf was never silent, bulging with static and wailing voices. A crank telephone hung beside the door. In a sideboard stood a forest of private bottles marked with initials and names.

Varn was at the oven bending for biscuits, dark and bandy-legged, Marion scraping milk gravy around and around the pan and jabbing a boil of halved potatoes. The coffeepot chucked its brown fountain into the glass dome of the lid.

"Dinner!" Varn shouted, dumping the biscuits into a bowl and taking a quick swallow from his little whiskey glass. "Dinner! Dinner! Dinner! Eat it or go hungry."

Ice stretched and got up, went to the door, coughed and spat.

They ate without talk, champing meat. There were no salads or vegetables beyond potatoes or sometimes cabbage.

Ice drank his coffee from the saucer as he always had. "Hear there was some excitement down Tie Sidin."

"Didn't take you long to hear it. Goddamn Tinsley kid that come back rode into Shawver's yard and jacked off in front a the girl. Matter a time until he discovers it's more fun a put it up the old snatch."

"Do somethin about that. Give me the relish," said Jaxon. "Sounds like nutty Mrs. T. drownded the wrong kid." He swirled a piece of meat in the relish. "God-damn, Varn, I am sure goin a miss this relish out on the road."

"Nothin a do with me. Buy yourself a jar—Billy Gill's Piccalilli. Get it at the store."

Around noon one day in the wide, burnt summer that stank of grasshoppers, Mrs. Tinsley heard the measured beating of a truck motor in the yard. She looked out. A roadster with a miniature windmill mounted in the trailer behind it stood outside, the exhaust from the tailpipe raising a little dust. There was a mash of hoppers in the tire treads, scores more in various stages of existence clogging the radiator grille.

"The windmill man is out there," she said. Horm turned around slowly. He was just getting over a cold and had a headache from the dust.

Outside Jaxon Dunmire in his brown plaid suit came at him with a smile. His dust still floated over the road. A grasshopper leaped from his leg.

"Mr. Tinsley? Howdy. Jax Dunmire. Meaning a come out here for two years and persuade you about the Mornin Glory windmill. Probably the best equipment on the market and the mill that's saving the rancher's bacon these damn dustbowl days. Yeah, I been meanin a get out here, but I been so damn busy at the ranch and then runnin up and down the state summers sellin these good mills I don't get around the home territory much." The smile lay over his face as if it had been screwed on. "My dad and my brothers and me, we got five a these Mornin Glories on the Rockin Box. Water the stock all over, they don't lose weight walkin for a drink."

"I don't do no ranchin. Pretty well out a the sheep business, never did run cattle much. I just do some truck gardenin, bees. Plan a get a pair a blue foxes next year, raise them, maybe. We got the well. We got the crick close. So I guess I don't need a windmill."

"Cricks and wells been known a run dry. This damn everlastin drought it's a sure thing. More uses to a mill than waterin stock. Run you some electricity. Put in a resevoy tank. That's awful nice to have, fire protection, fish a little. You and the missis take a swim. But fire protection's the main thing. You can't tell when your house is goin a catch fire. Why I seen it so dry the wind rubbin the grass blades together can start a prairie fire."

"I don't know. I doubt I could stand the expense. Windmills are awful expensive for somebody in my position. Hell, I can't even afford new tires. And those I need. Expensive."

"Well, sure enough, that's true. Some things are real expensive. Agree with you on that. But the Mornin Glory ain't." Jaxon Dunmire rolled a cigarette, offered it to Horm.

"I never did smoke them coffin nails." There was a ball of dust at the turnoff a quarter mile away. Windmills, hell, thought Horm. He must have passed the boy on the road.

Dunmire smoked, looked over the yard, nodding his head.

"Yes, a little resevoy would set good here."

Old Bucky rounded the corner, pounded in, lathered and tired and on him Ras, abareback, distorted face and glaring eye, past the windmill truck close enough for dirt to spatter the side.

"Well, what in the world was that," said Jaxon Dunmire, dropping the wet-ended butt in the dust and working the toe of his boot over it.

"That is Ras, that is my son."

"Packin the mail. Thought it might be that crazy half-wit got the women all terrorized wavin his deedle-dee at them. You hear about that? Who knows when he's goin a get a little girl down and do her harm? There's some around who'd as soon cut him and make sure he don't breed no more half-wits, calm him down some."

"That's your goddamn windmill, ain't it? It's Ras. Tell you, he was in a bad car wreck. There's no harm in him but he was real bad hurt."

"Well, I understand that. Sorry about it. But it seems like there's a part a him that ain't hurt, don't it, he's so eager a show it off."

"Why don't you get your goddamn windmill out a my yard?" said Horm Tinsley. "He was hurt but he's a man like anybody else." Now they had this son of a bitch and his seven brothers on their backs.

"Yeah, I'll get goin. You heard about all I got say. You just remember, I sell windmills but I ain't full a what makes em go."

Out in the corral Ras was swiping at old Bucky with a brush, the horse sucking up water. A firm man would have taken the horse from him. But Horm Tinsley hesitated. The only pleasure the boy had in life was riding out. He would talk to him in a day or so, make him understand. A quick hailstorm damaged some young melons and he was busy culling them for a few days, then the parched tomatoes took everything he had hauling water from the creek, down to a trickle. The well was almost out. The first melons were ready to slip the vine when the coyotes came after the fruit and he had to sleep in the patch. At last the melons—bitter and small—were picked, the tomatoes began to ripen and the need for water slacked. It was late summer, sere, sun-scalded yellow.

Ras sat hunched over in the rocking chair on the porch. For once he was home. The boy looked wretched, hair matted, hands and arms dirty.

"Ras, I need a talk to you. Now you pay attention.

125

You can't go doin like you been doin. You can't show yourself to the girls. I know, Ras, you're a young man and the juice is in you, but you can't do like you been doin. Now don't you give up hope, we might find a girl'd marry you if we was to look. I don't know, we ain't looked. But what you're up to, you're scarin them. And them cowboys, them Dunmires'll hurt you. They got the word out they'll cut you if you don't quit pesterin the girls. You understand what I mean? You understand what I'm sayin to you when I say cut?"

It was disconcerting. Ras shot him a sly look with his good eye and began to laugh, a ghastly croaking Horm had not heard before. He thought it was a laugh but did not catch the cause of it.

He spoke straight to his wife in the dark that night, not sparing her feminine sensibilities.

"I don't know if he got a thing I said. I don't think he did. He laughed his head off. Christ, I wish there was some way a tell what goes on in his mind. Could a been a bug walkin on my shirt got him goin. Poor boy, he's got the masculine urges and can't do nothin about it."

There was a silence and she whispered, barely audible, "You could take him down a Laramie. At night. Them houses." In the dark her face blazed.

"Why, no," he said, shocked. "I couldn't do no such thing."

The following day it seemed to him Ras might have understood some of it for he did not go out but sat in the kitchen with a plate of bread and jam before him, barely moving. Mrs. Tinsley put her hand gingerly to the hot forehead.

"You've taken a fever," she said, and pointed him up to his bed. He stumbled on the stairs, coughing.

"He's got that summer cold you had," she said to Horm. "I suppose I'll be down with it next."

Ras lay in the bed, Mrs. Tinsley sponging his scarred and awful face, his hands and arms. At the end of two days the fever had not broken. He no longer coughed but groaned.

"If only he could get some relief," said Mrs. Tinsley. "I keep thinkin it might help the fever break if he was to have a sponge bath, then wipe him over with alcohol. Cool him off. This heat, all twisted in them sheets. I just hate a summer cold. I think it would make him feel better. Them dirty clothes he's still got on. He's full a the smell of sickness and he was dirty a start with when he come down with it. He's just burnin up. Won't you get his clothes off and give the boy a sponge bath?" she said with delicacy. "It's best a man does that."

Horm Tinsley nodded. He knew Ras was sick but he did not think a sponge bath was going to make any difference. He understood his wife was saying the boy stank so badly she could no longer bear to come near him. She poured warm water in a basin, gave him the snowy wash-cloth, the scented soap and the new towel, never used.

He was in the sickroom a long time. When he came out he pitched the basin and the stained towel into the sink, sat at the table, put his head down and began to weep, *hu hu hu*.

"What is it," she said. "He's worse, that's it. What is it?"

"My god, no wonder he laughed in my face. They already done it. They done it to him and used a dirty knife. He's black with the gangrene. It's all down his groin, his leg's swole to the foot—" He leaned forward, his face inches from hers, glared into her eyes. "You! Why didn't you look him over when you put him to that bed?"

The morning light flooded the rim of the world, poured through the window glass, colored the wall and floor, laid its yellow blanket on the reeking bed, the kitchen table and the cups of cold coffee. There was no cloud in the sky. Grasshoppers hit against the east wall in their black and yellow thousands.

That was all sixty years ago and more. Those hard days are finished. The Dunmires are gone from the country, their big ranch broken in those dry years. The Tinsleys are buried somewhere or other, and cattle range now where the Moon and Stars grew. We are in a new millennium and such desperate things no longer happen.

If you believe that you'll believe anything.

The Bunchgrass Edge
of the World

THE COUNTRY APPEARED AS EMPTY GROUND, BIG sagebrush, rabbitbrush, intricate sky, flocks of small birds like packs of cards thrown up in the air, and a faint track drifting toward the red-walled horizon. Graves were unmarked, fallen house timbers and corrals burned up in old campfires. Nothing much but weather and distance, the distance punctuated once in a while by ranch gates, and to the north the endless murmur and sunflash of semis rolling along the interstate.

In this vague region the Touheys ranched—old Red, ninety-six years young, his son Aladdin, Aladdin's wife, Wauneta, their boy, Tyler, object of Aladdin's hopes, the daughters, Shan and (the family embarrassment) Ottaline.

Old Red, born in Lusk in 1902, grew up in an orphan home, a cross-grained boy—wrists knobby and prominent, red hair parted in the middle—and walked off when he was fourteen to work in a tie-hack camp. The year the First World War ended he was in Medicine Bow timber. He quit, headed away from the drought burning the west, drilled wells, prodded cattle in railroad stockyards, pasted up handbills, cobbled a life as though hammering two-bys. In 1930 he was in New York, shoveling the Waldorf-Astoria off the side of a barge into the Atlantic Ocean.

One salty morning, homesick for hard, dry landscape, he turned west again. He found a wife along the way and soon enough had a few dirty kids to feed. In Depression Oklahoma he bombed roosting crows and sold them to restaurants. When crows went scarce, they moved to Wyoming, settled a hundred or two miles from where he'd started.

They leased a ranch in the Red Wall country—log house, straggle of corrals that from a distance resembled dropped sticks. The wind isolated them from the world. To step into that reeling torrent of air was to be forced back. The ranch was adrift on the high plain.

There was the idea of running a few sheep, his wife's idea. In five years they built the sheep up into a prime band. The Second World War held wool prices steady. They bought the ranch for back taxes.

In August of 1946 a green-shaded lamp from Sears Roebuck arrived the same day the wife bore their last child. She named the kid Aladdin.

Peace and thermoplastic resin yarns ruined the sheep market and they went to cattle. The wife, as though disgusted with this bovine veer, complained of nausea as they unloaded the first shipment of scrubby calves. She stayed sick three or four years, finally quit. Red was a hard driver and of the six children only Aladdin remained on the dusty ranch, the giant of the litter, stubborn and abusive, bound to have everything on the platter whether bare bones or beefsteak.

Aladdin came back from Vietnam, where he flew C-123 Bs, spraying defoliants. Now he showed a hard disposition, a taste for pressing on to the point of exhaustion, then going dreamy and stuporous for days. He married Wauneta Hipsag on a scorching May morning in Colorado, the bride's home state. A tornado funnel hung from a green cloud miles away. Wauneta's abundant hair was rolled in an old-fashioned French knot. The wedding guests were her parents and eleven brothers, who threw handfuls of wheat, no rice available. During the ceremony, Wauneta's father smoked cigarette after cigarette. That evening at the Touhey ranch a few kernels of wheat shot from Aladdin's pants cuffs when he somersaulted off the porch, exuberant and playful before his new wife. The grains fell to the ground and in the course of time sprouted, grew, headed out and reseeded. The wheat seized more ground each year until it covered a quarter-acre, the waving grain ardently protected by Wauneta. She said it was her wedding wheat and if ever cut the world would end.

When he was twenty-six Aladdin wrenched the say of how things should go from old Red. Aladdin had been in the mud since blue morning digging out a spring. The old man rode up on his one-eyed mare. The son slung a shovelful of wet dirt.

"You ain't got it dug out yet?" the old man asked. "Not too swift, are you? Not too smart. Shovel ain't even sharp, I bet. How you got a woman a marry you I don't know. You must a got a shotgun on her. Must a hypatized her. Not that she's much, but probably beats doin it with livestock, that right?" The mud-daubed son climbed out of the hole, picked up clods, pelted his father until he galloped off, pursued him to the house and continued the attack with stones and sticks of firewood snatched up from the woodpile, hurled the side-cutters he always carried in a back pocket, the pencil behind his ear, the round can filled not with tobacco but with the dark green of home-grown.

Red, knot-headed and bleeding, raised one arm in sur-render, backed onto the porch. He was seventy-one then and called out his age as a defense. "I made this ranch and I made you." His spotted hand went to his crotch. Aladdin gathered can, pencil and side-cutters, and put the old man's horse away. He went back to the spring, head down, picked up the shovel and dug until his hands went nerveless.

Wauneta moved old Red's belongings out of the big upstairs bedroom and into a ground-floor room off the kitchen, once a pantry and still smelling of raisins and stale flour. A strip of adhesive tape held the cracked window glass together.

"You'll be closer to the bathroom," she said in a voice as smooth as gas through a funnel.

Wauneta taught her two girls to carry pie on a white plate to their grandfather, kiss him goodnight, while Tyler played with plastic cows and stayed up late. One forenoon she came in from hanging clothes and found four-year-old Ottaline gripped astraddle over old Red's lap and squirm-ing to get down. She ripped the child from him, said, "You keep your dirty old prong away from my girls or I'll pour boilin water on it."

"What? I wasn't—" he said. "Not—never did—"

"I know old men," she said.

"Potty!" screamed Ottaline, too late.

Now she warned the daughters from him, spoke of him in a dark tone, fine with her to let him sit alone in the straight-backed chair, let him limp unaided from porch to kitchen to fusty room. The sooner he knocked on the pearly gates the better, she told Aladdin, who groaned and rolled to his side, fretted by the darkness that kept him from work, a quick-sleeping man who would be up at three, filling the kettle, opening the red coffee can, impatient to start.

"Wauneta, what a you want me a do about it?" he said. "Drown him in the stock tank? He will kick off one a these days."

"You been sayin that for five years. He is takin the scenic route."

Time counted out in calving; first grass; branding; rainfall; clouds; roundup; the visit from Amendinger the cattle buyer; shipping; early snow; late blizzard. The children grew up. Aladdin got an old Piper Cub, swapping for it two bulls, a set of truck tires, a saddle, the rusted frame and cylinder of an 1860 Colt .44 he'd found at the root of a cedar. Wauneta's sandy hair greyed and every few months she went into the bathroom and gave it a maroon color treatment. Only old Red watched the progression of dates on his little feed-store calendar. He was older than kerosene now and strong to make his century.

Shan, the younger daughter, graduated from high school, moved to Las Vegas. She took a job in the package-design department of a manufacturer of religious CDs, quickly grasped the subtleties of images: breaking waves, shafts of sunlight denoted godly favor, while dark clouds with iridescent edges, babies smiling through tears represented troubles that would soon pass with the help of prayer. Nothing was hopeless and the money came in on wheels.

Ottaline was the oldest, distinguished by a physique approaching the size of a hundred-gallon propane tank. She finished school a year behind her younger sister, stayed home. She plaited her reddish-pink hair in two braids as thick as whip handles. In conversation a listener would look back and forth between the pillowy, dimpled mouth and crystal-crack blue eyes and think it a pity she was so big. The first year at home she wore gaily colored XXL skirts and helped out around the house. But her legs were always cold and she suffered from what Wauneta called "minstrel problems," a sudden flow that sent her running for the bathroom, leaving a trail of dark, round blood spots behind her varying in size from a dime to a half-dollar. After bare-legged wades through snow, after scaly chilblain, she gave up drafty skirts and housework, changed to ranch chores with Aladdin. Now she wore manure-caked roper boots, big jeans and T-shirts that hung to her thighs.

"Yes, keep her out a the house," said Wauneta. "What she don't break she loses and what she don't lose she breaks. Her cookin would kill a pig."

"I hate cookin," said Ottaline. "I'll help Dad." It was a fallback position. She wanted to be away, wearing red sandals with cork soles, sitting in the passenger seat of a pearl-colored late-model pickup, drinking from a bottle shaped like a hula girl. When would someone come for her? She was not audacious, not like her younger sister.

She knew her appalling self and there was no way to evade it.

Aladdin saw she was easy with the stock, where the boy Tyler whooped and whistled and rode like a messenger reporting a massacre.

"Had my way, ever hand'd be a woman. A woman got a nice disposition with animals." He intended the remark to sting.

"Oh, Daddy," said Tyler in comic falsetto. He was the horseman of the family, had slept out in the dilapidated bunkhouse since he was thirteen, Wauneta's edict.

"My brothers slept in the bunkhouse." There was in that flat remark all of Wauneta's childhood, sequestered, alert, surrounded by menace.

This only son, Tyler, was a huge, kit-handed youth of nineteen stout enough to frighten any father except Aladdin. The kid stamped around in dirty jeans and a brown hat. He was slack-mouthed in reverie, sported a young man's cat-fur mustache, cheeks marred by strings of tiny pimples. He was only one percent right about anything, alternated between despondency and quick fury. On Aladdin's birthday Tyler presented him with two coyote ears, the result of weeks of cunning stalk. Aladdin unwrapped them, laid them on the tablecloth and said, "Aw, what am I supposed a do with two coyote ears?"

"By god," screamed Tyler, "set one a them on your dick and say it won a fur hat in the church raffle. You are all against me." He swept the ears to the floor and walked out.

"He will be back," said Wauneta. "He will be back with dirty clothes and his pockets turned inside out. I know boys."

"I was the wanderin boy," old Red mumbled. "He won't be back. Takes after me. I cowboyed. I killed hogs. I made it through. Worked like a man since I was fourteen. Ninety-six years young. Never knowed my father. Carry you all to hell and spit on you." His finger dragged across the tablecloth, the long-ago self making a way. The old man showed a terrible smile, fumbled with his can of snoose.

Aladdin, face like a shield, curly hair springing, tipped his head toward the tablecloth, mumbled, "O bless this food." Heavy beef slices, encircled by a chain of parsnips and boiled potatoes, slumped on the platter. He had discovered two long-dead cows that afternoon, one bogged, the other without a mark of cause. He lifted a small potato and transferred it to his father's plate without looking at him, ignored the rattling of the old man's fork, though Wauneta, pouring coffee into heavy cups, frowned and said, "Watch it, John Wayne." A pastel envelope lay between her knife and a flat cake with sugar icing so thin it appeared blue.

"Somethin come from Shan."

"She comin back?" Aladdin crushed his potatoes, flooded them with skim milk. Game and Fish would pay for stock killed by grizzlies or lions. He had not seen lion sign for a decade and grizzly, never.

"Didn't open it yet," she said, tearing the end. There was a short and vague letter that she read aloud and, clipped to it, an astonishing photograph. It showed this daughter in a black bikini, greased muscles starkly outlined, exhibiting bulging biceps and calves, spiky crewcut hair whitened with bleach, her rolling, apricot-size eyes frozen wide open. In the letter, she had written, "Got into body building. Alot of girls here do it!"

"Whatever she has done to her hair," said Wauneta, "somebody talked her into it. I know Shan and that would not be her idea." When Shan left she had been an ordinary young woman with thin arms, blondish chew-ended hair. Her glancing unlevel eyes ricked from face to face. When she spoke, her hands revolved, the fingers flung out. The yearbook had named her "most animated."

"Bodybuildin." Aladdin's tone was neutral. He had the rancher's expectation of disaster, never believed in happy endings. He was satisfied that she was alive, not building bombs nor winking at drive-by johns.

Ottaline stared at her coffee. Floating on the surface was a spread-wing moth the shape of a tiny arrowhead. It pointed at her sister's empty chair.

Aladdin wore boots and a big hat but rarely mounted a horse. He missed the Piper Cub, which had seemed to him very like a horse. Someone had stolen it two years earlier, had unbolted the wings and hauled it away on a flatbed while he slept. He suspected Mormons. Now he was welded to the driver's seat of his truck, tearing over the dusty roll of land, and sometimes, drugged and fallen, he spent the night out in a draw, cramped on the front seat. The windshield glass, discolored by high-altitude light, threw down violet radiance. He had made the headache rack from poles cut on the ranch. He kept a bottle of whiskey, a rope behind the seat. The open glove compartment carried kindling, wrenches, bolts and nuts, several hundred loose fence staples, and a handleless hammer head. Wauneta tossed an old quilt in the cab and told him to wind up the windows when it rained.

"I know you," she said. "You will let the weather get you."

Every ten days or so Ottaline reared up and said she wanted to go to town and look for a job. Aladdin would not take her. Her weight, he said, ruined the springs on the passenger side. Anyway, there were no jobs, she knew that. She had better stay on the ranch where she didn't know how good she had it.

"I don't know why you would want a leave this ranch."

She said he should let her drive in alone.

"I will tell you when I am ready for advice," he said. "I am steerin my own truck for now. If you want a drive a truck then buy one."

"I am about a million dollars short." It was all hopeless.

"What a you want me a do, rob a bank for you?" he said. "Anyway, you're comin a the bull sale. And I'll give you a pointer you don't want a forget. Scrotal circumference is damn important."

What was there for Ottaline when the work slacked off? Stare at indigo slants of hail forty miles east, regard the tumbled clouds like mechanics' rags, count out he loves me, he loves me not, in nervous lightning crooked as branchwood through all quarters of the sky.

That summer the horses were always wet. It rained uncommonly, the southwest monsoon sweeping in. The shining horses stood out on the prairie, withers streaming, manes dripping, and one would suddenly start off, a fan of droplets coming off its shoulders like a cape. Ottaline and Aladdin wore slickers from morning coffee to goodnight yawn. Wauneta watched the television weather while she ironed shirts and sheets. Old Red called it drip and dribble, stayed in his room chewing tobacco, reading Zane Grey in large-print editions, his curved fingernail creasing the page under every line. On the Fourth of July they sat together on the porch watching a distant storm, pretending the thick, ruddy legs of lightning and thunder were fireworks.

Ottaline had seen most of what there was to see around her with nothing new in sight. Brilliant events burst open not in the future but in the imagination. The room she had shared with Shan was a room within a room. In the unshaded moonlight her eyes shone oily white. The calf-skin rug on the floor seemed to move, to hunch and crawl a fraction of an inch at a time. The dark frame of the mirror sank into the wall, a rectangular trench. From her bed she saw the moon-bleached grain elevator and behind it immeasurable range flecked with cows like small black seeds. She was no one but Ottaline in that peppery, disturbing light that made her want everything there was to want. The raw loneliness then, the silences of the day, the longing flesh led her to press her mouth into the crook of her own hot elbow. She pinched and pummeled her fat flanks, rolled on the bed, twisted, went to the window a dozen times, heels striking the floor until old Red in his pantry below called out, "What is it? You got a sailor up there?"

Her only chance seemed the semiliterate, off-again, on-again hired man, Hal Bloom, tall legs like chopsticks, T-

shirt emblazoned *Aggressive by Nature, Cowboy by Choice*.
He worked for Aladdin in short bursts between rodeo
roping, could not often be pried off his horse (for he
cherished a vision of himself as an 1870s cowboy just in
from an Oregon cattle drive). Ottaline had gone with him
down into the willows a dozen times, to the damp soil and
nests of stinging nettles, where he pulled a pale condom
over his small, hard penis and crawled silently onto her.
His warm neck smelled of soap and horse.

But then, when Ottaline began working on the ranch
for hard money, Aladdin told Hal Bloom to go spin his
rope.

"Yeah, well, it's too shit-fire long a haul out here any-
ways," Bloom said, and was gone. That was that.

Ottaline was dissolving. It was too far to anything.
Someone had to come for her. There was not even the
solace of television, for old Red dominated the controls,
always choosing Westerns, calling out to the film horses in
his broken voice, "Buck him off, kick his brains out!"

Ottaline went up to her room, listened to cell-phone
conversations on the scanner.

*"The balance on account number seven three five five nine is
minus two hundred and oh four . . ."*

"Yes, I can see that, maybe. Are you drinkin beer already?"
"Ha-ha. Yes."

*"I guess maybe you didn't notice." "It wasn't all smashed flat
like that, all soft. I took it out of the bag and it was—you goin a
carve it?" "Not that one. It's nasty."*

"Hey, is it rainin there yet?"

"Is it rainin yet?" she repeated. It was raining everywhere and people were alive in it except in the Red Wall
country.

★

Ottaline studied Shan's photograph, said to her mother, "If it kills me I am goin a walk it off."

"Haven't I heard that before?" said Wauneta. "I know you."

Ottaline marched around outside the house for a few days, then widened the loop to take in the corrals, the toolshed, the root cellar, circumambulated the defunct gravel quarry where Aladdin dragged worn-out equipment, a sample of tractors, one a 1928 blue Rumely OilPull tractor on steel with a chokecherry tree growing through the frame, beside it old Red's secondhand 1935 AC with the four-cylinder overhead valve engine, paint sun-scalded white. Half-buried at the foot of a caving bank lay the remains of a stripped Fordson Major, grille and radiator shroud smashed in, and next to a ruined stock tank stood the treacherous John Deere 4030.

She was walking through the rain-slick wrecks when a voice spoke, barely audible. "Sweetheart, lady-girl."

The low sun poured slanting light under the edge of a cloud mass so dark it seemed charred, the prairie, the tractors, her hand beyond the wrist hem of the yellow slicker, all gilded with saffron brilliance. Colors of otherworld intensity blazed in the washed air, the distant Red Wall a bed of coals.

"Sweet," the voice breathed.

She was alone, there were no alien spacecraft in the sky. She stood quite still. She had eaten from a plateful of misery since childhood, suffered avoirdupois, unfeeling parents, the hard circumstances of the place. Looniness was possible, it could happen to anyone. Her mother's brother

Mapston Hipsag had contracted a case of lumpy jaw from the stock and the disease took him by stages from depress-ive rancher to sniggering maniac. The light glided down to a dying hue and the wrecked machines sank into their own coffee-brown shadows. She heard nothing but mos-quito whine, small wind that comes with approaching darkness.

That night, listening to the ramble of talk on the scan-ner, she wondered if hunger had prompted an invisible voice, went to the kitchen and ate all of the leftover pork roast.

"I'm worried about you. I hope nobody tries to kill you or something." "Don't miss me too much."

"Nothin been hit." "It just rained like a bastard up here." "Rained like shit, here too." "No point stayin here."

Nothing happened for weeks, common enough in that part of the state. On a roaring noon she went again to the gravel pit.

"Hello, sweetheart. Come here, come here." It was the 4030, Aladdin's old green tractor, burly but with forward-raking lines that falsely indicated an eagerness to run. The machine had killed a ranch hand years earlier in a rollover accident at the weed-filled irrigation ditch— Maurice Ramblewood, or what? Rambletree, Bramble-food, Rumbleseat, Tumbleflood? She was a kid but he always flashed her a smile, asked her what was cooking, and on the fatal day tossed her a candy bar, pliable and warm from his shirt pocket, said she could borrow his sunglasses that turned the world orange. In late afternoon he was dead in bristle grass and spiny clotbur. His ghost.

"Maurice? That you?"

"No. No. It ain't him. That boy's a cinder."

"Who is talkin?"

"Two steps closer."

She stretched out her hand to the side grille. Yellow-jackets had built a nest in it and were creeping in and out of the grille's interstices, palping the air suspiciously. She stared fixedly at the insects.

"That is good," said the voice inside the tractor. "Get you a little stick and scratch where all that paint is blistered up." But she backed off.

"I'm just scared to pieces," she said, looking at the sky, the rise and fall of crested prairie, the bunchgrass edge of the world that flared like burning threads.

"Naw, now, don't be. This old world is full a wonders, ain't it? Come on, get up in the cab. Plenty a bounce left. The seat's still good. Pretend you're drivin right through L.A." The voice was hoarse and plangent, just above an injured whisper, a movie gangster's voice.

"No," she said. "I don't like this. I already got enough problems, not makin it worse by gettin in a old tractor cab that's ready to collapse."

"Aw, you think you got problems? Look at me, sweetheart, settin out here in the bakin sun, blizzards and lizards, not even a tarpolean over me, brakes wrecked, battery gone, workin parts seized up, no gas, surrounded by deadheads, covered with birdshit and rust. Here you are at last, won't even give me the time a day."

"It's six-twelve," she said and walked off, fingertips pressing her eyebrows. This was hallucination.

The voice called after her, "Sweetheart, lady-girl, don't go."

She craved to know something of the world, but there was only the scanner.

"Broken, threads stripped, had to take it up and get it welded. You know that fucker used a do that shit but he don't hang around here no more."

"—horns off the steers. I stopped by to see her." "Yeah? They told me you left before three." "I was there at three to change my clothes." "You know you're full a bullshit."

"It's fuckin pourin here, man." "I don't know what else. It was like—Whoa! Oh my god that was a big lightnin! Whoa! I got a get off the fuckin phone."

"I want a be with you, but I look at reality and I say to myself this fuckin woman wants a fuck everbody, I can't even get it on the couch, got a go in the fuckin bedroom." "Yeah, it's all my fault, right?"

It made her sick, it made her jealous to hear those quarrelsome but coupled voices.

She went again to the gravel pit. The choking rasp began when she was twenty feet distant.

"Maurice Stumblebum? Just forget him. Wrench your steerin wheel, jam the brakes, rev, rev, rev. Never change oil or filter, never check brake fluid, never got the ballast right, didn't bother a check the front-wheel toe-in, used a ride the clutch unmerciful, run in heavy mud and never think a the front wheel bearins. They're ground a dust. Jump around in the seat until it made me crazy. Aw, don't drum your fingers like that, take me serious."

She looked away to the Red Wall, something best kept at a distance. It was not a place to go. The distant highway flashed, the reflection from a bottle pitched out of a tourist's car.

"But that ain't why I killed him."

"Then why?"

"Over you," said the tractor. "Over you. I saved you from him. He was goin a get you."

"I could a saved myself," she said, "if I'd a wanted to."

At supper Wauneta opened a pink envelope from Shan.

"What I thought," she said. "I knew it. I knew Tyler'd show up." Shan wrote that Tyler had been living with her and her roommate for a month, that he was trying for a job with the BLM rounding up wild horses and, while he waited to hear, holding down a telephone job for a bill collector. He had bought himself a computer and in the daytime seemed to be studying electronics—the table was covered with bits of wire and tape and springs when she came home from the gym. They had become vegetarians, except Tyler, who ate shrimp and crab legs, foods he had never tasted until Las Vegas. He could not get enough of them. He had, wrote Shan, spent sixty-five dollars for a four-pound box of jumbo shrimp, had cooked and eaten them in solitary gluttony. "Ha-ha, not much has changed. He is still a pig," the letter ended.

Aladdin put a parsnip on old Red's plate.

"Shrimps'll make your pecker curl," said the old man. "Sounds like he's buildin a bomb with them wires."

"He's not doin no such thing," said Wauneta.

After supper Ottaline scraped the dishes, began to

snivel. Wauneta slung her hip against her, put her arm around the soft shoulders.

"What are you cryin about? That weight not comin off? Make up your mind to it, you are one a them meant to be big. My mother was the same."

"Not that. It seems like somebody is makin fun a me."

"Who? Who is makin fun a you?"

"I don't know. Somebody." She pointed at the ceiling.

"Well, let me tell you, that Somebody makes fun a everbody. Somebody's got a be laughin at the joke. Way I look at it."

"It's lonesome here."

"There's no lonesome, you work hard enough."

Ottaline went upstairs, set the scanner to rove and seek.

"Please enter your billing number now. I'm sorry, you have either misdialed or dialed a billing number we cannot accept. Please dial again."

"Why would it do that?" "Turn it off, turn it off."

"Hey, git doughnuts. And don't be squirtin around with twelve of em. Git a bunch. Don't be squirtin around, git two boxes."

"If that's fuckin all you have to say—then dang!"

Every day the tractor unloaded fresh complaints, the voice rough and urgent.

"Lady-girl, your daddy is a cucklebur. Get up and he don't get down. Stay in the seat sixteen hours. Aw, come here, I want to show you somethin. Look to the left a the cowl there, yeah, down there. What do you see?"

"Patch a rust. Big patch a rust."

"That's right. A big patch a rust. I won't tell you how that got there. I don't like to tell a girl somethin bad about her daddy. But in all the years I worked for your daddy I only once had a sweet day and that was the day I come here straight off the dealer's yard, fourth-hand and abused, and you was ten years old, your birthday. You patted me and said, 'Hello, Mr. Tractor.' Your daddy put you up in the seat, said, 'You can be the first one a sit there,' and your little hand was sticky with frostin and you wiggled around in the seat and I thought—I thought it was goin a be like that ever day and it never happened again, you never touched me again, never come near me, just that damn bony-assed Maurice couldn't be bothered a use the rockshaft lever, I got him with hydraulic oil under pressure, he got a infection. And your dirty dad. Broke my heart until now. But I'll tell you the truth. If your daddy was a get up here today I would hurt him for what he done a my brake system. I will tell you sometime about the beer and what he done with it."

"What?"

"I'd tell you, but I think it would disgust you. I won't turn a lady-girl against her family. I know you'd hold it against me and I don't want that. Tell you some other time."

"You tell me now. Don't go around talkin blah-blah. I hate that."

"All right. You asked for it. Stumblebum never bothered a check nothin. Finally brake fluid's gone. I'm out there with your daddy, on the slope, we was haulin a horse trailer. He's got his old six-pack with him, way he drinks he's alcoholic. He mashes his foot on the brake and we just keep rippin. No way he could stop me, not that I

149

wanted a stop. I didn't care. Slowed only when we come at a rise. He jumped off before the rollback, kicked a rock under a back wheel. What he done—poured warm beer in my master-brake-cylinder reservoir, pumped that beer down the brake lines. Yeah, he got enough pressure. But it ruined me. That's why I'm here. You hate me for tellin you, don't you?"

"No. I heard a worse crimes. Like killin somebody in a ditch."

"You goin a pout?"

Another day she stormed out to the gravel pit.

"Shut up," she said. "Don't you see I'm fat?"

"What I like."

"Why don't you fix your attentions on another tractor? Leave me alone."

"Now, think about it, lady-girl. Tractors don't care nothin about tractors. Tractors and people, that's how it is. Ever tractor craves some human person, usually ends up with some big old farmer."

"Are you like an enchanted thing? A damn story where some girl lets a warty old toad sleep in her shoe and in the mornin the toad's a good-lookin dude makin omelettes?"

"Naw. I could tell you they had a guy work at Deere a few years ago got fired out a the space program for havin picnics with foreigners and drinkin vodka but they couldn't prove nothin. He was cross-wired about it. It was around when they started foolin with computers and di-gital tapes. Remember them cars that told you to shut the door? Like that. Simple. Computers. He worked me up, fifteen languages. I could tell you that. Want a hear me say somethin in Urdu? Skivelly, skavelly—"

"You could tell me that, but I would not believe it. Some lame story." And it seemed to her that the inbuilt affection for humans the tractor harped on was balanced by vindictive malevolence.

"That's right, I was lyin."

"You got any kind a sense," she said, "you'd know people don't go crazy over tractors."

"Where you're wrong. Famous over in Iowa, Mr. Bob Ladderrung got himself buried with his tractor. Flat-out loved each other, he didn't care who knew it. And I don't just mean Iowa farmers. There's fellas can't keep away from us. There's girls fell in love with tractors all over this country. There is girls married tractors."

"I'm goin in," she said, turning away. "I'm goin in." She looked at the house, her mother's wedding wheat swaying yellow, old Red's face like a hanging skull in the window. "Oh, please," she said to herself, weeping, "not a tractor or nothin like it."

After supper, in her room, she wished for a ray gun to erase the brilliant needles of light from the isolate highway, silence the dull humming like bees in a high maybush. She wanted the cows to lie down and die, hoped for a tornado, the Second Coming, violent men in suits driving a fast car into the yard. There was the scanner.

"You think he's normal until you start to talk to him."

"I should a called the police, as mean and horrible as he is, but I'm not goin a do that. And this is what I'm thinkin. I'm goin a go after him even though we haven't been married that long. He's goin a pay. He's got it! He's makin two thousand a month.

Anyway, I got a headache every day a my life over this. But I'm fine. Just a little insane. Don't worry, I'm fine."

Aladdin lifted a wad of turnip greens from the bowl, lowered it onto Ottaline's plate.

"What are you doin out there in the gravel pit with them tractors? I was lookin for you half a hour."

"Thinkin," she said, "of maybe try a fix up that Deere. Like just mess around with it." That day she had climbed up into the cab, sat on the seat, feeling an awful thrill.

"I wouldn't spend a dime on that damn thing. It never run good."

"I'd spend my own money on parts. I don't know, maybe a foolish idea. Thought I might try."

"We had trouble with that machine from day one. Damn Morris Gargleguts got done, it wouldn't go much. We hauled that thing to Dig Yant, he replaced some a the wirin, cleaned the fuel tank, blew out the gas line, ten other things, rebuilt the carburetor. Then somethin else went wrong. Ever time they fixed it, it'd blow up somewhere else. They give me a hot iron on that one. I went to raisin heck and the dealer finally admitted it was a lemon. Give me a real good deal on the Case. Now, that's a tractor that's held up. You know, that 4030, you will be strippin it down to grit." He ate his meat loaf. He thought, said, "I could—might give you a hand. Haul it in that blue-door shed. Put a stove out there, run a pipe." He saw himself rising in the black wintry morning while his family slept, going out to the shed to stoke the fire, take a little smoke, and in the cozy warmth breaking loose rusty bolts, cleaning mucky fittings, pins, studs, screws, nuts soaking in a tub of kerosene while he waited for day-light and the start of the real day. "We'll get her in there tomorrow."

"Him," said Ottaline.

"You won't fix it," said old Red. "What you are tryin a fix ain't fixable."

"O.k.," she said, walking up to the tractor. "We are goin a move you into the blue-door shed and operate. My dad is goin a help me and you better stay hunderd percent quiet or it's all over."

"You want a know my problems? Brakes. Belts shot, block cracked, motor seized, everthing rusted hard, sludge, dirt, lifters need replacin, water pump's shot, camshaft bearins shot, seals shot, magneto, alternator fried—you look inside that clutch housin you'll see a nightmare. Clutch plate needs a be relined, got a replace the tie-rod ends, the fuel shut-off line is bust, the steerin-gear assembly wrecked, the front axle bushings, spindle bushings all bananas and gone, you want a talk differential you'll be listin parts for fifteen minutes. The transmission clutch slipped bad before everthing went blank. I don't want your dirty dad a work on me. He already done that and look at me."

"Different now. Anyway, goin a be mostly me. I'm doin this. What gears was that tranny clutch slippin in?"

"You? You don't know nothin about tractor repair. I don't want you workin on me. I want you should take me a Dig Yant—he's a tractor man. It's men that fixes trac-tors, not no woman. First and third."

"You don't got much choice. Tell you one thing, I

didn't take home ec. I took mechanics and I got a B. First and third? Seal on the underdrive brake piston or more likely the disks bad worn." She had brought a can of penetrating oil with her and began to squirt it on studs, bolts and screws, to rap on the rusted bolts with a heavy wrench.

"You make a wrong move I might hurt you."

"You know what? I was you I'd lay back and enjoy it." Something Hal Bloom had said.

The rain quit in September and the prairie began to yellow out. There were a few heated days; then the weather cooled and an early storm hoop-rolled out of the northwest, slinging a hash of snow, before they got the tractor dismantled to frame, motor and transmission.

"We got a get a engine hoist in here," said Aladdin, coughing. The first night of the storm he had got wasted and slept out in his pickup, window down, the snow carousing over him. He woke shuddering, drove home and heard they were out of coffee, drank a glass of cold water, told Wauneta he could not eat any break-fast. By noon he was feverish and strangling, took to the bed.

"That coughin drives me into the water and I don't swim," said old Red. "Better off just smother him, be done with it."

"There is somebody else at the top a my smotherin list," said Wauneta. "I knew this was goin a happen. Sleep in a truck." Aspirin, poultices, glasses of water, steam tent, hot tea were her remedies, but nothing changed. Aladdin roasted in his own dry heat.

"What's tomorrow," he said, rolling his aching head on the hot pillow.

"Friday."

"Bring me my calendar." With swimming eyes he studied the scrawled notes, called for Ottaline.

"She's out feedin. It snowed wet, froze hard crust out there, they can't hardly get grass. Supposed a warm up this weekend."

"God damn it," he whispered, "when she comes in send her here." He shivered and retched.

The snow rattled down on Ottaline in the cab of Aladdin's big Case tractor, a huge round bale on the hydraulic-lift spear. It could keep snowing until June the way it was coming down. At noon she drove back to the house, ravenous, hoping for macaroni and cheese. She left the Case idling.

"Dad wants you," said Wauneta. It was beef and biscuits. Ottaline took a pickle from the cut-glass dish.

She sidled into her parents' bedroom. She was one of those who could not bear sick people, who did not know where to look except away from the bloodshot eyes and swollen face.

"Look," he said. "It's first Friday a the month tomorrow. I got Amendinger comin out at eight o'clock. If I ain't better"—he coughed until he retched—"you are goin a deal with him, take him out there, he can look them over, see what we got, make you a offer." Amendinger, the cattle buyer, was a dark-complexioned man with sagging eyes, a black mustache whose ends plunged down to his jawline like twin divers. He wore black shirts and a black hat, gave off an air of implacable decision and control. He had no sense of humor and every rancher cursed him behind his back.

"Dad, I am scared a death a that man. He will get the best a me. He will make us a low offer and I will get rattled and say yes. Why not Ma? Nobody gets on her bad side."

"Because you know the animals and she don't. If Tyler was here—but he ain't. You're my little cowgirl. You don't have to say nothin. Just take him around, hear his offer and tell him we'll get back to him." He knew that Amendinger did business on the spot; there was no getting back to him. "I get better of this I am goin a buy a plane I been lookin at. It's the only way to work this big of a ranch. A truck ain't no good, windows and all."

"I could bring him in here, Dad."

"Nobody outside a my family sees me layin flat. God damn it." He coughed. "Ain't that how it goes, first your money and then your clothes."

She had the poorest kind of night and in the morning rose groggy and in a mood. The snow had quit and a warm chinook blew. Already the plain was bare, the shrinking drifts lingering in cuts and folds of land. They were still out of coffee. Upstairs Aladdin wheezed and panted.

"He don't look good," said Wauneta.

By eight the cattle dealer had not arrived. Ottaline ate two oatmeal cookies, another slice of ham, drank a glass of milk. It was past nine when the dealer's black truck pulled in, Amendinger's black hat bent down as he reached for papers. There were three hound dogs in the back. He got

out with the clipboard in his hand, already punching figures on a handheld calculator. Ottaline went outside.

It was not the cattle dealer but his son, Flyby Amendinger, big-nostriled, heavyset, a cleft in his stubbly chin, as
quiet as three in the morning.

"Mr. Touhey around?" he asked, looking at his boots.

"I'm showin you the stock," she said. "He got the flu.
Or some kind a thing. We thought you would come at
eight. We thought you was goin a be your father."

"I missed a couple turns. Dad's over in Hoyt." He
fished in his shirt pocket, drew out newspaper clippings,
showed her an ad, Amendinger & Son Livestock Dealers.
"I been workin with Dad almost nine years, guess I got a
idea what I am doin by now."

"I didn't mean you didn't," she said. "I'm glad it's you.
Your dad's mustache scares me." She pictured him driving
the red roads to the ranch, roads like heavy red marker
traced over the map, cutting the circle of horizon.

"Scare the hell out a me, too, when I was a little kid."
He looked at the porch, the house, the wedding wheat,
the blue-door shed.

"Well," she said. "Here we go."

"That wheat needs cuttin," he said.

She drove and he stared at the far horizon visible
beneath the bellies of cows. They bounced over pasture,
the dust in the truck cab shaken loose and suspended in a
fine sparkling haze as though an emanation from their private thoughts that might coalesce into audible statement.
He opened the gates. Ottaline thanked him, pointed out
the good qualities of the cattle, the trim, heavily muscled
bodies on straight legs, the rib-eye bulge on each side of
the backbone, their large size. He murmured at a coarse-

fronted cow with a steery look to her, pointed out some small and sickle-hocked steers with flat loins. He counted, made notes and added figures, offered a fair price.

"You are a knowledgeable girl," he said, "and a damn good-lookin one, though upholstered. Care for a beer?"

Ottaline spent the morning tipping back beer bottles with Flyby, who described the lonely life of a cattle dealer's son, illustrating his sad sentences with long, flat gestures of his hand. It was noon when he left.

She gave the figures to Aladdin from the bedroom doorway, hanging back. Dazed and fiery, bursting with tea, he nodded, said all right. It was all right. He did not need a computer to know the margin to a penny. It was all right, and wasn't that a sad relief. He couldn't say as much for himself.

That night old Red woke from his shallow sleep to a stiff, whistling risp he dreaded to hear. His heart beat, he rose and felt his way to the pantry window. The dirty moonlight fizzed through shredded clouds, glanced off a swinging scythe blade, though it was not Death come for him this time but a man in a dark hat cutting the wedding wheat in hissing swathes, stopping at the end of every row to swig from a bottle. He saw his granddaughter Ottaline, mouth cracked wide, her hundred teeth glinting like a mica bed, leaning against the doorframe of the blue-door shed. She hurled a piece of oily metal into the sky, where it twisted and fell, stooped for another, sent it flying.

Old Red watched, summed it up. "I drove teams. I cowboyed. Worked since I was a kid. Run sheep and run cows. Still present, fork end down, ready as a dog with two dicks. I ain't finished my circle yet."

Tyler and Shan were far away hoping for good luck, but here was Ottaline and her hay maker. He wouldn't waste his dear breath laughing.

There was a wedding in September and a tremendous picnic under the Amendinger cattle-sale canopy, red and white stripes that cast a rose flush, trestle tables in the side yard, pork barbecue, a baron of beef pit-roasted, spitted lamb, prairie oysters, sweet corn, giant shrimp in Tyler's ketchup sauce, oven rolls, a keg of sour pickles, melons, ripe Oregon peaches made into deep-dish pies, and a three-tier wedding cake with pale-blue frosting topped by a tiny plastic bull and cow. The day was hot and clear and the Red Wall trembled on the horizon. Out beyond the fence the stripped frame of the 4030 lay where Aladdin had dragged it, on its side in the sagebrush. Wauneta wept, not for her daughter but for the cut wheat. Tyler inspected the ranch, looking it over with a displeased eye. Everything was smaller and shabbier. Why had he wanted this? He had a cell phone and sat on his horse talking to someone far away. Wauneta told Shan she intended to come out to Las Vegas and visit one of these days.

"Not if I got somethin to say about it," said Aladdin.

The guests dragged the folding chairs back and forth, and when Ottaline smoothed the rayon satin of her dress over her knees she felt the grit, saw the glinting dust caught in the weft. A spot of barbecue sauce marked the bosom. At last she changed into the new aquamarine pants suit and drove away with Flyby Amendinger for a four-day honeymoon among the motels of Nebraska.

Where wheat once grew a row of doghouses stood. There were two trucks in the driveway. Old Red in his pantry wished for deafness when the bedsprings sang above. Otherwise all was the same.

Aladdin applied for a bank loan for another plane. "I said if the Lord spared me I'd get it." He was dreaming of a 1948 Aeronca Sedan, a loose, big-cabined thing with feminine curves and a split crankcase to be replaced with an undamaged one from Donald's Cowboy Junkyard.

"She's so roomy, if I had to I could put a couple calves in her, bales a hay, cake, just about anything, even Ottaline, ha-ha."

The bank approved the loan and on a quiet and grey morning, the wind lying low, Aladdin started his truck, got halfway down the drive, backed up, parked and came into the kitchen. Old Red dunked his toast in black coffee.

"I am goin a fly that plane home," he said. "I will land in the Triangle pasture. Preciate it you was all out there watchin. You, too, bubba," he said to his son-in-law.

"I got a go look at Trev's cows this mornin." Flyby Amendinger did not like living under the thumb of Aladdin Touhey. In the night he complained to Ottaline that Aladdin was worse than his mustachioed father.

"My block don't fit his tackle," he whispered.

"It sure fits mine," she whispered back.

"Call Trev up. Say you'll come a little later. He won't give a shit. I want a see everbody out wavin. Cause for celebration get a plane on this damn place again. Goin a teach Ottaline how to fly it."

It was mid-morning when they heard the drone of the engine.

"Ma!" shouted Ottaline into the house. "He's comin."

Wauneta came outside and stood with Ottaline and Flyby staring at the horizon. Old Red hobbled onto the porch. The wind had come up and was gusty and chill, the distant line of cliff marking a dull red break in the sere plain. Wauneta ran back into the house for her jacket.

The plane flew over and headed toward the Red Wall, turned and came again in their direction, very much lower. It passed over them twenty feet off the ground. Aladdin's head was barely visible in the smoke from home-grown that clouded the cabin. The plane soared up, shaking in the wind. It rose in a steep climb, leveled out and sailed away. When it was only a distant speck it turned and came toward the ranch again, curving and sliding, coming low. At a certain angle it resembled a billboard in the sky.

"He is actin up," said Wauneta. She watched the plane roar in low like a crop duster.

"I think he is goin a land," said Flyby, "or take a soil sample. Or stake out a homestead."

"He is actin up. I know him. YOU GET DOWN HERE!" Wauneta shouted at the plane.

As though obeying her, it touched the ground, sending up a puff of dust, bounced back into the air, and made two more prodigious hops before the left wheel caught the iron frame of the abandoned tractor and the plane fell on its face, crumpled into a mash of cloth, metal and rancher. There was an explosion like a mighty backfire, but no flame. A ball of dust rose.

Flyby dragged Aladdin to safe ground. His father-in-law's head lolled at an unusual angle.

"He is dead, I think. I think he is dead. Yes, he is dead. His neck is broke."

Wauneta shrieked.

"Look what you done," said Ottaline to her. "You killed him."

"Me! That's what cuttin the wheat's done."

"He done it hisself," called old Red from the porch. It was clear to him the way things had to go. They'd plant Aladdin. Ottaline and her scytheman would run the ranch. Wauneta would pack her suitcase and steer for the slot machines. The minute she was out of sight he intended to move out of the pantry and back upstairs. The main thing in life was staying power. That was it: stand around long enough you'd get to sit down.

Pair a Spurs

The Coffeepot

THE COFFEEPOT SOUTHEAST OF SIGNAL HAD BEEN an o.k. little ranch but it passed down to Car Scrope in bad times—the present time and its near past. The beef-buying states, crying brucellosis which they fancied cattle contracted from Yellowstone bison and elk on the roam, had worked up a fear of Wyoming animals that punched the bottom out of the market. It showed a difference of philosophies, the outsiders ignorant that the state's unwritten motto, *take care a your own damn self,* extended to fauna and livestock and to them. There was a deeper malaise: all over the country men who once ate blood-rare prime, women who once cooked pot roast for Sunday dinner turned to soy curd and greens, warding off hardened arteries, *E. coli*–tainted hamburger, the cold shakes of undulant fever. They shied from overseas reports of "mad cow" disease. And who would display evidence of gross carnivorous appetite in times of heightened vegetarian sensibility? To counteract the anti-meat forces Scrope contributed ten dollars toward the erection of a roadside sign that commanded passersby to EAT BEEF and, at the bottom, bore the names of the seventeen ranchers who paid for the admonition.

It was a bitter winter and a late spring; he was feeding into May waiting for green grass. Every ranch was out of hay and the nearest source was a long day's journey to eastern Nebraska where the overall boys squeezed them hard. Ten days before June a blizzard caromed over the plains, drifting house-high on lee slopes, dragging a train of arctic air that froze the wet snow, encased new calves in icy shells. For a week the cold held under glassy sky, snow-scald burning the cows' udders; it broke in minutes under a chinook's hot breath. Meltwater streamed over the frozen ground. The bodies of dead stock emerged from fading drifts, now you don't, now you see em, a painful counting game for ranchers flying over in single-engines. Scrope's yard flooded, a mile of highway disappeared under a foot of water while they held his mail at the post office, but before it ebbed another storm staggered in from the west and shucked out six inches of pea hail, a roaring burst that metamorphosed into a downpour, switched back to hail and finally made a foot of coarse-grained snow. Two days later the first tornado of the season unscrewed a few grain elevators from the ground.

"I never seen so goddamn much weather packed into two weeks," said Scrope to his neighbor, Sutton Muddyman, the two mud-speckled pickups abreast on the chewed-up road, tailpipes rattling. The dogs in the truck beds ran back and forth in parallel tracks and grinned at each other.

"Spanked us around pretty good," said Muddyman. "What worries me is the snowpack. There's still the bulk a the snowpack up in the mountains and when she starts to melt we'll see some real water. That EAT BEEF sign puttin you in the money yet?"

"The only people see it is the ones live on Pick It Up. All two a them. I suppose we should a put it on a blacktop highway where there's some traffic." He scratched the rashy hollow of his throat. Blond stubble glinted on his cheeks. "Hell," he said, "it's all hard times in this business. You was smart to get out."

"Car," said Muddyman, "don't think for one minute that I got it easy. I get the rough end a the pineapple ever day. I guess I better get goin. Inez's ice cream's meltin out a the bag."

"Take it on home, Sutton," said Scrope stepping gingerly on the gas prong, the pedal gone for months, while Muddyman eased south in his gravelly ruts.

Scrope, forty years old, had lived on the Coffeepot all his life and suffered homesickness when he went to the feed store in Signal. He'd acquired a morbid passion for the ranch as a child when he believed he could hear its grass mocking him. This ability had come the year Train, his older brother, died in some terrible and private way in the bathroom where their mother found him, an event he had never understood and still did not. In that time he couldn't grasp what was going on or might happen next, for his parents said nothing to him, but stayed close to each other whispering and weeping. He would hear them in the kitchen, their low voices trickling on and on like two water seeps, but when he stepped in, boots squeaking, they fell silent. Train's name could not be mentioned, that much he knew. Later they lied to him about such inconsequentialities as the names of weeds, the freshness of the butter on the saucer, how much school a ranch boy needed—not much, his father said, then complained years later that Car had not become a banker or insurance man. After his father's funeral he asked his mother straight-out, "What was all that stuff you and Da used to talk about? Was it about Train? What happened to him, anyway?" but she looked away from him and through the window, her gaze traveling out to the red hoodoos and the crumpled sky beyond and she said nothing at all.

The grass, on the other hand, never shut up, making a kind of hissing snicker like sawed-off John Wrench in high school days in the last row of the movies when he asked a girl to have some of his popcorn, his penis thrust through the bottom of the box up into the greasy kernels. Scrope's ex-wife Jeri had had some of that popcorn. *Best one lost, worst one stays,* hissed the grass.

The Coffeepot was small but well-balanced, eight sections of mixed range, some irrigated hay ground (not enough), grazing rights to BLM land. Bad Girl Creek watered the ranch, in low ground twisted into a slough improved by beaver to three small ponds. A dusty driveway, intersected by a line of power poles slung with a single wire, wandered in from the main road, numerous side-branches cutting toward the far parts of the ranch. Eighty yards west of the ranch house Mrs. Freeze's house trailer rested on cinder blocks in the shade of a cottonwood. An arrangement of corrals and fences led to a mild slope and at the height of the rise Scrope had put up a calving barn.

Scrope's old man had built the log ranch house after World War Two, and the son had changed nothing, not the faulty plumbing with its mineral-clogged pipes, nor the rusty porch swing that had stained Jeri's flowery skirts.

The entryway was as much dog kennel, opened into the kitchen. A photograph of the ranch taken in 1911 hung above the table, gaunt Scrope ancestors grinning in front of their dugout, the shadow of the photographer touching their feet. It had been there so long Scrope couldn't see it, yet was aware of it in the same way he was aware of oxygen and daylight—he'd notice if it was gone.

The southeast corner of the ranch was high bony ground populated by a pair of bobcats, a few rattlesnakes; the distinctive features were a big wash and red crumbling hoodoos that sprouted fossils after heavy rain. Once a desperate runaway from the juvenile detention home hid out beneath an overhang for a week. In the rags-and-blood sunset Car had caught him sneaking burned carrots and beef tallow out of the dog's dish, invited him in, learned his name was Benny Horn, slid him a plate of beans, candy bar for dessert, pointed out a tick on his neck and talked him into giving himself up, promised a below-minimum-wage, part-time, seasonal job when he got out.

"I knew your daddy," he said, remembering a shiftless loudmouth. When the kid left so did a stack of change on the windowsill and two mismatched socks from the back of a chair.

For twenty years the Coffeepot's foreman had been a woman, Mrs. Freeze, a crusty old whipcord who looked like a man, dressed like a man, talked like a man and swore like a man, but carried a bosom shelf, an irritation to her as it got in the way of her roping. The old man had hired her a few months before he crossed the divide and at first local talk was that he'd lost his mind.

The terrain of Scrope himself consisted of a big, close-cropped head, platinum-blond mustache, a ruined back from a pneumatic drill ride on the back of a sunfishing, fence-cornering, tatter-eared pinto that John Wrench, two decades earlier, had correctly bet he couldn't stay on, feet wrecked from a lifetime in tight cowboy boots, and simian arms whose wrists no shirt cuffs would ever kiss. His features, a chiseled small mouth, water-colored eyes, had a pinched look, but the muscled shoulders and deep chest advertised a masculine strength that had, over the years, attracted not a few women. His marriage, brief and childless, fell apart in half an hour. Then he looked at the moon through a bottle every night, watched pornographic videos, ate, in addition to large quantities of beef and pork, junk food from plastic sacks which set off itchy rashes and produced bowel movements containing long orange strands as though he had swallowed and digested a fox.

THE BOX HAMMERHANDLE

Directly south of the Coffeepot lay the Box Hammerhandle—Sutton and Inez Muddyman's place. Sutton Muddyman, of bunchy muscle and oily black curl, claimed dude ranching was hard work made harder by the need for intense and unremitting cheeriness, and although he and Inez weren't suited to the constant company of urban strangers it paid the bills and brought them more Christmas cards than they could open. Their daughter Kerri was a pastry chef in Oregon and living with a reformed gambler of whom they wanted no news. They kept thirty or so horses on the ranch, a small band of sheep, pack llamas and a pirate's crew of dogs constantly in trouble with skunks and porcupines, once with the bob-cats who gave them lasting memories of a trespass in the hoodoos.

Scrawny and redheaded, a little savage with an early change of life, Inez Muddyman had been one of the Bibby girls and raised, as she said, on a horse from breakfast to bed; it was she who took the dudes up into the mountains where tilted slopes of wild iris aroused in them emotional displays and some altitude sickness. She had been a good barrel racer and roper as a girl, made a few points and a little cash on the weekend circuit but hung that up when she married Muddyman. Off a horse she was awkward and stave-legged, dressed always in jeans and plain round-collared cotton blouses stained light brown from the iron water. Her elbows were rough, and above her amorphous face frizzed bright hair. She didn't own a pair of sun-glasses, squinted through faded eyelashes. In the bathroom cabinet next to Sutton's kidney pills stood a single tube of lipstick desiccated to chalk in the arid climate.

Three routes connected the Coffeepot and the Hammerhandle: a plank bridge over Bad Girl Creek—the joint property line—but that way involved opening and closing fourteen gates; a water crossing useable only in early spring and late summer; and the five-mile highway trip, one that Scrope avoided because of bad memories as it was at the highway bridge he had nearly killed his wife and broken so many of his own bones that he was now held together with dozens of steel pins, metal plates and lag screws.

SHOOTING

He wouldn't give up. Still in casts and marked with hot pink scars he had telephoned Jeri at the midnight hour, ricocheting between sore anger and yearning. As he spoke he watched the naked woman on the television screen cock one leg and brandish an object that might have been a potato masher.

"Jeri, where's your grit? Don't you want a make the whistle? I know you think you're ridin a dirty one but don't you want a make the whistle? You ain't a quitter."

"This is the whistle. I had it."

"We could have some kids. I wish we'd make some kids. We'd be o.k. then." He heard himself whining. He turned his back on the potato masher woman.

"The needle's on empty for that one," she said. "I wouldn't have a kid a yours for a million dollars."

"You don't come back to me and turn this damn divorce thing around I'm goin a have to shoot you." The telephone sucked his words down like a drain.

"Car," she said, "you leave me alone."

"Hey, woman. You don't see it yet, do you? It's me or nothin. You get your ass back out here or you'll find out what real trouble is," knowing that he was the one with trouble.

She began to cry, an angry weeping with a lot of spit in it. "You son of a bitch. Leave me ALONE."

"Look!" he shouted. "What you done with John Wrench is over and done. I forgive you!" He could almost lick her raw salt tears. Then he was sure she was not crying, but laughing.

She hung up. He tried to call back but got the rasp of the busy signal. *Best one lost.*

He drank some more, took his father's shotgun out of the cabinet, drove to Signal's only apartment building where her car was parked at the side, shot up the windows and tires of the vehicle he'd paid on for two years.

"Find the joke in that," he said.

The act released vengeful thoughts and on the way home he detoured to the Wrench ranch. John Wrench's pickup, the hood still warm, stood in the drive, curved metal naked under the moon. Scrope reloaded, blasted rubber and glass, fired into the dashboard shouting, have some popcorn, John!, threw his shirt on Wrench's front seat as a calling card. For the first time he wanted to kill them both, to kill something, if only himself. The upstairs lights glowed and he roared away, bare-torsoed, bottle to his mouth and drops of whiskey sparkling in his chest hair, hoping for a jackrabbit in the headlights.

When Jeri moved back to South Dakota he knew Inez had been in on it, the bowlegged old bitch, but they were neighbors and for Muddyman's sake he was civil.

Wrench, that curly wolf, kept scarce after the truck-shoot and Scrope couldn't stir up enough anger to file his teeth again. In younger days they had traded dozens of girls, fresh-used and still swimming with the other's spermy juice—old steadies ready for the discard heap, new girls, Wrench's sister Kaylee—sometimes back and forth and back again, easy trades with no rancor. But Wrench, never married, missed the difference between those girls and a wife.

They'd been high ace in each other's hand since baby days when Scrope's mother took care of infant Wrench.

They had shared a playpen, Scrope's brother Train making faces at them through the bars or lying under the table within their eyeshot and fooling with his plastic horses. Jeri had been Scrope's little South Dakota bird who'd perched a while and flown off, but John Wrench went back to the beginning and one of them would hoist the other's coffin.

THE SPUR-MAKER

A few Californians drifted into Signal, including cranky Harold Batts, his receding hairline eked out in a thin ponytail, and his wife, Sonia, who had been a car saleswoman until the salesmen got the better of her with jibes and innuendo. In his coastal days Batts had been a metallurgical engineer for Pacific Wings, suddenly pink-slipped with five hundred others in a company downsize. He became interested in prophecies, signs that the end was near and other eschatological fancies, told Sonia that until the final trump they were going to live a simple life in a simple place. He thought of blacksmithing, said he wanted to be useful to society as long as it lasted; the millenarian farrier's life would suit. He shied at the last minute and apprenticed to a spur-maker up in Oregon for a year, spent his weekends in retreat with a coming-end sect known as Final Daze.

In Signal—a town Batts chose by stabbing a fork into a road map—he opened his shop. In the workroom at his sparking grinding wheel or in the dark corner of the forge working adversarial steel, sweaty face reflecting the hot light as a chrome mask, he illustrated metal with coiled snakes and kissing birds. He scavenged scrap from abandoned ranches: old gates, rusted buggy leaf springs, coil springs, harrow teeth, odds and ends. Most of his work was in mild or high carbon tool steels but he experimented with unorthodox admixtures of nickel, chromium, copper, tungsten; played with molybdenum, vanadium, cobalt; set rich low brass, bronze, nickel silver against duller metal. Those who favored silver-crusted acanthus leaves and florid carving eschewed his work as "too modren." His best work was spurs, no design ever repeated, his distinctive style recognizable from a distance and costing the moon.

That late, hard spring he finished a pair of spurs with half-drop shanks in steel blued to the iridescent flush of ripe plums. The line was severe and elegant. The silver buttons, the silver-overlaid blunt-star rowels and shank tips held the same pale gleam as twilight water. Silver comets whose tails flowed into the shanks ornamented the heel bands. He added a playful note in a pair of jinglebob stars pendant from the rowel pins, the source of a shivering metal music pleasing to horse and rider.

"There's some power in these," he said to Sonia's cat, sleeping on top of the shop radio. "Somebody's going to Connect." He went home then, counting at the side of the road a dead deer, and on the road a dead coyote, a dead rabbit, another, another, dead rattlesnake, live rattlesnake in the sun soon to be dead, smear of blood, half a dead antelope.

No Surprise

Scrope walked in on them, a day of violent wind, willows along the creek in lashing motion, heaving themselves out of the soil.

He and Mrs. Freeze and the two hands, Benny Horn and Cody Joe Bibby, had ridden out early to drive two hundred animals north to Scrope's BLM lease. The undulating grass made the plain shudder as an animal's hide rolls in fly season. On the way Benny Horn lost his jacket and his teeth rattled.

"Good thing your balls is in a bag," said Mrs. Freeze, "or you'd a lost them."

A few things had gone wrong; hats blew off, dust irritated their eyes. Jeri did not meet them with sandwiches and beer at Johnson's place on Pass Water Creek. Scrope said she probably couldn't get the truck started. At one o'clock Kyle Johnson and his youngest son, Pleasant, comfortably belching hot beef and horseradish fumes, joined them for the drive across Johnson property, but the cows spooked when a tourist van blared through, spooked again at the bridge and the hollow clopping of their own hooves on it and ran in twelve directions, crisscrossing the freshly tarred highway, so deep a black the yellow stripes seemed to float above the surface; it stank of asphalt and yielded unpleasantly beneath hooves. When they had them bunched and moving again Cody Joe started one of his fits and went off his horse.

"Busted his collarbone," said Mrs. Freeze, easing him up, hearing the bone ends grate.

Johnson had business in town, said he would drive Cody Joe to the Knife & Gun Club. "You want," he said, "leave your animals until mornin. Give you a chance a rustle up some help." Scrope hated to take him up on the offer—there would be weighty payback.

Nothing to do but ride to the Coffeepot and get on the phone. Benny yammered, Scrope said, shut up, let me think. The wind made their ears ache, stirred up the horses' tails. It was getting colder. Half a mile from the house they saw something blue and small caught on the barbwire fence, jerking in the wind. The peacock blue color was familiar to Scrope. He rode up and pulled it from the barbs—Jeri's fancy panties—they'd had a fight over them, seventy-five dollars for a scrap of silk. Benny and Mrs. Freeze looked away to spare him embarrassment. Scrope knew the garment had not blown off any clothesline—he was still paying for the dryer. He unbraided the possibilities in the time it took to reach the house.

It wasn't much of a surprise to see John Wrench's truck in the yard, driver's door open, and, given that, no surprise at all to find him in the bed, working hard at the cowboy wiggle. He heard his wife say, keep goin, don't stop, and then she saw him. He didn't say anything, backed out and went down to the kitchen and tilted the whiskey bottle while he listened to Jeri wailing and John Wrench getting dressed, coming downstairs. From the door Wrench said, Car, it's not like you think, nosir.

Scrope did not feel much at first, and when feeling came suffered the flashing cuts of betrayal, swallowed the jealous acids, but Jeri, afire with guilt, called a showdown, screamed divorce. Scrope said that was a crazy thing to say. In the half hour since he'd walked into the bedroom he'd never thought they were at the end of anything, just at a washout in the road, get through the ditch and go on.

His blue-white eyes watered. He wanted to tell her that it was only John Wrench. Look, he wanted to say but could not, I done it a few times on the side too. Where would that get him? He thought nothing had to change, did not yet know it was impossible to dodge torment; like a heat-seeking missile it finds the radiant core.

"Let's talk about it," he said, "let's just drive around and talk about it," slugging whiskey fast and straight, his shirt-front drenched with it, and finally prodded his wife into the truck where all he said was let's talk and all she said was divorce. They couldn't get past that. Somehow they had ended up beneath the highway bridge, the truck wheels in the air and Scrope broken and crushed into a painful space the size of a footlocker, Jeri calling for help which he couldn't give.

By the time he was out of the hospital and able to lift a spoon again she had moved to Signal and the divorce kettle was on high boil, nothing of hers left in the house but a half-empty box of tampons on the bathroom shelf and a pair of snow boots in the entryway.

PAIR A SPURS

Sutton Muddyman brewed his own beer in the cellar and on a dust-shot day he went to town to pick up a few cans of malt. He slouched along the sidewalk, his 4-X cattle-man crease pointed against the gritty wind, past the computer store with its sun-faded boxes of obsolete software, past the lawyer's office with the blue shade drawn. He stopped in front of Batts's window and gazed at the spurs artfully laid out on a weathered plank: an unornamented pair of saddle bronc rider's spurs with wide heel bands and the shanks set off-center at a fifteen-degree angle, pure and functional in line; a pair of gal-leg spurs, the shanks ornate Victorian whore's stockings and high-buttoned shoes; another pair in bronze featuring straight shanks inlaid with turquoise chevrons, the rowel spokes in the shapes of tiny kicking boots. Nice, nice, nice, said Muddyman. He stepped inside, told himself he would get Inez a keychain for her birthday—the same thing he had given her two years running.

Sour Harold Batts stood behind the counter reading the Casper paper, mug of herb tea at his hand. Muddyman drifted along the showcase taking in the smell of oil and metal and leather, hibiscus and vanilla, stopped at the comet spurs.

"What do you want?" said Batts.

"Let's see them comet spurs," he said, pointing. Batts wrenched his lips, laid the spurs on the counter and began to twirl the end of his ponytail around a scarred finger.

"Pretty can openers," said Muddyman, pleased to see Batts clench and unclench his fist.

"That's the Hale-Bopp. I spent hours watching it that year—slept out on the deck. Cold, but I'd wake up and there was this thing up there. Beautiful. Terrible. The position of the earth in space is going to shift. There are forces coming that will make iron swim, cause a five-hundred-foot tsunami. We live in the final times—it's right in your face, the millennium, global warming, wars, horrible pestilences, storms and floods. The comet was the sign. Used one of those new little rotary chisels from Hines and Roddy over in Casper to cut the detail here."

Muddyman looked at the price tag. Three hundred—

he guessed the end wasn't quite in sight. He hadn't planned to spend more than twenty on his wife's present and said so. Said he'd read in the paper that comets, crammed with rich chemical molecules, were not signs of destruction but the seeds of life sowed through space.

"That's what *they* want you to believe," said Batts, smoldering, tapping his finger on the newspaper face of a woman politician as well known for her wild-eyed rants as for her stupidity. "So, don't buy them. Somebody will." The light from the street falling through the front window metalized strands of his hair. With his arms bent akimbo he was beginning to take on the shape of a pair of spurs himself.

His indifference goaded Muddyman. He wrote a check, cleaned out their tax return money.

It was almost worth it. Inez said, "Guess I will wear them to bed tonight," and she did until cold steel touched him and, laughing, he pulled off her boots, threw them jingling into the corner.

"He he he," said Muddyman, "here comes the comet." But afterwards lay awake wondering how to cook the books and keep her from finding out.

On Wednesday, the strong heat of the sun soaking into cold bones, wind flat and distant grass showing young green, Inez rode to Car Scrope's place. For years they had brought horseback dudes over to the Coffeepot for a fake roundup and a chuckwagon plate of beans and that was on her mind. A tractor passed her at the turn-in, Mrs. Freeze in the cab and driving; on the long flatbed bounced Cody Joe Bibby and a few empty mineral supplement tubs.

Cody Joe was her cousin, smart enough once, once of sweet disposition, but his brains scrambled four or five years before when a thousand-pound hay bale tipped off a stack onto him and his horse. He was strong, bull-shouldered like all the Bibbys, yet good for nothing now but simple jobs. She waved and there was no recognition in his scarred face, the stringy hair badly cut at home by his wife and whipping in the wind. He had been the best-looking boy in the world when they were kids, she thought, stiff, wheat-colored hair and darkest blue eyes. Look at him now, though she couldn't stand to do so.

When she rode up Cody Joe was dropping the tubs off the flatbed and Mrs. Freeze telling Scrope they had a bull with hoof rot in the creek pasture, too lame to be driven in for treatment, they'd have to go out with the truck and get him.

Scrope looked up at Inez, his expression in neutral.

"How you doin, Car?" Her red hair was whichaway, hat on the rack at home.

"Good enough. You?"

"We're good. Sutton wanted me come by ask you if Saturday be o.k. for us a bring the dudes over instead a Friday? He got a sit down with the tax man on Friday. They don't give you a choice a days. They are callin our place a entertainment ranch."

"Way it's goin, might as well call them all entertainment ranches. I'm sure entertained. We was just goin in, have a shot a coffee," said Car. "Park your horse."

"Beaut spurs," Mrs. Freeze said. She had the lean of an old fence post, had to be close to seventy years old, Inez figured, grey hair chopped short, hands as calloused and corded as any old cowpuncher's. Car said that what the old girl didn't know about stock could be written on a cigarette paper with room left over for Bible verses. Nobody knew where Mr. Freeze was—killed and kicked under the rug, maybe. There was something about Mrs. Freeze that Inez didn't like and never had; the hard old woman was like a rope stretched until there was no give left.

Scrope had to limp over, touch a rowel. He craned up at Inez, opened his mouth to say something smart, stopped, scratched the back of his welted neck. A mixed buzz like radio static got in his head.

"Sutton give em to me for my birthday about two weeks after the fact." Inez dismounted and followed them into the confused kitchen. "Figured I'd get out while it's quiet. Box elder bugs all over the dudes' cabins and I said to Janey she could get em with the vacuum if she wants to. Gives me a queasy feelin to hear them bugs rattlin up the hose, no way out. What they must be thinkin—end of the world, I guess." She looked over the kitchen, noticed one table leg shored up with a boot heel.

Scrope began to grind coffee beans in an old mill that threw up a cloud of fine dust. His head ached ferociously but he kept looking at her, somehow excited, forgetting his grievance over Jeri.

Inez regarded the cast-iron skillet half-filled with congealed bacon grease, evidence of innumerable fryings. There were sacks, empty and half-full, of curls, crackers, crunches, triangular corn chips, empty pots of dip, lumpish stale pastry rinds, gnawed tarts, empty pudding cans. Car Scrope might not have had a hot meal in the two years since Jeri left. A bluebird flew angrily at the window, defending territory from its own reflection. "Car, you ought a let me get Janey Bucks over here and clean this place up for you. She gets ten an hour but she's worth it." The floor was spotted with mashed food, the whole place an old boar's nest. She wondered how Mrs. Freeze could crush womanly concerns so thoroughly that it didn't bother her.

Scrope produced his strangled laugh. "She'd die a shock." He wouldn't explain the lonesome gnaw a clean kitchen brought him, worst when wholesome wheat cereal was cooking, the sun hitting a white plate—he could howl. "So, what d'you want a do Saturday? Make noon at Dirty Water or Mud Suck, which? There's about fifty head loose out there should a been shipped, we held off the fall market it was so bad. Worse now. They got this new Northern Plains beef co-op they're startin up but I doubt it's goin a help. If we could put them EAT BEEF signs up right across the country, New York to San Francisco, it'd call people's attention a beef. What a you say, Mrs. F.? O.k. with you for Saturday?" He shook a handful of objects like orange larvae from a plastic bag and chewed them, mustache absorbing the color.

Inez hardly knew where to look there were so many things wrong with the room and the people in it, settled her gaze on a dog in the yard beyond the window, murmured, "Dirty Water's better. Got a nicer view."

She thought Car Scrope was on his way downhill. He could end like that crazy old bristle on All Night Creek when she was a kid. She'd ridden out with her father and brothers, and miles from home they had come on a tumbledown place along the creek. A wild man came out of the door and confronted them, food-plastered whiskers sprouting stiff, his eyes crusted, and a stink coming off him that hit thirty feet away. Her father began to say who they were, the old guy mumbling eh? eh? and they all saw his pants suddenly glisten to the knees with fresh wet. Her father wheeled around and led them up a hill but the day was spoiled. "Jeez, did you see that," said her brother Sammy, "he just let go right in his pants. Smells like he poops in em, too."

"He used a be a pretty good rancher, but his wife died and he's a dirty old boar in a boar's nest now," their father had said. "Stay away from there." Men had that flaw in them, Inez thought, to go over the cliff of events and fall precipitously into moral ruin.

"My god," said Scrope. "I got a bear of a headache." He reached on top of the dish cupboard and fumbled for the aspirin bottle, dry-swallowed four, stubbed out his cigarette in a dirty saucepan. A cloud of steam rose from the coffeepot as he poured the boiling water over the grounds. He rinsed out stained cups under the faucet and filled them with the fresh coffee. His head pounded and he felt hot and strange as though a djinn had flown out of the kettle spout and up his nose. He gripped the back of a chair as if it could help him.

They went outside again to watch the grass grow, stood with their backs against the warm barn logs, a few early flies roaring around. Cody Joe drifted away toward the stack-yard with his coffee cup, stepping high over invisible furrows. Car shifted close to Inez, talk racing out of his mouth about the heavy snowpack in the mountains, saying Bad Girl Creek was up and likely to run over its banks if the warm weather held. The titanium plates holding his bones together were hot.

"It'll hold and it'll flood," said Mrs. Freeze, striking a

kitchen match on her thumbnail. She disliked idle chatter.

The coffee was too strong, bitter and scalding. "Whoa!" Inez said. "*That's* coffee!"

"Ain't it the truth," said Mrs. Freeze, setting her half-empty cup on the upturned box. "That coffee'll clean you out better than a chimney brush." She headed toward her house trailer.

As soon as she was out of sight Scrope seized Inez's hand, pressed it against what Jeri had called a dead sardine that night in the truck, comparing it, he thought then, to John Wrench's equipment, but when he had suggested that might be the case she had answered, don't say that scum's name.

"You set a match to me," he said now to Inez. "Let's go do it."

"For god's sake, Car. You out a your mind?" Her neck and cheeks flamed, she wrestled her hand loose. It was almost noon. Their shadows slid beneath their feet like spilled paint.

"Come on, come on," he said, pulling her toward an open door. The rank animal was out of him and in the open.

"Get ahold a yourself."

"*You* get ahold," and he was rubbing her flat buttocks, pressing against her, the breath whistling in his nose. "Come on."

She jabbed her chapped elbow into his throat, twisted up his arm, ducked and ran for the mare.

"I'm not quittin," he shouted after her. "I'm goin a get you. I'm goin a get in there before you can say 'sheep shit.'" Standing in her cloud of dust he knew something iron had thrown a lever while he poured the coffee.

Mrs. Freeze came back from the trailer, jamming her shirt into her jeans. "Where's Inez?" she said in her rough voice. Scrope smelled the drift of fresh-swallowed whiskey.

"She had a go." He stared south, colorless eyes watering from the pain of the headache. He could feel every piece of metal in his body straining after the ringing spurs.

"Probly the coffee," said Mrs. Freeze. "Hope she makes it."

"Tell you somethin, I could go for that." And he cupped his hands under two imaginary breasts and jiggled them.

Mrs. Freeze wrinkled her face. "Inez? A wall got more tit than Inez."

"Anyway, them's pretty spurs."

"You got that right. Beauts."

The Wolf

Car Scrope became a nuisance to her, plotting her day and appearing whenever Sutton was somewhere else; he telephoned at strategic hours. He followed her into town, once or twice got on a horse and angled his ride to coincide with the dudes and Inez on the trail to Rabbitheels. And at those times he stared at her with lustful, white-eyed gaze and talked filth *sotto voce*.

"You keep it up and I am goin a say somethin to Sutton. I don't believe you'd like that. He seems to you like maybe just a good old fella you knew for years but when Sutton gets mad he's mean."

"I can't help it," he said. "Inez, I don't hardly even like

you when you ain't around but when you are around I feel like somebody shoveled hot coals in my shorts. You make my head ache I want it so bad. Come on, send these dudes ahead and let's you and me get up behind them rocks and fuck." He pursed his mouth and made kissing noises under the platinum mustache.

She shuddered. "I could rope you," she said, "and drag you to a dishrag. Maybe that'd get the message across. Maybe you'd like that."

"What I'd like," he said, "is a good, juicy bareback ride. What I'd like is to put my dick right where it wants to go. What I'd like is to bounce you until your eyes cross. What I'd like—"

She started on Sutton the next morning when he came in for daybreak breakfast, their early hour before the dudes winced across the porch in their new boots, stretching their arms and saying how good the air smelled. Outside the wind was slapping the faded grass. She knew better than to tell him what to do in the morning but couldn't keep it back.

"I hate to say this, Sutton, but Car Scrope's been makin passes and ugly remarks to me for two weeks. I thought he'd calm down and quit, why I didn't say anything, but he keeps on."

He laid a bloody patch of wool on the table. "Somethin's at the sheep. Two dead and one mostly eat, one dragged off and one crippled." He picked up his coffee cup, blew and sucked at it as though it were hot solder, smell of sage rising from his hands.

"You hear what I said about Car Scrope? About what he's been tryin a do to me? He's just as rammy as he can be."

"I think dogs. The prints are twict the size of a coyote's."

"I told him I was goin a tell you, you'd straighten him out. But he don't seem to get the message."

"I hope to Jesus it ain't our dogs. I don't see Posy last couple days."

"I got a hard enough life I don't need a put up with a sex maniac neighbor comin at me. I expect my husband a take the matter in hand pronto."

He got up, went to the porch, came back to the table. "Well, it's not Posy. She's on the porch with that infected leg. I forgot that leg. Wasn't her." The dog had looked at him and yawned, one ear up, one down, left eye catching the sun as a glassy red ball.

"You need a go up there and give him what-for. You need a put some steel in sight, he knows you mean it. How you think I feel with him rubbin his wrinkly old thing up against me?"

"Yeah. I could go up to Car's, find if he seen anything, had any calf loss."

"You do that," said Inez. "You do that," voice like that of a shot crane, recalling it had sometimes been a trio in the old days, Wrench, Scrope and Muddyman out having themselves a high-heeled time, the rotten pigs.

In the late morning a trio of New York women lawyer dudes called on the cell phone that Sutton said they must carry when they went walking, that or hold on to a long string attached to the porch rail, a rule laid down in the wake of a grass fire set by a strayed guest who had depended on smoke signals to show his whereabouts.

"Inez, we are lost," said a cross voice as though she had set them wandering. "And there's wolves out here." Fast breathing came through the receiver. Sutton scratched sums on his Big Chief tablet.

"Coyotes. Describe what's around you and we'll figure out where you're at," and listened to the voice saying big orange rocks, barbwire fence and empty space.

"Fence in good shape or is it all wrecked?"

"Well, it just looks like a fence." A whistling sigh, or was it the wind? Bills and letters and tax information brochures covered the table, a month's work and all in red.

"Big rocks. They're big."

"I think they're out on the edge a Car's hoodoos," she said to Sutton. "I'll ride out and point them back. But if *he's* out there I ought a take the .30-.30."

"Take the truck. If the ladies're walkin, it's four miles back." The feed bill glared PAST DUE.

"Teach em a lesson." But she knew it wouldn't and said Muddyman could drive out there himself if he wanted, pack in the front seat with three women, be a treat for him, take them to see Car Scrope, maybe he'd fix on one and get off her case. She wanted to ride and she would. She touched the feed bill, said, lucky we got that tax return.

The women swore wolves. They were dressed in stiff, stacked jeans and roper boots, Santa Fe jackets and silk neckrags. The wind tangled their hair into mops.

"I know what I'm talking about," said lawyer Glacken. "I've seen hundreds of hours of wolf tapes in a case I had

189

where a man was keeping a wolf in his walkup and trying to pass it off as a seeing-eye dog. DNA, the whole bit. I *know*. We saw a wolf."

"Well, the ranch is that way. See the smoke blowin up? That's the fireplace chimney. You'll come on the ranch road, walk south, close the gates behind you. Sutton'll be along with the truck. Remember about the gates."

She rode up the wash. To her right in a clump of rabbitbrush a large female wolf appeared, watching her with yellow cross-eyes. Its fur shivered in erratic gusts. Without thinking she uncoiled her rope, made a loop and threw. As she took a few dallies around the horn the wolf leaped straight up into the air and the dun mare reared. The wolf hauled back, squatting on its haunches, and the mare reared a second time, walked backward on her hind feet like a circus horse, dropped, put her head down and bucked violently; Inez went through the windshield, landed on her chin and skidded, neck broken, mouth open, lower teeth plowing red dirt. The dallied rope pulled free and the wolf bolted away through sagebrush that wagged stiffly in the wind.

The week after the funeral Sutton Muddyman put the ranch on the market and made ready to move to Oregon near his daughter. His sister and her husband drove up from Rock Springs to help him pack and sort out things for the auction.

"What about these spoons, this red pillow, these spurs, Sutty? They're real handsome with the little comets on them. Though muddy."

"She was wearin them goddamn things when it happened. They're bad luck." His voice shook, thickened in his throat. "I don't want a see em. Put em with the rest a the auction stuff." It had been Sutton, truck full of dude women, who'd found his wife, her teeth dug into the state of Wyoming. He'd shot the mare in front of them.

Local opinion discounted the dudes' identification of a wolf as eastern hysteria; it was no wolf but a dog loose from some tourist's camper and how pleased the owner must have been when he saw Inez's nice grass rope.

TEXAS BOYS

The Muddyman place was renamed Galaxy Ranch. Frank Fane, the new owner, played a Jupiterean warlord in a science-fiction television series but preferred the western theme in private life. He stocked the place with cutting horses and hired a crew of Texans headed up by the snuff-dipping, pole-legged, stretched-out foreman, Haul Smith, face decorated with a frothy beard, ringlets the size and color of ginger ale bubbles.

Smith came into the Firehole bar in Signal one Saturday night with a few of his Texas brush-poppers, called drinks for the house on him, said they were looking to shoot a little eight ball, and they stayed until closing time showing whatever they knew about horses, and that was not a little, might be secondary to what they knew about green felt and cue balls. Haul's style was a slow walk around the table while he fluffed his beard, bending and scrutinizing, then making a difficult yet showy shot that rarely failed. When he missed he slammed the butt of the cue on the floor once, *bang*.

"You play Cowboy here?" said Haul. "Nice game. Little change a pace. Play to a hunderd points and hunderd and one wins but the last shot got a be the cue ball on a carom off the one ball into a called pocket and no nickin no other ball."

Serious play had come to Signal and after a while there was some talk of a winter-long tournament and maybe some good prizes, something better than a six-pack or a can of Copenhagen. There were a few sullen remarks from the unemployed about Frank Fane bringing in Texas men when he could have had a heart's pick of Wyoming, or at least that part of it.

"Mr. Fane didn't know nobody here and he known me from when he come out to Texas on a film shoot. They picked Texas for Mars. But as these boys"—jerking his thumb at his crew—"drops off and goes home we're replacin with local guys. Things'll work out."

They'd have to wait and see if that was true. At the moment it didn't look like any of the weasel-headed Texans were missing their flatland southern home, roiled as it was with whirlwinds and secessionists.

Mrs. Freeze, red-faced and quiet, sat with her back to the bar drinking whiskey, her legs stretched out, watching the table action.

Haul looked over a few times, said, "Them's a pair a spurs you don't see ever day. Lady, you think about sellin them I'd want a buy. Go good at the Galaxy, the comets and stars and all."

Mrs. Freeze snorted. "They come from there, from when Muddyman had it. Not for goddamn sale."

John Wrench, short and stocky, so close-shaved his face seemed polished, said in his deep voice, "She got em at the auction. The auctioneer says, What'll you give me for this box a old rope? Them spurs was way down in there and she says two dollars and she got it all. What'd you do with that rope, Mrs. F., stuff a pillow?"

"Stuff your ass," said Mrs. Freeze.

She put out one foot and wagged it to see the light play over the comet. She drank her whiskey, left at ten-thirty to catch what she said was some beauty sleep.

Haul said, "She's a piece a work, ain't she?"

"Top hand. Kept Car Scrope's Pot cookin for years."

"Tough as they come and good as a man."

"*Three little girls from Sheridan,*" sang John Wrench softly, chalking a cue and handing it to the short-shanked girl with him, a tourist in red boots, "*Drinking beer and wine, One said to the other one, Your ass twict as big as mine.*" He looked at the balls on the table and said, "Look what that fuckin Texas man done left us."

"Mrs. Freeze, now," said the old range cootie, Ray Seed, "what, must be almost thirty years ago I worked on the Double Eight, she was the cook. We was in the middle a shippin cattle and terrible shorthanded. Boss man says to her, you ride a horse? She threw down that apron, pulled on a pair a boots and been lookin at the world through a pair a horse's ears ever since."

"Mr. Freeze around them days?"

"Nope."

"Oh my, oh my, I do like em slender and tender," John Wrench said, patting Red Boots on her pockets.

"Like Car Scrope's wife? Car must a been pretty faded let you pick that little apple off his tree."

"We ain't goin a talk about that. And don't say nothin else unless you are ready for a new set a teeth. I'll crawl all over you." Finally he had gone out to Scrope's place. Car told him how much he wished John had been in his truck the frothy night he had ventilated it; John said he wished he had, too, that what he'd done was nothing beyond a reflexive deed; Scrope said I know it, and they drank until it was clear that Jeri had caused the trouble and all the sad consequences.

"Well, excuse me all to hell. Cole, draw me another, will you? I'm goin a fight John I might as well have some a that liquid bobwire first."

Ray Seed wasn't ready to move off his subject. "Mrs. Freeze, now, there was a few tried to make up to her back then. She kept a bullwhip handy and she'd crack it around. Course she was never much to look at so she wasn't troubled too much. She had some kind a fever once made all her hair fall out. I don't think there ever was no Mr. Freeze."

"Maybe she's one a them tongue-and-groove women."

"No. She got as much use for the females as she does for the men. What she likes is cows and horses. She growed up in North Dakota. Seven girls in the family. They could ride and rope and ranch, ever one a them."

John Wrench wedged into a corner with Red Boots and the bar talk turned to one-legged Don Clow who had backed his truck over a cliff on a dark night while navigating by flashlight and accidentally shot himself on the way to the ground, probably a good thing he only had one leg now, keep him out of trouble, a fellow as irresponsible for his personal health as he was. And look at Car Scrope, filled with medical metal, another example of self-ruin. It was good to have an audience that hadn't heard the local history.

MRS. FREEZE MOVES FIVE MILES OFF

They were in the stock truck, one Angus and two Hereford bulls in back, the comet spurs on Mrs. Freeze's small boots catching at the floor mat. She swore under her breath, eased the truck into the ruts leading to the upper pastures. The wind bounced a tumbleweed over the hood. Two redtails cruised the high thermals.

"What a you think then," said Scrope, chewing a strip of antelope jerky. "Them Texas boys say a few words about what Mr. T.V. Fane is goin a do over there? He ain't come by to say his howdys or nothin like it. You suppose he wears them wax ears in daylight?" He looked at her boots.

"Lives in California, just comes out here now and then. What a you hear from Muddyman?" The back of the truck shook. "Damn bulls." She stepped suddenly on the brake, sent the fighting animals lurching and staggering to keep their feet, sexual rivalry set aside in favor of personal balance. The truck ground forward. "He say how he liked it out there?"

"Sent me a e-mail on the computer. Said he should a moved a Oregon twenty years ago. No wind, plenty a rain, nice neighbors for a change, grass to yer ass and good-lookin women, by which I take him to mean he got one picked out. Old Inez must be a-rollin." He shifted closer to Mrs. Freeze, already pressed against the door.

"*You* was pretty crazy about her there for a while."

"Yeah. Poor old bowlegged Inez. I don't know what it was. I admit it, I was hot. But it passed over when she did. I come to realize that what counts is you and me, I mean, how we been together through thick and thin for quite a few years." He edged west again and all at once threw his rank and heavy arm over Mrs. Freeze's shoulders. "I think a good deal of you, Mrs. F.," he said, puffing humid breath.

Mrs. Freeze drove her elbow into his ribs. "Goddamn, get over, will you, you got me half out a the truck."

Scrope moved less than an inch, reluctantly and slowly.

"All right, *you* drive, then," said Mrs. Freeze, putting on the brake and getting out, going around to the passenger side. "I don't like bein crowded, Car." She didn't get in until Scrope was behind the wheel. "I'm ridin out after we get these bulls scattered. Cody Joe and me's got fence work out in the hoodoos. When Mr. Fane comes by you ought a ride the line. These Texas boys is shy about the fence so far."

"Fence? I'm comin with you," said Scrope, shifting into second. "Fence work is what I need. Benny was here I'd get at the paper but he ain't been in this week."

"They got him in jail for burglary," said Mrs. Freeze. "Robbin the cigarette machine at Higgins." She put down the passenger window and the wind banged through like a plank.

They rolled into the yard in eddies of dust. Cody Joe Bibby sat on the porch steps, a length of binder twine in his hand, dazed and uncomprehending.

"Tell you what, this got a be the most fucked-up ranch operation in Wyomin. I'm gettin sick a this," Scrope said.

Mrs. Freeze said, "He don't look good for fencin. I better take him home."

She was back in forty minutes, two empty beer bottles rolling on the pickup floor, an inch out of the whiskey bottle under the seat. This day was slow in getting to its end.

"Wife says he's gettin worse."

"If we get real shorthanded—" said Scrope. "Damn it to hell and back again."

"Have to wait and see." Mrs. Freeze threw rolls of wire into the truck, glanced at the wind-scratched sky. "Weather comin."

"What else?" said Scrope. "I got a take me some aspirin."

Up in the red hoodoos Scrope leaned too close. He'd torn his hands on barbwire. The aspirin was useless. His veins and arteries pulsed.

"Hey," he said, his voice slurred and heavy, "why don't we—?" and mumbled.

"What? What did you say to me?" Mrs. Freeze stood away from the fence, the dry, set face reddening. Wind jerked the rag-ends of her torn jacket.

"Come on," Scrope said. "Come on, now." He stretched out his bloodied hand.

"Keep off from me." Mrs. Freeze jumped back, comet spurs ringing once, her whole body giving off dangerous rays. "There isn't no fella on this earth goin a put no moves on me. I'll kill you flat dead." She backed to her horse, gathered the reins.

"Aw, now. It ain't—don't you run out on me, Mrs. F.," said Scrope, "or I'll fire your ass. You don't need a blow up and throw a fit. Just hold on a minute," but he groaned and rubbed his thighs with both hands when the jinglebobs sounded, angled toward the woman who, one foot in a stirrup, swung into the saddle, turned to look and saw satyr-faced Scrope glaring crazily, point of his tongue thrusting into the blond mustache.

"I quit!" shouted Mrs. Freeze and took off for the ranch.

"You're fired," answered Scrope in agony.

In her trailer house Mrs. Freeze belted down a good drink, telephoned Haul Smith, hearing the wind over at the Galaxy whistling in Smith's cell phone.

"Hey, Mrs. Freeze. You sound a little hot. Hope we don't got my horses busted through. Been meanin a get in touch with you, work out somethin on that fence."

"Callin to see you got a openin. You said somethin the other week about hirin local help? I been here over twenty goddamn years. Time to get out."

Haul sounded doubtful.

"Well, I don't know. Never had a woman work for me."

"You ain't spent much time in Wyomin. Half the hands is women nowadays and not paid near as good as the men."

"Matter a fact I couldn't offer you much. And I'll say it, you're considerable older than the rest a the boys. And I don't know how they'd take to it anyway. Oh, I know you got a good name for bein a hand, I'm bringin up the arguments."

There was an eloquent silence.

"On the *other* hand Mr. Fane's been talkin about buffalo. If you feel a callin for buffalo." He droned on. "Maybe work somethin out there. I'm losin two a the boys, goin on one a them damn historic cattle drive things they got worked up, drive longhorns through the traffic and sell rawhide hair ribbons. I got a ask why you want a leave a job where you been for all those years." The wind between them whistled like a bird.

"I can't take that son of a bitch Scrope no more. Man's crazy. Buffalo? Hell, I dream about em."

"I had some unusual dreams myself over the years but buffalos has figured in damn few. Make you a deal. And it's goin a cost you. I want them comet spurs. I went down and seen that ponytail freak but he said those're the only comets he ever will make. Seemed to enjoy sayin no. Told me Muddyman paid three hundred for them babies and I know you got em for nothin so I'll swap you for a job buildin up Mr. Fane's nonexistent buffalo herd. Think about it, give me a call."

"I don't need a think about it," said Mrs. Freeze. She dropped the cap of the whiskey bottle, kicked it under the chair. She didn't need that either.

Car Scrope again, pulled up beside her truck, watching her shove boxes into it. He ached all over, felt the metal plates straining against his skin, the screws pulling out of his bones. He slammed the truck door.

"Mrs. F., I don't know. Don't know what's eatin at me. Somethin come over me. Hell, you been workin for me forever, never thought nothin about you that way, know what I mean? Hey, you're old enough almost a be my grandmother. I rather eat rat jelly than—"

But he was edging closer and Mrs. Freeze saw his trick and the red-flushed neck swelled like that of an elk in mating season, the face beaded with desperate sweat. Scrope was getting close enough to jump. Mrs. Freeze dropped the box she was carrying and took up the shovel leaning against the trailer. "Get the fuck away from me, Car Scrope."

Scrope touched his forehead delicately with his fingertips, said, "My goddamn brains is blowin up," and stumbled toward the house. A little later Mrs. Freeze heard a cry and crashing sounds from the kitchen. It sounded as though the dish cupboard had gone over. She leaned the shovel against the wall.

Then Scrope came once more to the house trailer, nearly emptied of Mrs. Freeze's meagre belongings, raised his shotgun and said, "You are not sayin no to me about nothin. Not today, not tomorrow, not next week—"

The shovel shot forward as though a javelin, struck Scrope's shoulder and the shotgun fell clattering. Mrs. Freeze jumped for it. Her thumb lay on the safety. She looked at Scrope with hard, bright eyes.

"Don't say nothin about a headache, Car, or I'll sure fix it for you. You are all messed up. You get on away from me. I'm gone you can come and get your gun. I'll lay it on the bunk."

Scrope threw one hand out in a furious gesture, went to the cab of his truck where he sat with the door open, watched Mrs. Freeze load her horse.

Everybody left him. Jeri had taken with her the soft heat of morning, the faint scream of her heels sliding up the sheet, thighs falling open for him like a book to the wet crease, her purple-red nail drawing along his belly from sex to nipple, and afterwards in the shining kitchen the wheat cereal smacking in the pot like a hungry dog, like John Wrench's sap-sticky talleywhacker slapping into Jeri and there he was back at the same damn corner. He couldn't bear the loneliness but the place had its claim on him and there was no leaving unless through his brother's door.

"What the fuck do you know about nothin, you sanctimonious dried-up old shit of a bitch? Get the hell off my place!" he shouted at the old woman's horse trailer, now dwindling south.

Deep Waters

The snowpack began to melt rapidly the second week in June, a blaze of hot temperatures into the nineties, and while Scrope's hat felt like a plugged-in hot plate on his head, the terrible headaches evaporated when Mrs. Freeze left. He'd carried eighteen empty whiskey bottles out of the trailer, and guessed there might be a thousand underneath it with the rattlesnakes. By the weekend water coursed over the tile-hard ground in sheets, creeks swelled to the size of rivers, and heavy mudslides choked roads. It was then, when he was desperately short of help, that Haul Smith telephoned and said he wanted to see what his share of the fence work amounted to, he'd be over in the morning.

On the Galaxy Ranch Mrs. Freeze listened to the bison specialist from the university drone on. He said in his dull, faint voice, larynx damaged in a childhood snowmobile accident, "That right, Mr. Fane wants to keep on with the cutting horse operation *and* run bison?" It was hard to believe he cared one way or another.

"What he says."

"It's a good move to go to bison, twice the profit, half the work. Labor costs are low because they only need a third a the feed the cow does. Rustle their own grass right through the snow, bring a beautiful $2.35 a pound. However. They need room. Big room. Which you don't got." His eyes roved over the bitten grass, the stamped dirt, pulling the distance close with a longsighted squint.

Haul Smith, beard like yellow foam, rode up on his roan gelding, a Texan beast with delusions of grandeur. "Mrs. Freeze, you got any messages for your old boss? On my way over there check that fence with him." The gelding danced crazily and Smith encouraged him, the comet spurs flashing.

"No." She spit. "Just watch out. He's a pisser."

"Ah, he's all right. He sounds all right," and he rode north toward the castellated hoodoo skyline.

At noon the specialist fanned his boiled-beet face with his hat, said yes to a cold one. They went into the kitchen where Janey was scraping carrots.

"This is some terrible heat for June," she said. "Haul with you? Car Scrope's called about five times wonderin where he's at."

"Ah, shit," said Mrs. Freeze.

"Last time he called he was real mad, said Haul could have the whole fence if he wanted a play games."

"A little after nine this mornin when we saw him," whispered the specialist, setting down the empty bottle. "How far is it?"

"Four, four and a half miles," Mrs. Freeze said, tracing

the distance in her mind, trying to count the hazards. Rattlesnake, gopher hole, spooked horse, heatstroke, heart attack, lightning bolt, willful departure, Car Scrope. "I better take the truck in case he's throwed and hurt. Which way he went I don't know—go out and scatter around until I cut sign, I suppose."

"Car said he was goin a meet him at the house," said Janey. "That's what made him so mad, he had a keep goin out to the fence, see if Haul was there, and comin back to the house, see if Haul was *there*. And he weren't. Said he's just havin a yo-yo day."

"I'll go with you," said the specialist. "Might take a man, lift him in the truck if he's down."

Mrs. Freeze said something to herself.

Mud-crusted from prying the truck out of sinks and gumbo washes they reached the high meadow. There was no sign of Haul Smith beyond the tracks his horse had made, heading straight down now to Bad Girl Creek, not toward the ranch bridge but in the direction of the ford.

"He didn't get across that," said Mrs. Freeze.

They skidded down the greasy slope. Bad Girl, a big, brindle, foaming torrent, bank full and over, was cutting a new route on the flats. The willow trees along the margin were in the water, some toppled into the current and filling the creek from bank to bank with tangled limbs, great strainers, others swept downstream to mass against the barbwire fence and at the place where the old railroad trestle had collapsed in the creek years before. The sun drove its glittering spurs through the wet branches.

"Scrope's dirt dam must a broke." She meant nobody had kept it in repair after she had left.

The bison man whispered, "You know, eighty-five

percent a Wyomin's stream water flows out a the state. It's the so-called—there is somethin hung up in that tree on the bend."

Mrs. Freeze knew damn well what it was. It was the crazy gelding, drowned, the reins streaming out in the current like insect feelers, no sign of Haul Smith. "There's Texas sense for you. He didn't need a cross water but he tried it anyway."

They scouted the bank, made their way back to the ranch kitchen and the phone. As they came down into the yard the specialist said in his weak voice, "It won't work to try and run bison with this horse operation."

"I know it. Whole setup makes me puke."

Haul Smith showed up when the water began to subside, wrapped and twisted in willow roots, half a mile below where they'd found the horse. His boots and shirt were gone, torn off by the force of the current. The three remaining Texans walked up and down the creek bank looking for the boots, saying the comet spurs would be a nice thing for his kids to have. They didn't find them, for the weighted boots had lodged under a sunken steel beam of the old railroad trestle, the spurs seeking sister metal.

THERE'S STILL WHISKEY

At the end of summer Fane was out of the ranch game, the Texans and the cutting horses were gone, and the Galaxy sold to a breakfast food mogul sworn to organically grown grains who said he wanted nothing more than to let the ranch "revert to a state of nature." Mrs. Freeze, out of a job unless she wanted to take up the apron again and cook, drifted down to the Firehole and drank whiskey. After a while a whiny voice beside her said, "Hello, Mrs. Freeze."

"Old jailbird Benny," looking out of the corners of her singeing eyes.

"Don't say nothin like that. I'm goin straight now. In fact, I got your old job. I'm the foreman now out at Car Scrope's place. Livin in that trailer." Thready stars of fox-tail barley seed hung from his sleeve.

"Jesus Christ."

They watched golfers. The television sound was turned off. Mrs. Freeze swallowed her whiskey, asked for water and another shot. Benny revolved his finger in his beer, licked it.

"There's somethin I want a know," said Mrs. Freeze. "He don't bother you?"

"Who? Car?"

"Yeah, son of a bitch Car."

"He don't bother nobody. Well, in a way he does. I mean, you're right, he is crazy, but it ain't wild or nothin. He just sets down by the creek all day long eatin tater chips. Goes down by the old railroad trestle right after breakfast with five, six little bags a chips and a bottle a aspirin. Got a kitchen chair in the willows. I have to bring him a sandwich at supper. And he comes back up around dark. He's got a headache ever day. Ask me he's got a brain tuber. Yesterday he gets a old range tent he found somewheres and he been tryin to set it up by the creek except some a the poles is missin."

"What the hell does he do down there?"

"Nothin. I told you. Don't do no work. It wasn't for me and Cody Joe that ranch'd go down the hole. He just sets there and stares at the water. Sometimes he dabbles his hand in it. Stuck his head down in it the other day. He don't fish, nothin like that. It's kind a funny. I don't know what he's goin a do when the cold weather comes."

"Nobody got a answer on that one," said Mrs. Freeze. She signaled for another glass of whiskey, something to hold on to, even in an apron, and that was more than Car Scrope had, ill-balanced on his sloping mudbank.

A Lonely Coast

YOU EVER SEE A HOUSE BURNING UP IN THE NIGHT, way to hell and gone out there on the plains? Nothing but blackness and your headlights cutting a little wedge into it, could be the middle of the ocean for all you can see. And in that big dark a crown of flame the size of your thumbnail trembles. You'll drive for an hour seeing it until it burns out or you do, until you pull off the road to close your eyes or look up at sky punched with bullet holes. And you might think about the people in the burning house, see them trying for the stairs, but mostly you don't give a damn. They are too far away, like everything else.

. The year I lived in that junk trailer in the Crazy Woman Creek drainage I thought Josanna Skiles was like that, the house on fire in the night that you could only watch. The reason for it seemed to be the strung-out, buzzed country and the little running grass fires of the heart, the kind that usually die out on their own but in some people soar into uncontrollable conflagration.

I was having my own troubles then, a problem with Riley, my old boy, something that couldn't get fixed. There was a feeling of coming heat and whirlwind. I didn't have a grip on much.

The house trailer I rented was old. It was more of a camper you'd tow behind a car, so small you couldn't cuss the cat without getting fur in your mouth. When the wind blew I'd hear parts coming off it and banging along the ground. I rented it from Oakal Roy. He said he'd been in the big time back in the 1950s, been a stunt man out in Hollywood. He was drinking himself down. A rack-sided dog hung around—I guess it was his—and once I drove in late at night and saw it crouched and gnawing at a long, bloody cow bone. He needed to shoot that dog.

I had a junior college certificate in craft supply merchandising—silk flowers, macramé, jewelry findings, beads, quills, fabric paints, that stuff. Like a magpie I was attracted to small bright objects. But I'd married Riley the day after graduation and never worked at the beads and buttons. Never would, because there weren't any craft shops in a radius of 300 miles and I wasn't going to leave Wyoming. You don't leave until you have to. So two nights a week I waitressed at the Wig-Wag Lodge, week-ends tended bar at the Gold Buckle, and the other nights I sat in the trailer doing crossword puzzles and trying to sleep, waking always at the same hour the alarm went off at the ranch, the time when Riley would be rolling out and reaching for his shirt, and in the window the hard little dot of Venus rising and below it the thin morning.

Josanna Skiles cooked at the Wig-Wag. She'd had the job for seven or eight months. Most people quit after a few weeks. You had to learn how to make sushi and some kind of sticky rice. The owner was Jimmy Shimazo. Fifty

years ago in World War Two he was a kid in the intern-
ment camp at Heart Mountain, and he said that when his
family went back to California with its cars and money
and the bright coast, he missed Wyoming, its hardness
imprinted on him. He came back years later with enough
money to buy the Wig-Wag, maybe suffering some per-
verse need for animosity which he did find here. None of
the others came back and who can blame them? All his
guests were Japanese tourists who wandered through the
lodge looking at the old saddles and cow skulls, in the gift
shop buying little six-guns and plastic chaps for their kids,
braided horsehair key rings made at the state pen. Jimmy
was a tough one to work for, short-fused, but careful to
pick women to yell at after the maintenance man, an ex-
ranch hand from Spotted Horse, beat the piss out of him
with a fence post and left him half-dead next to the
dumpster. Josanna never had a run-in with him until the
end, but she was good at cooking that Jap food and out
here everybody knows to leave the cook alone.

She had two women friends, Palma Gratt and Ruth
Wolfe, both of them burning at a slower rate than
Josanna, but in their own desperate ways also disintegrating into drifts of ash. Friday night was what they called
girls' night out, margaritas and buffalo wings at the Gold
Buckle while they read through the personal ads in the
paper. Then they went to the Stockman for ribs.
Sometimes Palma brought her kid along. The kid would
sit in the corner and tear up paper napkins. After the pra-
line cake and coffee they saw the movie at the Silver
Wing, and they might come back to the Buckle or not.
But Saturday night was their big night when they got into
tight jeans and what Josanna called dead nigger shirts, met

at the Rawhide or Bud's or Double Shot or Gold Buckle and acted wild.

They thought they were living then, drank, smoked, shouted to friends, and they didn't so much dance as straddle a man's thigh and lean in. Palma once stripped off her blouse to bare tits, Josanna swung at some drunk who'd said the wrong thing and she got slugged back, cussing pure blue through a split lip, kicking at the cowboy held tight by five or six of his delighted friends who urged her on. Nothing was too bold, nothing not worth the risk, they'd be sieving the men at the bar and cutting out the best three head, doing whatever drugs were going in the parking lot, maybe climb on some guy's lap in the cab of his truck. If Josanna was still around at two in the a.m. she looked like what she was, a woman coming into middle age, lipstick gnawed off, plain face and thickening flesh, yawning, departing into the fresh night alone and sorry. When Elk came along she had somebody to go home with, and I thought that was the point.

Every month or so she went up to the Skiles ranch south of Sundance with a long-shot view of Black Buttes. She had a boy there, sixteen, seventeen years old, in and out of the detention home. Her folks had come through rocky times. She told me that their herd had carried the gene for dwarfism since her grandparents' day, back in the forties. They'd been trying to clean the snorters out for two generations, little by little. They should have sold every one of them for beef, started over, but somehow couldn't do it. The gene had showed up while her grandmother was running the ranch, the grandfather off to World War Two with the Powder River Cavalry, the famous 115th. The government took their horses away and gave them trucks, sent those good horsemen to desks and motor pools. He came back home to stumpy-leg calves and did his best. In 1960 he drowned in the Belle Fourche River, not easy to do, but, Josanna said, her people had always taken the gritty way.

She brought me a jar of honey from their hives. Every ranch keeps bees. Me and Riley, we had twenty hives and I told her one time I missed the honey.

"Here," she said. "Not much but it's something. I go up there," she said. "That damn kind a life. Clayton wants a get out—he's talkin about goin down to Texas but I don't know. They need him. They'd take it wrong, I suppose, give me the blame if he went. Hell, he's pretty much growed up, let him do what he wants. He's headed for trouble anyway. Pain-in-the-ass kid."

Riley and me never had any kids, I don't know why. Neither one of us would go to a doctor and find out. We didn't talk about it. I thought it was probably something to do with the abortion I'd had before I knew him. They say it can mess you up. He didn't know about that and I suppose he had his own ideas.

Riley couldn't see blame in what he'd done. He said, "Look, I seen my chance and I taken it," reverting to Sweetwater home talk, where he comes from, and that was his last word on the subject.

Who knew better than me that he had a love spot on his body? She might have touched it. If she did he couldn't help it. Riley is just slat and bone, he has a thin, mean face, one of those mouths like a paper cut and he doesn't say much. But you touch that love spot, you get

213

him turned on, you lie down with him, his mouth would get real swollen, I'd just come apart with those thick, wet kisses and how big he got. Out of his clothes, horse and dog and oil and dirt, out of his clothes his true scent lay on his skin, something dry like the pith of a cottonwood twig when you break it at the joint disclosing the roan star at the center. Anyway, there's something wrong with everybody and it's up to you to know what you can handle.

In nine years married we had only one vacation, to Oregon where my brother lived. We went out on a rocky point and watched the rollers come in. It was foggy and cold, there wasn't anybody there but us watching the rollers. It was dusk and the watery curls held light as though it was inside them. Up the lonely coast a stuttering blink warned ships away. I said to Riley that was what we needed in Wyoming—lighthouses. He said no, what we needed was a wall around the state and turrets with machine guns in them.

Once Josanna gave me a ride in her brother's truck—he was down for a few days to pick up pump parts and some pipe—and it was sure enough a down-home truck, pair of chaps hanging over the seat back, chain, beat-up hat on the floor, a filthy Carhartt jacket, seven or eight torn-up gloves, dog hairs and dust, empty beer cans, .30-.06 in the rear window rack and on the seat between us in a snarl of wire, rope, and old mail unopened, a .44 Ruger Blackhawk half out of the holster. Let me tell you that truck made me homesick. I said something about her brother had enough firepower, didn't he, and she laughed and said the Blackhawk was hers, she kept it in the glove compartment of her own truck but it was in the shop again that day with the ongoing compression problem they couldn't seem to fix; it was on the seat because she didn't want to forget it when her brother went back.

Long hair, frizzled and hanging down, was the fashion, and in the tangled cascades women's faces seemed narrow and vulnerable. Palma's hair was neon orange. Her brows were plucked and arched, the eyes set wide, the skin below dark and hurt-looking. Her daughter lived with her, a mournful kid ten or eleven years old with a sad mug and straight brown hair, the way Palma's would be if she didn't fix it up. The kid was always tearing at something.

The other one, Ruth, had the shadow of a mustache, and in summer heavy stubble showed under her arms. She paid forty-five dollars twice a month to have her legs waxed. She had a huge laugh, like a man's.

Josanna was muscular like most country women, tried to hide it under fuss-ruffle clothes with keyhole necklines. Her hair was strawberry roan, coarse and thick and full of electricity. She had a somewhat rank odor, a family odor because the brother had it too, musky and a little sour, and that truck of his smelled the same way. With Josanna it was faint and you might mistake it for strange Jap spices, but the aroma that came off the brother was strong enough to flatten a horse. He was an old bachelor. They called him Woody because, said Josanna, he'd come strutting out into the kitchen raw naked when he was four or five years old showing a baby hard-on and their old man had laughed until he choked and called him Woody and the name persisted forevermore and brought him local fame. You just couldn't help but look once you heard that, and he'd smile.

All three women had been married, rough marriages full of fighting and black eyes and sobbing imprecations, all of them knew the trouble that came with drinking men and hair-trigger tempers. Wyos are touchers, hot-blooded and quick, and physically yearning. Maybe it's because they spend so much time handling livestock, but people here are always handshaking, patting, smoothing, caressing, enfolding. This instinct extends to anger, the lightning backhand slap, the hip-shot to throw you off balance, the elbow, a jerk and wrench, the swat, and then the serious stuff that's meant to kill and sometimes does. The story about Josanna was that when she broke up with her ex-husband she shot at him, creased his shoulder before he jumped her and took the gun away. You couldn't push her around. It gave her a dangerous allure that attracted some men, the latest, Elk Nelson, whom she'd found in the newspaper. When they set up together he collected all the cartridges in the house and hid them at his mother's place in Wyodak, as if Josanna couldn't buy more. But that old bold Josanna got buried somewhere when Elk came around.

"Listen, if it's got four wheels or a dick you're goin a have trouble with it, guaranteed," said Palma at one of their Friday-night good times. They were reading the news-paper lonely hearts ads out loud. If you don't live here you can't think how lonesome it gets. We need those ads. That doesn't mean we can't laugh at them.

"How about this one: 'Six-three, two hundred pounds, thirty-seven, blue eyes, plays drums and loves Christian music.' Can't you just hear it, 'The Old Rugged Cross' on bongos?"

"Here's a better one: 'Cuddly cowboy, six-four, one hundred and eighty, N/S, not God's gift to women, likes holding hands, firefighting, practicing on my tuba.' I guess that could mean noisy, skinny, ugly, plays with matches. Must be cuddly as a pile a sticks."

"What a you think 'not God's gift to women' means?"

"Pecker the size of a peanut."

Josanna'd already put an inky circle around *Good-looking, athletic build Teddy Bear, brown-eyed, black mustache, likes dancing, good times, outdoors, walking under the stars. Lives life to its fullest.* It turned out to be Elk Nelson and he was one step this side of restless drifter, had worked oil rigs, construction, coal mines, loaded trucks. He was handsome, mouthy, flashed a quick smile. I thought he was a bad old boy from his scuffed boots to his greasy ponytail. The first thing he did was put his .30-.30 in the cab rack of Josanna's truck and she didn't say a word. He had pale brown eyes the color of graham crackers, one of those big mustaches like a pair of blackbird wings. Hard to say how old he was; older than Josanna, forty-five, forty-six maybe. His arms were all wildlife, blurry tattoos of spiders, snarling wolves, scorpions, rattlesnakes. To me he looked like he'd tried every dirty thing three times. Josanna was helpless crazy for him from the first time they got together and crazy jealous. And didn't he like that? It seemed to be the way he measured how she felt about him and he put it to the test. When you are bone tired of being alone, when all you want is someone to pull you close and say it's all right, all right now, and you get one like Elk Nelson you've got to see you've licked the bottom out of the dish.

I tended bar on the weekends at the Gold Buckle and watched the fire take hold of her. She would smile at what he said, listen and lean, light his damn cigarette, examine his hands for cuts—he had a couple of weeks' work fencing at the 5 Bar. She'd touch his face, smooth a wrinkle in his shirt and he'd say, quit off pawin me. They sat for hours at the Buckle seesawing over whether or not he'd made a pass at some woman, until he got fed up enough to walk out. He seemed to be goading her, seeing how far he could shove before she hit the wall. I wondered when she'd get the message that she wasn't worth shit to him.

August was hot and drouthy, a hell of grasshoppers and dried-up creeks. They said this part of the state was a disaster area. I heard that said before any grasshoppers came. The Saturday night was close, air as thick as in a closet with the winter coats. It was rodeo night and that brings them in. The bar filled up early, starting with ranch hands around three in the afternoon still in their sweaty shirts, red faces mottled with heat and dirt, crowding out most of the wrinkle-hour boys, the old-timers who started their drinking in the morning. Palma was there a little after five, alone, fresh and high-colored, wearing a cinnamon red satin blouse that shined with every move she made. Her arms were loaded with silver bracelets, one metal ring on another clinking and shifting. By five-thirty the bar was packed and hot, bodies touching, some fools trying to dance—country girls playing their only card, grinding against the boys—people squeezed eight to a booth meant for four, six deep at the bar, men hat to hat. There were three of us working, me and Zeeks and Justin, and as fast as we went we couldn't keep up. They were pouring the drinks down. Everybody was shouting. Outside the sky was green-black and trucks driving down the street had their headlights on, dimmed by constant lightning flashes. The electricity went off for about fifteen seconds, the bar black as a cave, the jukebox dying *worrr,* and a huge, amorous, drunken and delighted moan coming up from the crowd that changed to cussing when the light flickered back on.

Elk Nelson came in, black shirt and silver belly hat. He leaned over the bar, hooked his finger in the waistband of my jeans and yanked me to him.

"Josanna in yet?"

I pulled back, shook my head.

"Good. Let's get in the corner then and hump."

I got him a beer.

Ash Weeter stood next to Elk. Weeter was a local rancher who wouldn't let his wife set foot in a bar, I don't know why. The jokers said he was probably worried she'd get killed in a poolroom fight. He was talking about a horse sale coming up in Thermopolis. Well, he didn't own a ranch, he managed one for some rich people in Pennsylvania, and I heard it that half the cows he ran on their grass were his. What they didn't know didn't hurt them.

"Have another beer, Ash," Elk said in a good-buddy voice.

"Nah, I'm goin home, take a shit and go to bed." No expression on that big shiny face. He didn't like Elk.

Palma's voice cut through a lull, Elk looked up, saw her at the end of the bar, beckoning.

"See you," said Ash Weeter to no one, pulling his hat down and ducking out.

Elk held his cigarette high above his head as he got through the crowd. I cracked a fresh Coors, brought it down to him, heard him say something about Casper.

That was the thing, they'd start out at the Buckle then drive down to Casper, five or six of them, a hundred and thirty miles, sit in some other bar probably not much different than the Buckle, drink until they were wrecked, then hit a motel. Elk told it on Josanna that she got so warped out one time she pissed the motel bed and he'd had to drag her into the shower and turn it on cold, throw the sheets in on top of her. Living life to its fullest. He'd tell that like it was the best story in the world and every time he did it she'd put her head down, wait it out with a tight little smile. I thought of my last night back on the ranch with Riley, the silence oppressive and smothering, the clock ticking like blows of an axe, the maddening trickle of water into the stained bathtub from the leaky faucet. He wouldn't fix it, just wouldn't. Couldn't fix the other thing and made no effort in that direction. I suppose he thought I'd just hang and rattle.

Palma leaned against Elk, slid back and forth slowly as if she was scratching her back on his shirt buttons. "Don't know. Wait for Josanna and see what she wants a do."

"Josanna will want a go down to Casper. That's it, she

will because that's what I want a do." He said something else I didn't hear.

Palma shrugged, shifted out into the dancers with him. He was a foot taller than she, his cigarette crackling in her hair when he pulled her close. She whipped her hair back, slammed her pelvis into him and he almost swallowed the butt.

There was a terrific blast of light and thunder and the lights went off again and there was the head-hollowing smell of ozone. A sheet of rain struck the street followed by the deafening roar of hailstones. The lights surged on but weak and yellow. It was impossible to hear anything over the battering hail.

A kind of joyous hysteria moved into the room, everything flying before the wind, vehicles outside getting dented to hell, the crowd sweaty and the smells of aftershave, manure, clothes dried on the line, your money's worth of perfume, smoke, booze; the music subdued by the shout and babble though the bass hammer could be felt through the soles of the feet, shooting up the channels of legs to the body fork, center of everything. It is that kind of Saturday night that torches your life for a few hours, makes it seem something is happening.

There were times when I thought the Buckle was the best place in the world, but it could shift on you and then the whole dump seemed a mess of twist-face losers, the women with eyebrows like crowbars, the men covered with bristly red hair, knuckles the size of new potatoes, showing the gene pool was small and the rivulets that once fed it had dried up. I think sometimes it hit Josanna that way too because one night she sat quiet and slumped at the bar watching the door, watching for Elk, and he didn't come in. He'd been there, though, picked up some tourist girl in white shorts, couldn't have been more than twenty. It wouldn't do any good to tell her.

"This's a miserable place," she said. "My god it's miserable."

The door opened and four or five of the arena men came in, big mustaches, slickers and hats running water, boots muddy, squeezing through the dancers, in for a few quick ones before the rodeo. The atmosphere was hot and wet. Everybody was dressed up. I could see Elk Nelson down the bar, leaning against Palma, one arm over her satin shoulder, big fingers grazing her right breast, fingernail scratching the erect nipple.

They were still playing their game when the door jerked open again, the wind popping it against the wall, and Josanna came through, shaking her head, streaming wet, the artful hair plastered flat. Her peach-colored shirt clung to her, transparent in places, like burned skin where it bunched and the color doubled. Her eyes were red, her mouth thin and sneering.

"Give me a whiskey, celebrate a real goddamn lousy day."

Justin poured it high, slid the glass carefully to her.

"Got a wee bit wet," he said.

"Look at this." She held out her left hand, pulled up the sopping sleeve. Her arm and hand were dotted with red bruises. "Hail," she said. "I spun my truck in front a Cappy's and nicked a parking meter, busted the hood latch. Run two blocks here. But that's not hardly the problem. I got fired, Jimmy Shimazo fired me. Out a the clear blue sky. Don't anybody get in my way tonight."

"You bet," said Justin, pressing against me with his thigh. He seemed to want to get something going, but he was going to be disappointed. I don't know, maybe I'd think the score was even. But it wouldn't be.

"So I'm goin a have a drink, soon's the rain stops I'm goin a get me some gone, try Casper is any better. Fuck em all, tell em all a kiss my sweet rosy." She knocked back the whiskey, slammed the glass down on the bar hard enough to break it.

"See what I mean?" she said. "Everything I touch falls apart." Elk Nelson came up behind her, slipped his big red hands under her arms, cupped her breasts and squeezed. I wondered if she'd seen him feeling up Palma. I thought she had. I thought he wanted her to see him handling her willing friend.

"Yeah," he said. "What a you want a do? Casper, right? Go get something a eat, I hope. I'm hungry enough I could eat a rancher's unwiped ass."

"You want some buffalo wings?" I said. "Practically the same thing." We called across the street to Cowboy Teddy for them and inside an hour somebody brought them over. Half the time they were raw. Elk shook his head. He was fondling Josanna, one hand inside her wet shirt, but looking at the crowd behind him in the bar mirror. Palma was still at the end of the bar, watching him. Ruth came up, slapped Josanna on the butt, said she'd heard what Shimazo did, the little prick. Josanna put her arm around Ruth's waist. Elk eased back, looked at Palma in the mirror, cracked that big yellow smile. There was a lot going on.

"Ruth, babe, I'm tired a this bullshit place. How about go down a Casper and just hang around for a while. I'm just goin a say fuck him, fuck Jimmy Shimazo. I said, hey, look, at least give me a reason. I put too much wasabi on the goddamn fish balls? Shit. He just fired me, I don't even know why."

Elk put in his dime's worth. "Hell, it's only a shittin job. Get another one." Like jobs were easy. There weren't any jobs.

"The latch on my truck hood is busted. I can't get it to stay shut. If we're goin a Casper it's got a be fixed." Josanna's truck had a crew cab, plenty of room for all of them. They always went in her truck and she paid for the gas, too.

"Reef it down with a little balin wire."

At the cash register Justin murmured to me what he'd heard at the back booths—Jimmy Shimazo had fired Josanna because he caught her in the meat cooler snorting a line. He was death on that. For now he was doing the cooking himself. He was talking about getting a real Jap cook in from California.

"That's all we need around here," said Justin. They say now the Japs own the whole southwest part of the state, refineries, big smokestacks.

Something happened then, and in the noise I didn't see them go, Josanna, Elk, Palma, Ruth and somebody she'd picked up—Barry, romping on his hands with whiskey. Maybe they left before the fireball. There is a big plate glass window at the Buckle onto the street, and outside a wooden ledge wide enough to set beer bottles on. Mr.

Thompson, the bar owner, displayed his collection of spurs, coils of rope, worn boots, a couple of saddles, some old woolly chaps so full of moths they looked like a snowstorm in reverse in spring, other junk inside the window. The window was like a stage. Now a terrific, sputtering ball of fire bloomed on the ledge throwing glare on the dusty cowboy gear. It was still raining. You could hear the fireball roaring and a coat of soot in the shape of a cone and peck-speckled with rain was building up on the glass. Justin and a dozen people went out to see what it was. He tried knocking it off the ledge but it was stuck on with its own burning. He ran back in.

"Give me the water pitcher."

People at the front were all laughing, somebody called, piss on it, Justin. He poured three pitchers of water on the thing before it quit, a blackened lump of something, placed and set afire by persons unknown. There was a sound like a shot and the glass cracked from top to bottom. Justin said later it was a shot, not the heat. It was the heat. I know a shot when I hear one.

There's a feeling you get driving down to Casper at night from the north, and not only there, other places where you come through hours of darkness unrelieved by any lights except the crawling wink of some faraway ranch truck. You come down a grade and all at once the shining town lies below you, slung out like all western towns, and with the curved bulk of mountain behind it. The lights trail away to the east in a brief and stubby cluster of yellow that butts hard up against the dark. And if you've ever been to the lonely coast you've seen how the shore rock drops off into the black water and how the light on the point is final. Beyond are the old rollers coming on for millions of years. It is like that here at night but instead of the rollers it's wind. But the water was here once. You think about the sea that covered this place hundreds of millions of years ago, the slow evaporation, mud turned to stone. There's nothing calm in those thoughts. It isn't finished, it can still tear apart. Nothing is finished. You take your chances.

Maybe that's how they saw it, gliding down toward the lights, drinking beer and passing a joint, Elk methed out and driving and nobody saying much, just going to Casper. That's what Palma says. Ruth says different. Ruth says Josanna and Elk had a bad fight all the way down and Palma was in the middle of it. Barry says they were all screwed out of their skulls, he was only drunk.

We had a time with the calving, Riley and me, that spring. A neighbor rancher's big Saler bulls had got into our pastures and bred some of our heifers. We didn't know it until the calving started although Riley remarked once or twice that some of the heifers had ballooned up really big and we figured twins. We knew when the first one came. The heifer was a good one, too, long-bodied, meaty, trim and with a tremendous amount of muscle, but not double muscled, sleek and feminine, what we wanted in our mother cows, almost torn in half by the biggest calf either one of us had ever seen. It was a monster, a third of the size of its mother.

"That bastard Coldpepper. Look at that calf. It comes from them fuckin giant bulls, the size a tanks. They must a got in last April and you bet he knew it, never said a word. I guess we are goin a find out how many."

The weather was miserable too, spring storms, every kind of precip. We got through the first ten days sleepless, wet and cold, especially Petey Flurry who'd worked for us for nine years, out ahorseback in the freezing rain driving the heifers into the calving yard. Wouldn't you know, he got pneumonia when we needed him the most and they carted him off to the hospital. His wife sent the fifteen-year-old daughter over to help and she was a pretty good hand, ranch raised, around animals all her life, strong but narrow little hands that could work into a straining heifer and grasp the new hooves. We were all dead tired.

Around mid-afternoon I'd left them in the calving barn with a bad heifer, gone up to the house to grab an hour of sleep, but I was too tired, way beyond sleep, wired, and after ten minutes I got up and put the coffeepot on, got some cookie dough from the freezer and in a little while there was steaming coffee and hot almond sandies. I put three cups in a cardboard box, the cookies in an insulated sack, and went back out to the calving barn.

I came in with that box of coffee and cookies, pushed the door open gently. He'd just finished, had just pulled out of her, back up on his feet. She was still lying on a hay bale, skinny kid's legs bent open. I looked at him, the girl sat up. The light wasn't good in there and he was trying to get it back in his pants in a hurry but I saw the blood on him. The heat of the coffee came through the cardboard box and I set it on the old bureau that held the calf pullers and rope and salve and suture material. I stood there while they pulled at their clothes. The girl was sniveling. Sure enough, she was on the road to becoming a sleazy little bitch, but she was only fifteen and it was the first time and her daddy worked for the man who'd done it to her.

He said to her, "Come on, I'm gettin you home," and she said, "No," and they went outside. Didn't say anything to me. He was gone until the next afternoon, came back and said his few words, I said mine and the next day I left. The goddamn heifer had died with a dead calf still inside her.

Most things you never know what happened or why. Even Palma and Ruth and Barry who were there couldn't say just how it came apart. From what they remembered and what the papers told it seems like they were on that street full of cars and trucks and Elk tried to get around a trailer loaded with calves. There wasn't a vehicle on the highway until they turned onto Poplar, and then there was the backed-up traffic from the light that's east of the exit ramp, traffic all around them and with it a world of trouble. While he was passing the trailer a blue pickup passed him, swerving into the oncoming traffic lane and forcing cars off the road. The blue pickup cut sharp in front of the trailer-load of calves. That trailer guy stepped on the brake and Elk hit the trailer pretty hard, hard enough, said Palma, to give her a nosebleed. Josanna was yelling about her truck and the baling wire on the hood latch loosened and the hood was lifting up and down a few inches like an alligator with a taste in its mouth. But Elk was raging, he didn't stop, pulled around the calf trailer and went after the blue pickup which had turned onto 20-26 and belted off west. Josanna shouted at Elk who was so mad, Ruth said, blood was almost squirting out of his eyes. Right behind Elk came the calf trailer flicking his lights and leaning on the horn.

Elk caught the blue truck about eight miles out and ran him into the ditch, pulled in front and blocked him. Far back the lights of the calf hauler came on fast and steady. Elk jumped out and charged at the blue pickup. The driver was coked and smoked. His passenger, a thin girl in a pale dress, was out and yelling, throwing stones at Josanna's truck. Elk and the driver fought, slipping on the highway, grunting, and Barry and Ruth and Palma stumbled around trying to get them apart. Then the calf hauler, Ornelas, screamed in from Mars.

Ornelas worked for Natrona Power Monday through Friday, had a second job nighttimes repairing saddles, and on his weekends tried to work the small ranch he'd inherited from his mother. When Elk clipped him he hadn't slept for two nights, had just finished his eighth beer and opened the ninth. It's legal to drink and drive in this state. You are supposed to use some judgment.

The cops said later that Ornelas was the catalyst because when he got out of his truck he was aiming a rifle in the general direction of Elk and the pickup driver, Fount Slinkard, and the first shot put a hole in Slinkard's rear window. Slinkard screamed at his passenger to get him the .22 in his rack but she was crouching by the front tire with her hands clasping her head. Barry shouted, watch out cowboy, ran across the highway. There was no traffic. Slinkard or Slinkard's passenger had the .22 but dropped it. Ornelas fired again and in the noise and fright of the moment no one grasped causes or effects. Someone picked up Slinkard's .22. Barry was drunk and in the ditch on the other side of the road and couldn't see a thing but said he counted at least seven shots. One of the women was screaming. Someone pounded on a horn. The calves were bellowing and surging at the sides of the trailer, one of them hit and the smell of blood in there.

By the time the cops came Ornelas was shot through the throat and though he did not die he wasn't much good for yodeling. Elk was already dead. Josanna was dead, the Blackhawk on the ground beneath her.

You know what I think? Like Riley might say, I think Josanna seen her chance and taken it. Friend, it's easier than you think to yield up to the dark impulse.

The Governors of Wyoming

WADE WALLS

THE QUICK THUNDERSTORM WAS OVER, THE street wet and slices of tingling blue showing through bunched cloud. They waited in the truck. Roany had parked close to the newsstand, the stop for the Denver bus. A few final raindrops fell, hard as dice. At five thirty-five the bus pulled in, stinking, sighing. Eleven passengers descended, Wade Walls the last. He shot them a glance without turning his head when Roany put down the window and said his name. They watched him cross the street and go into the Ranger Bar.

"Is that him? Where is he going?" Renti chewed gum until it snapped for mercy. She was a small, grubby woman in black tights and construction worker boots, ingrained dirt on the backs of her arms, her face handsome and impatient. She stared after the man crossing the street, jumping a rill of water.

Her married sister, Roany Hamp, shrugged. Her hair, sleeked with rose oil, was twisted into a knot. Clean arcs divided the windshield into a diptych, and their faces flared through the glass.

"Maybe he wants a beer," said Renti, punching the radio buttons.

"He doesn't drink. Maybe he wants a kick in the butt." Roany turned the key and they heard the exhortations of a local announcer, the one who pronounced his own name as though he had discovered a diamond in his nostril.

"We supposed to wait for him or follow him in there?"

"Won't hurt to sit in the truck for a few minutes." She took a tube from her purse, squeezed a clot of unguent into her palm, scented and the color of bloodstained jelly. "*Black hat, black hat blues . . .*"

"He's trying to pretend like he's a spy or something."

They watched people go in and out of the bar. The door swung, slowed, swung again. "*Got those dirty old black hat blues . . .*"

"Uh-huh," said Roany, "doesn't drink and doesn't drive but he's happy to blow up a dam for you. How he got Shy mixed in his business I can't figure. Before I knew him. Shy is about as much of a—" The door latch clicked and Wade Walls slid into the crew seat. "*Don't put it on the bed . . .*"

"For god's sake. You gave me a heart attack," said Roany, "creeping up like that." She turned off the radio.

"I went out the back door and through the alley," he said. The cab smelled of attar of roses, the fruity gum.

"My sister Renti," she said. "Staying with us for a couple of weeks. From Taos. You think all this stealth is necessary, we're in the movies? You think they're following you or what?" She pulled into the traffic behind a pickup hauling a gooseneck trailer. They could hear his rapid breathing, like that of a dog, behind them. If it were a movie his signature music would be a huffed and spitty harmonica.

"I have been doing my deeds for seventeen years," he said, "and out of a dozen people that started with me I am the only one left. Because I'm careful."

"How come you went into the Ranger?"

"Bottled water. Drank about three of those little ones on the plane. Two more on the bus."

There wasn't much to say to that and they rode in silence. Wade Walls seemed to be in a coma until they turned onto the county road.

"It is dry," he said, dazed, trying to seem awake, caught in a half-nightmare about this place as though still on the bus and coming over the border through a fringe of billboards, cheap gas stations, cigarette and fireworks stores, then a few wind-scoured towns, ranches scattered like a shovelful of gravel thrown on rough ground.

"Welcome to Wyoming," said Roany in her arid voice. "Welcome to paradise."

But he knew all about the place, the fiery column of the Cave Gulch flare-off in its vast junkyard field, refineries, disturbed land, uranium mines, coal mines, trona mines, pump jacks and drilling rigs, clear-cuts, tank farms, contaminated rivers, pipelines, methanol-processing plants, ruinous dams, the Amoco mess, railroads, all disguised by the deceptively empty landscape. It wasn't his first trip. He knew about the state's lie-back-and-take-it income from federal mineral royalties, severance and *ad valorem* taxes, the old ranches bought up by country music stars and assorted billionaires acting roles in some imaginary cowboy revue, the bleed-out of brains and talent, and for common people no jobs and a tough life in a trailer house.

It was a 97,000-square-mile dog's breakfast of outside exploiters, Republican ranchers and scenery. The ranchers couldn't see their game was over. They needed a hard lesson and he was here to give one.

"It is dry. It's been a bad drought." Roany steered and the sister said nothing.

"Drought," he said as though trying a new word, her intricate hair and creamy nape in front of him.

"Spot shower before the bus came. Not out here, but in town. Not a drop out here."

The ranch was twenty-two miles south of Slope in mima mound country—what old men called biscuit land, low domes of earth cast up on the plain by ancient rodents or frost action, no one was sure—and to the west a fanged landscape that seemed to be coming at them. In this dry, heated year the grass was already yellow-bronze, the dusty earth quivering with grasshoppers in chirring flight, heads and thoraxes marbled hazel and drab. Cheatgrass crowded native bunchgrass, pernicious weeds grew. He knew before she made the turn that Roany would take the back way and the truck passed over metronomic shadows of telephone poles, then onto the washed-out gravel rut they called the Drunk Road.

Juniper Hamp had quarried the pale sandstone in 1882 and built the square, two-story ranch house with his six sons. There was a chimney at each corner rising above the mansard roof, tall windows and a high porch. The stone barn and springhouse, the stone-paved square courtyard at the back entrance had fairly well cleaned out the small quarry to the sons' relief—they joked that he would have built corrals with it if the stone had held out. Roany had pulled out old partitions, replaced ceilings, gutted the kitchen. Only the parlor was as it had been, with its glass-fronted cabinet and green velvet lounge.

In the kitchen Renti looked Wade Walls over: face somehow thick as if the flesh was dense, lower lip jutting like that of a grouper fish. His courtesy smile showed yellow teeth all the same size. From a distance, holding his non-leather briefcase, he resembled a water rights lawyer. Close to, he seemed odd, legs tight as though ready to leap, his strange suit made from a coarse fabric, sewed with crooked seams.

He could sense the femaleness of the house. "Where's Shy?" When he spoke his stiff face jerked as though moved with hooks and wires.

"I wish I knew. He took off early Tuesday. Didn't say where to."

"What do you mean?" They were standing in the kitchen and like cartoon figures only their mouths moved.

"I think maybe he's in Montana. He said something about Montana, I think. They're killing the bison up there." She might have said they were mowing lawns.

"That was two years ago. The remaining bison are alive and well so far. Until winter."

"Well, I don't know. He's got a thousand things. He's always sounding off about land swaps and ferrets, I don't know what else. Besides that crap he's got his business to run—I mean the horse insurance—and I've got mine. He does not sign out when he goes. There's times I only see him once a week." A fragment of her voice broke off.

"This sure sounds like fun," said Renti, hair crisscross, missing the sharp Taos nights, even the milling tourists half-blind from staring at silver jewelry, most of them oldies—matched pairs—traveling together, the men in the front seat where they could see everything, the women in back like dogs, getting flat side views of guardrails and roadside trash.

She had worked jobs: highway construction flagger, running a candle-wrapping machine, art sales in the lesser galleries, step-and-fetchit for a designer of stained glass, summer theatre stagehand, before Muleshoe Gallery took her on. There she glued muslin onto the backs of yellowed maps, replaced spring rollers and draw rods on old roll-ups, one slack afternoon climbed up on the map table with Pan, the manager, and copulated. There was enough to it to keep them going and in a month Pan wondered, bringing a present of two cold bottles and a plate of *chiles rellenos,* if they didn't have a relationship; she was raw, unbeautiful, but a stopper in a skinny long dress with a deep border of red. Twenty miles out toward Angel Fire they found a one-room adobe house with a trailer grafted onto the north wall. He dragged big orange pots onto the patio, she grew herbs, they took in an abandoned Alsatian wolfhound. The dog was obedient and mild, a backseat dog. There was nothing wrong, but after a year Renti had packed a bag, told him she would be back in a few weeks. She was going to Wyoming to see her sister. The next night she had suffered a terrible dream in which she stood a Chihuahua in a pot of boiling broth and when she ladled the broth into her bowl the burned animal spoke humbly, asking if it might be taken to the doctor, perhaps in the afternoon if she had time.

For a few days it was fine, all blood affection and the old familiar, then everything had been said. They'd reached the point in reminiscence where their lives had diverged and superficial accounts rather than shared intimacies were the most that could be expected. Renti said that the thing with Pan was turning a little gummy. Her fault, she was stone-hearted, didn't want what she got. Roany said Shy was two steps up from an idiot, but sweet, and though he slowed her down in every way, divorce wasn't worth the misery and he was too damn beautiful to lose. In a week they began to fight as they had when they were children and about the same things: which of them the parents had favored over the other, and why she, Renti, was such a dirty bird.

"You're like a greasy old crow," Roany said, "dressed in black all the time. You'd be good-looking if—"

"Dear sister, do not try to remodel me." In truth they were both slovenly, Roany, not in her person nor her shop, but in housekeeping. Though Shy Hamp, her husband, was, like many ranch-grown men, obsessively neat. The greasy sinks, the dust! He waited until she left for the shop, ignored his horse insurance business to attack the filth. Now, two sisters in the house, a knife clotted with orange jam as though used to crush some monstrous insect, dead flies on the bathtub surround, a window streaked with bird excreta seemed squalid evidence of his private longings.

Renti had looked forward to Wade Walls, supposed he would have arms as hard as wood, a menacing glint, but he was slump-shouldered, seemed to come from nowhere and belong to no one.

"It's not about fun." He sat in the chair, his hands

folded across his stomach. It had been made into a kitchen from a magazine, copper pans dangling from beams, a forest of arty vinegar and oil flasks.

Roany took a half-empty bottle of chardonnay from the refrigerator and poured a little in two wineglasses.

"He knows you're here. He's coming back today. Or tonight. Sometime today, right? I don't have any idea what you are doing and I don't want to know. I'm just the damn chauffeur." She drank some of the wine, threw another sentence his way. "You're in the room you had before, the cowboy room."

He went upstairs with his briefcase. This room was tricked out with cow skulls, grimy lariats, a digital reproduction of a chromolithograph showing a rustler caught in the act. Most of the furniture was stumpy wildwood. There was one Molesworth chest with painted longhorns marching across the drawer panels. Someone had tried to chisel off one of the longhorns, leaving a splintery scar.

Renti and Roany heard the toilet flush.

"Little bottles of water still coming through," said Renti.

He came down the back stair, clearing his throat. "I hate to trouble you girls but do you have anything to eat?"

"Didn't they give you something on the plane?"

"I don't eat airlines food—" He laughed a little, trying to hide his irritation. The two of them sat there drinking wine, making no dinner preparations.

"Tomato soup, eggs, grapefruit juice, bread." Roany waited a beat or two. The devil stirred in her. "There's some steaks in the freezer." That would wind him up.

"I don't eat meat. You know I don't eat meat. You're fighting the cattlemen but you support them by eating their beef?"

"I'm not fighting the cattlemen," said Roany. "That's you and Shy."

"It's in the freezer," said Renti. "It'll get freezer burn if nobody eats it." She had quickly hated him when he said "you girls."

"That makes it all right?"

"Look," said Roany. "It's not beef, Wade. It's buffalo. Nobody here eats beef. Anyway, what we eat hasn't got anything to do with whatever you and Shy have going."

"It has everything to do with it. These subsidized ranchers and their gas-bag cows destroying public range, riparian habitat, wiping out rare plants, trampling stream banks, creating ozone-destroying methane gas, ruining the National Forests that belong to the people, to all of us, stinking, polluting, stupid, world-destroying cows—and for what? A pitiful three percent of this state's gross income. So a few can live a nineteenth-century lifestyle." He stopped in a kind of despair. To have to explain it here. He looked down. The skinny dark one was wearing leather boots. He noticed now that they smelled of meat, the house stank of it. He opened the refrigerator with a wide exposing motion, saw two dark carrots, broccoli turning yellow, bottles of tonic and wine and beer, a basket of shriveled chilies, in the meat drawer packages wrapped in butcher paper, maroon blood on them.

"I'm not into cooking tonight," said Roany. "Everybody make their own."

He drank a glass of water while he waited for the soup to heat.

"I remember," he said to Roany in an almost tender voice, "the artichokes. Last year? You grilled those big California artichokes. I didn't know you could cook them like that. They were wonderful. All of us out on the deck watching the moon rise?" He had known she was drunk. The only time people liked him was when they were drunk.

"Yes," she said disinterestedly. "We can't get those artichokes now. I don't know why." An enormous heaviness was settling in the kitchen. That night a year ago, over the artichokes he had told Roany he had sewn the brown suit himself from New Zealand hemp. It would last forever. She had swallowed so much wine the suit seemed beautiful and Wade Walls a kind of hero. In the headachy morning he was just a man in a wrinkled jacket.

"So," he said, very quietly, "Shy went back to meat." Once, when Shy Hamp was a kid running cows in sorrow and frustration, he'd set him right. But that was a long time ago.

"He didn't 'go back to meat.' He never quit meat, only beef. And he said buffalo was different, it was o.k."

"Not o.k." He did not try to keep savagery out of his voice. "The domestication of livestock was the single most terrible act the human species ever perpetrated. It dooms everything living. The future of the earth is inescapable, a harsh, waterless desert littered with bones if we cannot stop—"

"Your broth is boiling, Wade," said Roany. She folded her lips in tightly, stood uncertain and half-turned from him, then, as though confronted with problems whose postulates changed constantly, gave up, poured wine into her sister's glass and into her own. She carried her wine out to the deck, sat in a canvas chair and smoked a cigarette. There she lounged beyond the open door, smoke pouring from her nose, red glass in hand.

"Wade," said Renti, "do you work for a real estate developer?"

"For god's sake, no. What gave you that idea?"

"You want to get rid of the cows, right? I mean, isn't that what it comes down to, cows or subdivisions? I mean, what happens to a ranch once the stock is gone? Development, right? What else is there? I mean, what are you trying to do?" Contempt came out of her like water from a firehose.

"I want to bring it back," he said. His voice swelled with professional passion. "I want it to be like it was, all the fences and cows gone. I want the native grasses to come back, the wildflowers. I want the dried-up streams to run clear, the springs to flow again and the big rivers run hard. I want the water table restored. I want the antelope and the elk and the bison and the mountain sheep and the wolves to reclaim the country. I want the ranchers and feedlot operators and processors and meat distributors to go down the greased pole straight to hell. If I ran the west I'd sweep them all away, leave the wind and the grasses to the hands of the gods. Let it be the empty place."

"Yeah. Why don't you blow up a meatpacker then instead of hammering ranchers? Why don't you wreck Florida ranchers? I bet there's more beef comes out of Florida than the west."

She walked out of the room with a haunchy slouch, not waiting to hear him say that western beef was the pivot point on which it all turned, that the battleground was the ruined land that belonged to the People.

BAD BEEF

They were the daughters of Tucson lawyers, Slinger & Slinger, brought up in comfortable style. Renti had majored in art at school in California, Roany in business at the University of Wyoming where she found Shy Hamp. He was a novelty; her mistake was in taking the possibilities all the way.

She knew she had business acumen and superior taste.

"They don't get it here," she said to Shy after Delong Teleger in the hardware store asked her to go back to the shelves and check the price of four Phillips-head screws she was trying to buy. She had dropped the screws and walked out.

"That man thinks because he's the only hardware store in town people have to buy from him. And then he whines when all the business goes to Denver or Billings or Salt Lake City."

"Well, Delong's got a bad hip. I bet he thought you could get to the shelf there and back quicker'n he could. And he sure knows you're not goin a Denver for four screws."

"He should have had the price in his head or on a computer. He is still writing everything down on a little pad. With carbon copies."

"Don't get all hard-breathin, Roany. Ease off."

Later, at a chain store in the mall, she bought inferior screws packaged in clear plastic and bearing a price sticker.

She intended to show them how to do it right. There was money in western goods—aromatic sage bath oil, yucca soap, the fragrant seeds of wild columbine, dried flowers of ladies' tresses, cedar potpourri for tourists who sniggered at drugstore lavender and cordovan hair dye. She'd carry hitched horsehair bracelets and keychains, a few hides and coyote pelts. The central business would be adaptations of antique western clothing—twill serge walking skirts, ranchers' vests, and a line of custom-made rodeo shirts. She would hire two or three women to sew. Minimum wage. And for the fun of it she would stock a cabinet with Cowboy Curls mane detangler, packets of wild bergamot the Cheyenne had used to perfume favorite horses, cans of herb chew, funky stuff nobody needed but that they would buy because it was funky stuff, as she had taken on Shy Hamp. He was champion of nothing, a kind of tame cowboy without the horse sweat and grit. What she loved was his sweet slowness.

"The customers are there," she told him, sharp and defiant, "but if you are going to mess with that ranch it won't be me keeping the books and calling the feed store. I've got my own life." Later, she wilted, went moody, despised her own furious impatience. "I don't know what's wrong. I get crazy," she said. "I can't—"

"It's all right," he said. Then, as if they had been talking of something else, "Don't worry, you big old pretty girl, I'll always make it back home." To say something like that he might have been planning a voyage to the Bellingshausen Sea. "Come on over here," he murmured, "little old crazy girl." But he was miles and miles back of home range. He was double-riding a ghostly thoroughbred from years ago, couldn't help it.

Shy Hamp had wanted not to ranch but to go to college—his nimble-blooded brother Dennis was the cowboy and welcome to it. It puzzled the family. Dennis was the smart one. Shy had struggled all the way through school and here he was, wanting more of it.

"You dipshit," his father said, "you couldn't pound nails in mud. Go get you some business education but I expect you will be back on the ranch one a these days."

They didn't know him, had never known him. From earliest childhood he had recognized his distance from them, embarrassed by his disinterest in land and stock.

He was not swift with the books but had stumbled along, no quitter. Then, halfway through his final year and engaged to Roany Slinger, the fatal snow brought everything down, knocked him off his feet and threw him back into ranch life.

The morning after the funeral he was throwing bales of hay off the back of the truck. There was no one else to do it. He looked up at the furious sky marked with a row of wave clouds in measured, curling peaks, shear layers near the jet stream, evidence of great turbulence aloft. The ranch was on the lee side of the range and all day the violent wind raged. If it had been that way on Saturday his people might have kept on playing cribbage, they might have lived. It was the sweet days that took you down, the bright square of sunlight that burned you alive.

After a few weeks on the ranch sidling through the interstices between grief and work, he went to the university to ask for a tuition refund, the dry socket of his heart choked. A woman with a wart between her eyes told him there was no hope of getting the money back.

"They got killed," he said, "my folks. I'm out there on my own, I'm busted and I can't get back to school."

"You'd be surprised," she said, "how many boys work

a ranch, take their classes and make good grades. You'd be surprised how many go right on to Harvard and Yale." Raised on sour milk and showing every spoonful.

"You bet I would be surprised." He closed the door with some force.

He put off starting the long drive to the ranch, dreading the house, silent and vague, the wind rustling dry snow through the grass, and drifted with a crowd to a public lecture billed provocatively as *Bad Beef*. The visiting speaker was Wade Walls. The audience interrupted constantly, hooting and razzing. Shy turned and said to the man beside him, a heavy-shouldered rancher who kept a stained hat on and a wad of tobacco in his cheek, "He's got a point." The rancher said nothing, got up and moved as though apostasy, like blackleg, was contagious.

After the lecture he was the only one who went up to the table where the speaker sat, bought a signed copy of the man's book and asked him to come have a drink at the Lariat.

"I don't drink alcohol but I'll take coffee." Walls was wound up. Shy drank two beers, switched to whiskey. Something in Walls's opinionated voice, something in the way the man leaned at him made him throw down his trouble.

"I'm tore up over my folks. Third a February. Dennis had a new machine. Beautiful day. Cold but no wind. Not a cloud. You couldn't get a better day. They told me it looks like about fourteen, fifteen miles from the pass they crossed a open slope, triggered a slab avalanche. That thing run them down into a aspen grove. The snow packed up as hard as cement. My family is gone, I'm out a school, I'm running cattle on the old ranch, I'm strapped for money, there's a hundred and fifty first-calf heifers coming due. I can't get no help. What the fuck am I supposed a do? What?"

"Get out of ranching. Think of your children," Walls said. "They'll know their father was a rancher, one of the men destroying the west. They'll blame you for it."

"I'm not even married yet. I don't have any kids. That I know of."

For his part, Wade Walls announced himself to Shy as a monkey-wrencher, a hard man who would hammer a spike into a tree without hesitation. "You know what Abbey said about cows, don't you—'stinking, fly-covered, shit-smeared, disease-spreading brutes.' But it's not the way they are that matters, it's what they do to the land. They've wrecked the west, they're wrecking the world. Look at Argentina, India. Look at the Amazon." He talked against cows for a long time.

"Listen," he said in his intense monotone, sloshing his coffee. "When kindness fails and persuasion doesn't persuade, you fight fire with fire. It's the only thing these people understand—force. Listen," he said, "we could use you." "We" was some complex acronym. In truth, there was no acronym; he was a solitary avenger, and maybe that was what drew Shy to him.

"Count me," said Shy, "count me in. I'll get rid a the fuckin cows." He was very drunk, getting close to the floor.

A LIVING

The summer after the accident he married Roany Slinger.

It had been a western wedding with a reception at the Hitching Post Motel in Cheyenne, Roany in her hand-made silk dress holding a bouquet of wilting wild roses, Shy ragged out in a wool frock coat that came to the knees. His cousin Huey said, "You look like General Sherman, yes suh." They drank champagne from glasses etched with ropes spelling out the words "Shyland & Roany." The two families sat apart, at different tables, talked among themselves. Huey and Hulse Birch drank themselves wolfish, filled a trash sack with motel forks and knives, tied the sack under the getaway car.

Hulse Birch had been his friend in the early grades. They rode their horses to the back of the Birch place where Pinhead Creek pooled, camped out for three or four days in the summers, living off half-roasted potatoes and trout. When they were eleven they discovered three or four caves up in the brittle limestone outcrops. In one, thick with dust, three saddles and bridles waited inside, the leather curled and hard.

"Train robbers," said Hulse, who aspired to be one himself. "They must a hid these saddles here. They'd steal some horses and come up here for the saddles and get away. I bet they tried a steal our horses and my dad or grandpa shot them dead as dirt."

They looked then for the cave where the robbers might have cached banknotes and bars of gold. Hulse's father got excited when he saw that one of the saddles was an old Cheyenne Meanea; it was stamped WYOMING TERRITORY, and the crooked initials *B.W.* had been punched with an awl on the edge of one fender. King Ropes in Sheridan offered them high money for it, but Hulse begged to keep it. After that it seemed they did nothing but look for caves until Shy got sick of bat-guano'd holes.

The plastic bag tore open on Interstate 80 with a sound that convinced him the engine had fallen out. His mustache was long, the ends waxed to needle-points, and the cake frosting had got into it. He stood at the side of the highway staring at the curving trail of utensils behind them, and Roany pointed at his sugary mustache, laughed herself wet.

"Looks like bird shit," she gasped.

He shaved it off a week after the wedding, about the time he gave up feeding cows and started killing them.

"At least I can make us a livin," he told Roany. He used part of the herd sale money to finish up his business degree, kicked a little into Roany's shop. He graduated, took a two-month course in Colorado in equestrian underwriting. His business cards read:

SHY W. HAMP
BIG HORSE EQUINE INSURANCE
FOR RANCH & FARM
SLOPE, WYOMING

A recorded message on his telephone began with a horse's whinny, and then his tense voice said, "Big Horse is dedicated to insuring your horse against mortality, fertility loss, barn fire, earthquake, lightning. Let us help you work out a equine health plan."

"I'll sell off the cattle," he told Roany. "But I won't

never sell the ranch. We been on the place seventy-five years. We'll damn well live on it even if we don't run cows. I'll lease it, sheep, maybe, but not cattle. Keep a few horses, only thing I ever liked about the ranch was the horses." Yet he had come up through 4-H, pledging Head, Heart, Hands and Health to something, to destruction, it seemed. Once or twice a year Wade Walls arrived and together they did harm where Walls said it would do the most good.

It was easy enough to lease out the land. Old Edmund Shanks, weasel-shrewd, took it up. His philosophy was well-known: why own anything when you can lease and control it for less than you'd pay in taxes.

The horse insurance game was slow going. Roany's shop put the crackers in the soup. He couldn't believe there were that many women anxious to spend good money on potions and pony-skin vests, that many cowboys who needed three-hundred-dollar shirts. She couldn't keep ahead of orders for the custom-made shirts. A famous calf-roper ordered a new one every month. Yet hadn't a penny of insurance on his horses.

All along Shy had expected her shop to fail—then she would keep the Big Horse books, answer the telephone, handle the paperwork. It was working out the other way. She had paid for the new truck, the ranch house renovation, she was talking lap pool. He was not doing much with horse insurance. He took his customers at their word on the health, ancestry, value and prowess of their horses and steadily lost money. In a world of liars and cheats he believed in handshakes although he was himself an advanced dissembler with a vile and criminal habit.

Once he said to Roany, "I can't *get* a holt on it. On

anything." She had no idea what he meant but made a soothing noise in her throat.

PORTUGEE PHILLIPS

When habits set fast in certain people they cannot be broken while breath is still drawn. Shy Hamp had a habit, tied to a journey in the back of Nikole Angermiller's grandfather's old sedan. For the rest of his life every nuance of touch, the feel of the scratchy velour seat, the fleering landscape, came vividly and instantly into his mind. It had been 1973 and he was twelve years old, Nikole Angermiller thirteen. They were in the seventh grade, research partners on a history project, the 1866 ride of Portugee Phillips from Fort Phil Kearny to Fort Laramie following the massacre of foolhardy Fetterman and his eighty misguided men.

"Granddad says it isn't possible—unless Phillips had a iron butt and a magic horse—to ride two hundred and thirty-six miles in two days. Through blizzards." She lived in town with her paternal grandparents. Her father, their only son, had died on the Ca Mau Peninsula in 1963 and her mother lived in Austin, Texas, with a sitar player whose name was unpronounceable.

"The horse died. He rode it to death. A thoroughbred horse." He wanted it to be true, that Portugee Phillips had made the heroic journey.

Nikole Angermiller was dark, olive skin and high-colored cheeks and mouth, beautiful but not popular. The shanky girls with their stick arms and man-sized feet hated her for her looks and the wart-fingered boys were afraid of her. Robert Angermiller, the pharmacist, was her grandfather, jovial, boisterous. Her grandparents took her everywhere, spoiled her with clothes purchased in Fort Collins and Denver, and the grandfather cut her hair himself. Everything about her was taut. She was allowed to wear colorless nail polish and her pointed fingernails flashed as though made of tin. Three copper bracelets on her left wrist insured health.

Nikole's grandfather said, "Sonny, you are growin so fast your head's pushin up through your hair. How's your folks?" Then, "Surprised you didn't pick a different project considering what you got at your place." There was a flash of gold from his mouth.

"What? What have we got?"

"Governors of Wyomin—photographs, all of them until your granddad died. You know, we got along good, your granddad and me. That's a treasure on that wall. But your old man didn't care much about it."

"Well, the teacher just passed out the assignments. Ours was the only Wyoming one except for a couple a others. The other kids got good ones like Scott dying at the South Pole, and shark attacks. We got Portugee Phillips."

He had barely noticed the photographs. He had been eight or nine years old when his grandfather died and the photographs had always been there, a kind of black-and-white wallpaper with sets of hooded eyes and thin lips. His grandfather's teeth still waited in a bureau drawer, his jacket with its tobacco smell hung in the entryway. The old man had pinned him and Dennis with his stories of the last wolf killed on the ranch, the neighbor woman who went blind when her eyes froze and who later burned to death in a grass fire, the buffalo powder horn he found in the creek, and how somebody in the family had gone to

Brazil to ranch, and eating something called squeaks and rattles. They couldn't wait to get away.

"And because it's Wyomin it don't seem so interestin to you?" Nikole's grandfather drew a bottle from an inside pocket, unscrewed the cap.

"Yeah. I guess so." The same grassy shadows, the same long wind, everlasting fence.

"Kid, let me tell you. Goddamn important things happened in this place." The glutch of swallowing.

To crown the project her grandparents drove them on a Sunday to the historical markers at each end of the famous ride—the Thoroughbred Horse monument at Fort Laramie and the Portugee Phillips plaque on its rubble-stone column near Fort Kearney. He snapped photographs with his mother's camera. None of them came out.

"I think it's retarded they would put up a monument for a horse," Nikole said.

"Christ, they got all kinds a monuments," said the grandfather. "Peace pipes, dude ranches, rocks, coal mines, sundials, dead ranchers, vigilante hangins, Masonic lodges, Indians, tie-hacks, firefighters, bath houses and little chirpin chickadees. There's Babe, the Little Sweetheart of the Prairie, oldest horse in the world. Died when she was fifty years old. And, a course, one for that horse's ass, the first woman governor of Wyomin."

"Robert," said the grandmother, for whom the barb was meant. She occasionally attended a women's group that honored Mrs. Nellie Tayloe Ross, a governor's widow elected in 1924 on the chivalric vote—though uneasy in her attendance because Mrs. Ross had been a Democrat.

On the way home from the Phillips monument, sun striking through the rearview window to color the backs of the grandparents' heads as yellow as wild canary breasts, the sedan passed through banded cliffs and the sagebrush on strange fire. To the east lay a cherry red wall of cloud. The sun went down, the fluid dusk dimmed the car interior. The grandfather raised a little bottle now and then and drank from it, exhaling the smell of whiskey, held it out to his wife who shook her head. Shy leaned against the seat back, drowsy from the long day. The radio played "I Shot the Sheriff" and darkness pooled around them.

He was not asleep, yet not awake, and he felt the heat of her fingers before she touched him. She placed her hand, still and hot, in his crotch. It was utterly unprecedented, phenomenal. As though in response to his sudden erection she moved her fingers, an infinitesimal movement but enough to bring him to his first orgasm. Still she did not remove her hand and after a while it happened again. He made no effort to touch her or even shift his position for he believed her hand was innocent. The sticky mess in his shorts, the heat of her fingers through the denim, the droning of the car engine, the smoke from the grandfather's cigarette made the backseat a cave, secret and sly. A tremendous feeling for Portugee Phillips and the thoroughbred horse overcame him. At the ranch he stumbled out of the car without looking at her and into the apron of light on the front porch, his hands beating at the storm of miller moths that struck him like soft bullets.

A long time later it occurred to him to wonder how she had known what she knew, for although when he was twelve he had believed her touch accidental, at thirty-seven he recognized the innocence had been his. She had hurled him into corruption, but who had thrown her into that pit?

FIDDLE AND BOW

At daylight on the Fiddle and Bow ranch old lady Birch sat in a straight-backed wooden chair, her son Skipper, himself grey-headed and aging, gently brushing her thin white hair, so long it nearly touched the linoleum. He stood the brush, handle down, in a black jar and began the first braid.

"Where's Hulse this mornin?" She wanted breakfast over and done with and it was a rule that they all ate together.

"They went out early, Mama."

"It's hard work, isn't it, savin the world." Now they'd have to wait for him. She could see someone moving around outside the corral, but too stout to be Hulse. "It's not how Birches have ever ranched. Your father would be mortified to see you makin those crooked fences, wastin time with government men."

"Showin results. Where we raked the hay into those little piles and left it—places where that hard old alkali ground's been bare since Birches come into the territory—it's softer, mellow. It's makin grass. You want a know how much the land and water's been run down, Mama, take a look at the county agricultural reports for back at the early part of the century—all the kinds a grass that growed here, all kinds a water. Now it's brittle. Hard

and brittle. The soil is crusted up. It's the long run Hulse
and me is thinkin about, seein that good grass bloom on
the stock."

"You can do all those fine things, Skipper, but I'll tell
you what—ranchers will do what they please. That's
your neighbors. And it's not the long run that's on their
minds. The long run is a luxury. You can drive a nail on
that."

"Hulse and me come to feel the long run is the only
thing that matters. Times change. You know better than
anybody what a hard business this is, workin with a
fingernail profit margin. We can't afford a let our range
run down no more. We got a do something. They are
cuttin back our allotment, that federal rangeland reform is
comin, we got irrigation problems. Comes right down a
dollars and cents. I don't want a say anything against Dad,
but the things he done and his father way back when,
drives what Hulse and me do now."

"Is that Bonnie out there?"

"Yes."

The first braid was smooth and hard, the end held with
a red rubber band. He worked swiftly, seeing Bonnie turn
toward the house. "She's comin in now. She'll get somethin goin. Get some fresh coffee goin anyway."

"That's all I want. And that dark bread. I hope we don't
have to sit and wait for Hulse."

"We can go ahead. He won't mind."

"Well, I mind. We'll wait. Hulse deserves that much
courtesy."

But they had not waited. At six-thirty Skipper pulled a
ham slice from the pan, laid a piece of black bread on it
and a fried egg, touched on a little *salsa verde* with a tiny

spoon stamped *Alberta,* sat at the table with his book open before him. He read in his soft voice,

> *"I drown, my Lord. What though the Streames I'm in*
> *Rosewater bee, or Ocean to its brinkes*
> *of Aqua Vitae where the Ship doth Swim?"*

Skipper had been married and a father himself years before but the two young sons, playing in the open trunk of the new car, had closed it on themselves while the parents carried in groceries. Cattle prices had been up that fall and they had paid cash for the sedan, meant for Ziona.

"Where are the boys?" she said. They ran here and there, calling, drove over the ranch shouting their names while the children suffocated. It had been the hottest day and afterwards he hoped they had quickly slipped into unconsciousness, unable to hear the anguished calling voices just a few feet away. Out there on the prairie something—the evasive turn of a harried bird with a motion like a convulsive kick?—had made him stop and open the trunk. In that airless oven they lay limp and blue. It was wrong what they said about grief. It augered inside you forever, boring fresh holes even when you were sieved. Ziona lived now in San Diego, remarried, and with other children, but he was still here seeing the places they had been every day. The pastor had given him—he who had never read a poem since grade school—an unlikely book, the meditations of a seventeenth-century metaphysical Calvinist in the wilderness of Massachusetts. The first lines he read began with the same burning question whose wick had flared when he raised the trunk lid.

Under thy Rod, my God, thy smarting Rod,
  That hath off broke my James, that Primrose, Why?

The minister's three-hundred-year-old grief and his bony kneeling on it, grief like gravel under his kneecaps, gave Skipper's smarting heart if not ease, then company, united his vague thoughts on the conjunction of God and Nature into belief. In the years since, he had read the meditations many times, coming from them with the sense of divine order in a chaotic universe. It could not be otherwise.

Old lady Birch sipped at her black coffee and watched the gate.

"There he is. There's Hulse. Get a cup for your husband, Bonnie, he likes his coffee scalding."

Hulse, his leather jaw clean-shaven, came in with a handful of wild chives for Bonnie, said, "Why in hell didn't you wait for me?" He tipped his hat back on his round, close-shorn head. The thick neck sloped into colossal shoulders and arms so developed in muscle that they could not hang straight. His face seemed compressed into heavy cheeks and a blunt nose, a serious man with a tight smile. His enemies knew him to be a curly-headed, rank son of a bitch with severe ways.

The two cowboys, Rick Fissler, straight out of the box and needing assembly, and Noyce Hair, right half of his face puckered with scars, followed him in, washed at the kitchen sink. Skipper had hired them on when they changed the way they ranched. The new way meant keeping the stock moving so they would not overgraze nor bunch for long weeks at water points and shade, meant drifting small bunches instead of driving the big herd up into the Forest allotment. They needed cowboys, were surprised to find them a scarce commodity.

"Hell," said Skipper. "Maybe we can train one." He went to the local high school's Career Day, set up a card table and a sign:

LEARN TO BE A COWBOY,
ROPE AND RIDE ON THE FIDDLE & BOW.
THIS IS THE REAL THING
DAY WORK OR AUTHENTIC BUNKHOUSE.
3 SQUARES AND A STRING OF HORSES.
SUPPLY YOUR OWN SADDLE.
RANCH BACKGROUND PREFERRED.

It brought him a lot of laughs and Rick Fissler, an emaciated kid from the trailer slums out by the mines.

"You ride?"

"No. I was goin a try out for the navy but I rather be a—do this." He pointed at the sign. "You can't git a chance at a horse you don't grow up on a ranch."

Skipper took the kid's name, told him to show up on Saturday morning but doubted he'd see him. Fissler rode up on a kid's bicycle, knees out like a grasshopper, multicolored streamers at the handle grips. Skipper sent him in to breakfast.

"That poor Rick is half-starved," Bonnie said after supper when the new hand had gone down to the bunkhouse. "He ate just everythin this mornin. Seven or eight pieces a toast, three eggs and bacon, home fries. He drank a quart a milk. And look what he put away tonight—six helpins a potatoes."

"He fell off his goddamn horse about six times, too," said Hulse. "It's goin a be a long time makin him a hand."

Hulse stood as thousands of men in the west, braced against the forces bending him, pressing him into a narrow chute. He was in a hurry. He struggled with the semiarid climate, the violent weather, government rules and dense bankers, alien weeds, the quixotic beef market, water problems, ornery fellow ranchers. There was not much give in him. He could make it work if things would clear out of his way.

"What did you see this mornin, Hulse," asked his mother. "Did you see if the eagles are nestin on the butte again?"

"I didn't look. But I doubt it because the sheep is up there. Hazy from them fires in Oregon. Didn't get to see much because I spent the whole damn time listenin to Shot Matzke. His brother-in-law down Tie Sidin just sold out a some corporation for two and a half million dollars. That's a lot a money but not as much as it's worth. Goddamn pirates're subdividin, stockin 'the common land' with tame elk. Half the people buyin into it are telecommuters. That's your New West. Christ, they're not even suitcase ranchers. They don't need a run no cattle, make more money just settin on their ass than we'll ever see. Drinkin cappuccino while they watch the elk. Shot said his brother-in-law had plastic diaper trouble quite a few times last year. Buggers threw them over the fence where the cows got them. Lost seventeen head. Wouldn't be surprised if it was goons hired by the corporation a force a sale. By god, I could use another cup a coffee. Rick and Noyce, you guys want coffee?" But Noyce wanted grapefruit juice and Rick went for cola with ice. The men sat together at the south end of the table.

"Grinning at you with his butter teeth, that Shot Matzke. You know," said old lady Birch, "I am coming to believe that there is a conspiracy. There is a powerful international group of men who want to control the ranchers and the farmers—to control the food supply of the world. Ultimately they will decide who lives and who dies."

Bonnie passed a pan of hot biscuits, said, "You don't believe that."

"Kids not up yet?" Hulse looked at the three porridge bowls.

"They're scufflin around up there," said Bonnie, pushing a platter of eggs toward him.

Hulse roared at the ceiling, "Rattle your hocks and get on down here. We got a busy day."

Skipper slid two biscuits onto his plate. "*Angells bread of Heavens wheate . . .*" he murmured. "That poor old doe out there, I ought a shoot her. Ears hangin down, got screwworm sure as—hangs around behind the aspen."

"I know it," said Noyce. "I seen her this mornin. She'll just die slow."

"Not enough a rancher has to take care a cows, you got the wild stuff too," said Hulse. "The main thing about ranchin," he went on, "last as long as you can, make things come out so's it's still your ranch when it's time a get buried. That's my take on it." Though he had rarely seen an old rancher die on his place; they always sold out and moved to town, got themselves planted in Santa Monica or Tucson. Better to have a shotgun accident climbing over a fence.

"Amen," said old lady Birch.

There was giggling at the head of the stairs.

"What's so funny up there?" said Bonnie.

"It's Cheryl, what she's got on." Two bare feet and legs descended a few steps. They saw the youngest girl, clad in white underpants and the pink bra Bonnie had left to dry on the shower rod. The garment hung like some outlandish harness. Rick Fissler shot a look at Bonnie and blushed.

"You got one hell of a long ways to go before you fill that out," said Hulse. "Now get on the prod."

"You know," said Skipper. He poured more coffee in Hulse's cup, his own. "It's not like things don't happen around here. Not plastic diapers but gates that somebody opened. Remember last summer, a dozen gates opened in the night? That wasn't no accident. And over by Casper they have cut fence. Oh, they're up here too."

"They are, and it's probably not a bad idea we spent a little time out under the stars these nice nights. Take a bedroll and a rifle and sleep out. Take turns. Wouldn't hurt. You never see the bastards in winter." He looked at the moist breath of the coffee rising above the cup.

Old lady Birch left the table, hunting her magazine, *Today's Christian Ranchwoman*. Bonnie stirred the kids' porridge, looked at a papaya that was shriveling on the windowsill. Why had she bought it? She disliked the womb-shaped fruits with their middles full of seeds.

THE GOVERNORS OF WYOMING

Wade Walls sat on the old sofa, drumming his fingers on his knee, glancing up now and then at the faces of dead politicians on the wall, the mass of them diffusing an oppressive mood. Many of the photographs were inscribed with sentiments—*To Monty Hamp, my old pard,* and *Takes an SOB to know one.* The living room held the bitter odor of dyed leather and dead ash.

Roany put down a plate of crackers and cheese. Renti dipped a cracker in her glass of wine.

"The food here is sickeningly bland."

"You can find Mexican in Slope," said Roany. "That's what you miss."

"That stuff out of a jar. No. I want some *pozole rojo* and a salad with fresh *nopales*. I want a turkey leg with roasted peppers. God."

A little after nine Shy walked in.

Walls had never seen a more ghastly shirt, a western cut of deliberately mismatched plaids overstitched with green and orange diagonal stripes.

Renti was hit once more by her brother-in-law's classic western good looks; long-legged, with a sharp-beaked, handsome face, a mask of reddish stubble. He hardly glanced at her; she was what he did not like in women.

"Where have you been, Shy," said Roany. "Wade's been here since this afternoon. We picked him up in town."

"Tell you what, Roany, I expected you would do that. I had a go to North Dakota. Protestin a damn dog shoot. Should a seen it—thirty guys shootin prairie dogs and about thirty big old deputies keepin us back," he lied. He had been two nights with a very young girl in a cabin in the Wind Rivers, a Shoshone girl from the reservation. To get to the cabin they had walked through yellow alpine lilies at the base of melting drifts. A stairway cascade of glassy meltwater trickled over and between the rocks, through brilliant clusters of split-leaf paintbrush, clouds of mosquitoes and midges rising from shaken plants. He was covered with mosquito bites. The child had said little, slapped at her arms and legs. There was a stick of insect repellent in his jacket, something he carried for Roany. He held it out to the girl. She shook her head. There was no repellent that could keep him off her. He couldn't think about it now. A wash of shame, an intention to do it again.

"How was the trip?" he said to Wade Walls.

"Turbulent. Very bad turbulence over the mountains. They kept us circling DIA for half an hour. Worst part of it." The clay face fixed, sentences coming out as coins returned from a pay phone.

"I sure hope that's right." He went into the kitchen where Roany was foraging in the refrigerator for another bottle of wine. "You got anything to eat?" He wasn't looking at her.

"Tomato soup. *Canned* tomato soup. And the *buffalo* steaks in the freezer. We had a discussion about the buffalo steaks."

"What, with Wade?"

"You bet."

"Shit. What did you say?" He took the bottle from her, twisted in the point of the corkscrew. The composition cork squealed out. He must have opened a thousand bottles for her in sixteen years. Two thousand.

"Said you said buffalo was different. Than beef." She leaned against the counter, braced hands. The position emphasized the width of her broad butt. Her nails were cut straight across in the French style, varnished a milky rose.

"What'd he say?"

"Oh, he was stern. He said, 'Once a rancher always a meat-eater,' or something like that. He's like a teacher, always watching and correcting you. This's the last time I'll put up with it. He can stay at a motel you keep doing this stupid stuff. God, I am tired."

"We'll talk about it. He's a little hard a take, I guess. I'll have some a that soup, couple pieces a toast. Whatever you got. We'll be goin out tonight. You want a drink?" Whiskey might get him through these complexities.

"No, I'm staying with the wine. You do what you want. You fix it yourself. I'm going to bed." Her hands rose, pulled pins from the twist, shook the dark cascade of hair from which emanated the sudden full scent of roses, a scent he detested. She filled her glass. She was afraid of the dark and slept with the light on. Wine, she said, helped her sleep.

One of the lesser pleasures of his nights with the young girl was the deep, rich darkness which encouraged the imagination, submerged the foreboding prescience of discovery and punishment.

Faintly, from the big room down the hall, came the needle sound of Renti's voice talking long-distance on the cordless phone. She made a sound like a barking dog, laughed.

★

"What did they charge you with?" said Wade Walls in the living room. He had gone upstairs and changed the hemp suit for black pants and hooded sweatshirt.

"What?" He hated drinking soup out of a mug.

"Didn't they arrest anybody? Who were you with, Prairie Dog Defense League?"

"No. I was somewhere else. Nothin a do with fuckin prairie dogs. Personal stuff. I was with somebody."

"Look—" said Wade Walls.

"I don't want a talk about it. It's personal stuff. It's personal stuff, just tears and years of old stuff." He had been twelve years old again, excited, but supine, letting something happen. It was complicated. He became the child and the girl the adult. That was much of it, revulsion and excitement rubbing against each other. This business with Wade Walls, which he had never thought out nor weighed beyond believing it a kind of good, served him as the balance column in the ledger of his own evil doings. He had not lost the knack for ranching because he'd never had it. The subversion had been simple enough—opening gates, letting stock amble onto the highway, tossing out molasses-coated sheets of plastic.

Wade Walls took from his backpack a stack of small yellow cards and a marking pen, sat at the small table in the living room and began to print in block letters: RANCHERS OFF FEDERAL TIT. TIME TO END RANCHER TAKEOVER PUBLIC RANGE. NO COWS ON PUBLIC LAND. GOOD RIDDANCE WELFARE COWBOYS. As he finished each card he put it into the backpack.

"Those photographs," he said, writing cards. "Every time I'm here I mean to ask you. I don't think I've ever seen a more—who's that one," pointing at an unfocused face swimming above a sprawled signature. His hand was reflected in the glass.

"Governors. The governors of Wyoming. Roany wanted a take them down, we first got married, but they've always been here. Granddad was in the legislature and he went after them, after ever one he could get, like a blind dog in a butcher shop."

"A kind of political rogues' gallery."

"I guess. Here's Doc Osborne, first Democratic governor. A lynch mob hung Big Nose George Parrott back in the 1870s. Doc got the body, skinned it, tanned the hide, made himself a medical bag and a pair a shoes. Wore the shoes to his inauguration. They don't make Democrats like that anymore."

"For god's sake," said Wade Walls. "And this one?" A prissy face glared from an oval, the face askew in a stellate tear.

"Supposed to been a fight with another legislator over a water bill—way the hell back. One smashed this photograph over the other's head, said he wouldn't hang on the same wall with such a damn fool."

He pointed at the beard-scribbled face of a man, the photograph plowed by bullet holes. "A Kansas Democrat appointed by Grover Cleveland. You might a liked Governor Moonlight—he hated big ranch outfits, gloated over the boys that went under in the winter of 1886. He pushed for deeded ranches—little pocket-watch ranches—on river and stream bottom lands. That pissant hundred and sixty acres easterners always had stuck in their pinheads."

"Look at that idiot." Walls nodded at a photograph of a man upside-down high above a large blanket gripped by sixty men in cowboy hats, heads tipped back, mouths open, watching the man fly up, dark suit wrinkled, polished shoes flashing in the sunlight. "Tossed in a blanket."

"Governor Emerson."

"What was the point? Is that how you get votes in good old Wyoming? Play the fool?"

"I suppose they were voters—I know what it means but I can't explain it."

"It doesn't mean anything. It's just a fool playing up for political advantage. I'm with Roany. You should throw them all out."

"You know, they weren't all fools. They weren't all bad."

Wade Walls snorted. "All right," he said. "Maybe you'd better tell me about the meat in the freezer."

"No, I guess not. What we eat isn't your business, Wade." Here it came.

"As I said to your lovely wife, it is very much my business. We're trying to close down the beef ranchers. You are part of the action. Any idea how the publicity would hurt us if they found out that one of our militant activists was a meat-eater?"

"Aw, come on. Let's figure out this thing we're supposed a do and that's all."

Walls opened his map, hand-drawn, fence lines meticulously marked, and the boundaries of deeded private property, BLM land, state land outlined. It took a minute for Shy to see it.

"Wade," he said. "That is right around here."

"I know. It's a test of principles. You can always say no."

"No. I'm not goin a cut my neighbors' fences, I don't

care if they're raisin wolves or weeds." A doubt, a cloudy scrim lowered over the column of good in his interior ledger.

Wade Walls said nothing, leaned back.

"Anyway, what's the point a cuttin fence that adjoins public land? The damn stock just gets onto the public land. Or off it. Dependin where they are when you start."

"It's not so much the logic of the act as the action of the act, the point made." He spoke patiently. He always had to explain it.

"I guess I'm not smart enough for this fuckin stuff," said Shy. "I don't like this fence cuttin."

"You're smart enough," said Wade Walls, ramming his arms into the sleeves of a black jacket.

IN WAIST-HIGH GRASS

He first saw the girl's brother stumbling through the grass. He had been driving into the reservation on his way to Dubois, a high rough day with blown sand, saw a squat figure moving through the waist-high fescue at the side of the road, an Indian with hair to his shoulders, his lopped gait harsh and crippled, keeping well away from the road. Shy drove past in a rush that set the grass waving and in the side mirror he watched the figure toil on. Hours later, his business finished, he approached the reservation from the west. About ten miles out of Fort Washakie he was amazed to see the man lurching toward him. He was closer to the road and Shy saw the broad face clearly, sweaty, numb. The Indian pitched along, left, right, left, right. Then Shy was past again, but moved by something.

He turned around, drew up beside the man who did not stop walking. He drove slowly, the window down.

"Hey buddy, you want a ride?" The sky showed a scraped nakedness, hard, and with a stain along the southwest horizon from the Utah refineries.

The man said nothing, swiveled on his heel, opened the door and got in. There was a smell of grass and crushed leaf and sour, unwashed clothes.

"How far you goin?"

"Nowhere. Takin a walk. I don't know. Somewhere. Where you goin?"

"Well, I was headin to Slope, thought I'd turn around, give you a ride. Seen you on my way west this mornin."

"I seen you too. I'm not goin nowhere."

The car, pointed in the wrong direction, was idling at the side of the road. The man didn't want to go anywhere. The situation was awkward. Would he just sit and talk?

"Well, I guess then I better turn around and head for home. If you're not goin anywhere."

"Yeah." But made no move to get out.

"Guess this is where we part ways."

"Not yet." The man stared straight ahead. He was muscular and broad, but there was nothing threatening in his posture, his big hands lay open and loose on his knees. "How come you stopped?"

"Hell, I thought you needed a ride. You been walkin a long way."

"You want somethin. What a you want? What do you think you want from me?"

"Shit, I don't want a thing from you. I was goin a give you a ride." The truck idled.

So quickly that he did not see the man's hand move the keys were out of the ignition, locked in the Indian's thick fingers. "No. You want somethin. You never talked about it to no one. But you want it bad enough to come here and turn around for me. Because you want to ask me."

And he had blurted it out. A girl. Thirteen. To fuck. He would pay. He would pay the man, he would pay the girl.

Christ, why hadn't he kept his mouth shut, or been born dead?

RICOCHET

It was a dry night with a green moon, a few clouds like toppling pillars. The roads were long and washboarded, gravel spurting from the tires and making a ceaseless rattle, dust in the cab, in their mouths with its stony taste. The turnoff roads narrowed, rose higher, gullied and strewn with loose rocks the size of Dutch ovens. The headlights shone on chop of boulders, the truck ground forward; the flashlight beam quivered over the map, Wade Walls saying, here, and they got out and cut fence in the soft darkness. Walls pushed the message cards under rocks, forced them between twisted strands of wire. They cut, drove on to the next mark.

The night silence rang hard, Wade Wall's breathing magnified. He was exultant, charged with the rush of destruction, the hidden self emerged, Wade Walasiewicz, avenging son of an assembly line butcher, his father the head boner inserting his knife in the mouth cavity, trimming ropy veins and bruises from the stiff tongue, cleaving the skull to remove brain and pituitary, shearing the horns away and dead at forty-two from some malignant infection.

Shy squeezed the wire cutters, feeling the resistance and then the give with a faint jangle of free wire. They'd been at it for hours. They were working up a steep slope. It would have been a chore, putting this fence in. The sky paled in the east.

"Half hour," panted Walls. He could cut for days, weeks.

There was enough light to see the landforms though lodgepole and tumbled rock were black. The arid cold proved the inexorable shortening of days, the weight of it pulling under the false heat of afternoon.

Shy straightened, put a hand in the small of his back and leaned into the ache. The horizon seemed to be filling with bright water, the level rising as he watched. There was the dull cry of some bird, coyote calls chipped out of distance. His senses sharpened in the fresh stirring of air. To the north a cliff snouted out of the darkness. He could make out the black holes of caves. The click of blades, stiff scrape of sagebrush against his boots made him listen uneasily for something. It seemed he might have ridden through this country a long time ago.

When the shot came he heard it with a kind of satisfaction that his sense of disturbed air had been true. The bullet hit the cliff and ricocheted. Two sounds seemed simultaneous, the flat whine and his own falsetto gasp, like that of a man dropped overboard into Arctic water. There was a huge incandescence in his hip, a numb fire. He was on the ground, his good foot kicking against a steel post, the end of the cut wire rattling.

Someone below them was shouting, "You son of a bitch, you get down on the road with your hands up. Right now. And bring them fuckin wire cutters with you. We been watchin you an hour. Hurry up or I'll make it a little closer." The tinny voice was hysterical with rage.

Wade Walls crouched beside him, said, "You're shot. You're shot."

The voice came again, "Son of a bitch, I have to come up there you'll come down wearin a bobwire necktie."

Another voice said, hold it.

Shy felt the wire cutters still in his hand. Below, flashlight beams bobbed, weakened by the remorseless dawn. His leg might have been made from cardboard. He let the wire cutters fall, touched his hip, the gluey warmth of blood and a sharp, rough thing that was in him, wedged deep into the hip joint. Touching it set off mean ridges of pain. The climbers below were in a gully, hidden from view. Wade Walls moved away from him.

The sun's orange light arrived, transformed a moth on a stem in front of him into glowing parts.

"Wade," he said. "I think it's a splinter of rock. I'm not shot." But Wade was scrambling away toward the opening into the National Forest. He was gone.

"Wade," he said.

The sun flooded up, immediate and strong. His eyes watered. He was slumped against a mass of rabbitbrush, seemed almost to be in the backseat of a sedan, light coming from all sides. He could see through the roof, and there was Governor Emerson up in the air, past his apogee and falling, sidewise and awkward. It was wonderful to him how clear it was: you were tossed up and out of the blanket, you rose, you hung in the air, faces grinned or scowled at you, you fell, you hit the blanket and that was it.

He got ready to smile at the voters.

55 Miles to the Gas Pump

RANCHER CROOM IN HANDMADE BOOTS AND FILTHY hat, that walleyed cattleman, stray hairs like curling fiddle string ends, that warm-handed, quick-foot dancer on splintery boards or down the cellar stairs to a rack of bottles of his own strange beer, yeasty, cloudy, bursting out in garlands of foam, Rancher Croom at night galloping drunk over the dark plain, turning off at a place he knows to arrive at a canyon brink where he dismounts and looks down on tumbled rock, waits, then steps out, parting the air with his last roar, sleeves surging up windmill arms, jeans riding over boot tops, but before he hits he rises again to the top of the cliff like a cork in a bucket of milk.

Mrs. Croom on the roof with a saw cutting a hole into the attic where she has not been for twelve years thanks to old Croom's padlocks and warnings, whets to her desire, and the sweat flies as she exchanges the saw for a chisel and hammer until a ragged slab of peak is free and she can see inside: just as she thought: the corpses of Mr. Croom's paramours—she recognizes them from their photographs in the paper: MISSING WOMAN—some desiccated as jerky and much the same color, some moldy from lying beneath roof leaks, and all of them used hard, covered with tarry handprints, the marks of boot heels, some bright blue with the remnants of paint used on the shutters years ago, one wrapped in newspaper nipple to knee.

When you live a long way out you make your own fun.

Brokeback Mountain

ENNIS DEL MAR WAKES BEFORE FIVE, WIND ROCKING the trailer, hissing in around the aluminum door and window frames. The shirts hanging on a nail shudder slightly in the draft. He gets up, scratching the grey wedge of belly and pubic hair, shuffles to the gas burner, pours leftover coffee in a chipped enamel pan; the flame swathes it in blue. He turns on the tap and urinates in the sink, pulls on his shirt and jeans, his worn boots, stamping the heels against the floor to get them full on. The wind booms down the curved length of the trailer and under its roaring passage he can hear the scratching of fine gravel and sand. It could be bad on the highway with the horse trailer. He has to be packed and away from the place that morning. Again the ranch is on the market and they've shipped out the last of the horses, paid everybody off the day before, the owner saying, "Give em to the real estate shark, I'm out a here," dropping the keys in Ennis's hand. He might have to stay with his married daughter until he picks up another job, yet he is suffused with a sense of pleasure because Jack Twist was in his dream.

The stale coffee is boiling up but he catches it before it goes over the side, pours it into a stained cup and blows on the black liquid, lets a panel of the dream slide forward. If he does not force his attention on it, it might stoke the day, rewarm that old, cold time on the mountain when they owned the world and nothing seemed *wrong. The wind strikes the trailer like a load of dirt coming off a dump truck, eases, dies, leaves a temporary silence.*

They were raised on small, poor ranches in opposite corners of the state, Jack Twist in Lightning Flat up on the Montana border, Ennis del Mar from around Sage, near the Utah line, both high school dropout country boys with no prospects, brought up to hard work and privation, both rough-mannered, rough-spoken, inured to the stoic life. Ennis, reared by his older brother and sister after their parents drove off the only curve on Dead Horse Road leaving them twenty-four dollars in cash and a two-mortgage ranch, applied at age fourteen for a hardship license that let him make the hour-long trip from the ranch to the high school. The pickup was old, no heater, one windshield wiper and bad tires; when the transmission went there was no money to fix it. He had wanted to be a sophomore, felt the word carried a kind of distinction, but the truck broke down short of it, pitching him directly into ranch work.

In 1963 when he met Jack Twist, Ennis was engaged to Alma Beers. Both Jack and Ennis claimed to be saving money for a small spread; in Ennis's case that meant a tobacco can with two five-dollar bills inside. That spring, hungry for any job, each had signed up with Farm and Ranch Employment—they came together on paper as herder and camp tender for the same sheep operation north of Signal. The summer range lay above the tree line on Forest Service land on Brokeback Mountain. It would be Jack Twist's second summer on the mountain, Ennis's first. Neither of them was twenty.

They shook hands in the choky little trailer office in front of a table littered with scribbled papers, a Bakelite ashtray brimming with stubs. The venetian blinds hung askew and admitted a triangle of white light, the shadow of the foreman's hand moving into it. Joe Aguirre, wavy hair the color of cigarette ash and parted down the middle, gave them his point of view.

"Forest Service got designated campsites on the allotments. Them camps can be a couple a miles from where we pasture the sheep. Bad predator loss, nobody near lookin after em at night. What I want, camp tender in the main camp where the Forest Service says, but the HERDER"—pointing at Jack with a chop of his hand—"pitch a pup tent on the q.t. with the sheep, out a sight, and he's goin a SLEEP there. Eat supper, breakfast in camp, but SLEEP WITH THE SHEEP, hunderd percent, NO FIRE, don't leave NO SIGN. Roll up that tent every mornin case Forest Service snoops around. Got the dogs, your .30-.30, sleep there. Last summer had goddamn near twenty-five percent loss. I don't want that again. YOU," he said to Ennis, taking in the ragged hair, the big nicked hands, the jeans torn, button-gaping shirt, "Fridays twelve noon be down at the bridge with your next week list and mules. Somebody with supplies'll be there in a pickup." He didn't ask if Ennis had a watch but took a cheap round ticker on a braided cord from a box on a high shelf, wound and set it, tossed it to him as if he weren't worth the reach. "TOMORROW MORNIN we'll truck you up the jump-off." Pair of deuces going nowhere.

They found a bar and drank beer through the afternoon, Jack telling Ennis about a lightning storm on the mountain the year before that killed forty-two sheep, the peculiar stink of them and the way they bloated, the need for plenty of whiskey up there. He had shot an eagle, he said, turned his head to show the tail feather in his hatband. At first glance Jack seemed fair enough with his curly hair and quick laugh, but for a small man he carried some weight in the haunch and his smile disclosed buckteeth, not pronounced enough to let him eat popcorn out of the neck of a jug, but noticeable. He was infatuated with the rodeo life and fastened his belt with a minor bullriding buckle, but his boots were worn to the quick, holed beyond repair and he was crazy to be somewhere, anywhere else than Lightning Flat.

Ennis, high-arched nose and narrow face, was scruffy and a little cave-chested, balanced a small torso on long, caliper legs, possessed a muscular and supple body made for the horse and for fighting. His reflexes were uncommonly quick and he was farsighted enough to dislike reading anything except Hamley's saddle catalog.

The sheep trucks and horse trailers unloaded at the trailhead and a bandy-legged Basque showed Ennis how to pack the mules, two packs and a riding load on each animal ring-lashed with double diamonds and secured with half hitches, telling him, "Don't never order soup. Them boxes a soup are real bad to pack." Three puppies belonging to one of the blue heelers went in a pack basket, the runt inside Jack's coat, for he loved a little dog. Ennis picked out a big chestnut called Cigar Butt to ride, Jack a bay mare who turned out to have a low startle point. The string of spare horses included a mouse-colored grullo whose looks Ennis liked. Ennis and Jack, the dogs, horses and mules, a thousand ewes and their lambs flowed up the trail like dirty water through the timber and out above the tree line into the great flowery meadows and the coursing, endless wind.

They got the big tent up on the Forest Service's platform, the kitchen and grub boxes secured. Both slept in camp that first night, Jack already bitching about Joe Aguirre's sleep-with-the-sheep-and-no-fire order, though he saddled the bay mare in the dark morning without saying much. Dawn came glassy orange, stained from below by a gelatinous band of pale green. The sooty bulk of the mountain paled slowly until it was the same color as the smoke from Ennis's breakfast fire. The cold air sweetened, banded pebbles and crumbs of soil cast sudden pencil-long shadows and the rearing lodgepole pines below them massed in slabs of somber malachite.

During the day Ennis looked across a great gulf and sometimes saw Jack, a small dot moving across a high meadow as an insect moves across a tablecloth; Jack, in his dark camp, saw Ennis as night fire, a red spark on the huge black mass of mountain.

Jack came lagging in late one afternoon, drank his two bottles of beer cooled in a wet sack on the shady side of the tent, ate two bowls of stew, four of Ennis's stone biscuits, a can of peaches, rolled a smoke, watched the sun drop.

"I'm commutin four hours a day," he said morosely. "Come in for breakfast, go back to the sheep, evenin get em bedded down, come in for supper, go back to the sheep, spend half the night jumpin up and checkin for coyotes. By rights I should be spendin the night here. Aguirre got no right a make me do this."

"You want a switch?" said Ennis. "I wouldn't mind herdin. I wouldn't mind sleepin out there."

"That ain't the point. Point is, we both should be in this camp. And that goddamn pup tent smells like cat piss or worse."

"Wouldn't mind bein out there."

"Tell you what, you got a get up a dozen times in the night out there over them coyotes. Happy to switch but give you warnin I can't cook worth a shit. Pretty good with a can opener."

"Can't be no worse than me, then. Sure, I wouldn't mind a do it."

They fended off the night for an hour with the yellow kerosene lamp and around ten Ennis rode Cigar Butt, a good night horse, through the glimmering frost back to the sheep, carrying leftover biscuits, a jar of jam and a jar of coffee with him for the next day saying he'd save a trip, stay out until supper.

"Shot a coyote just first light," he told Jack the next evening, sloshing his face with hot water, lathering up soap and hoping his razor had some cut left in it, while Jack peeled potatoes. "Big son of a bitch. Balls on him size a apples. I bet he'd took a few lambs. Looked like he could a eat a camel. You want some a this hot water? There's plenty."

"It's all yours."

"Well, I'm goin a warsh everthing I can reach," he said, pulling off his boots and jeans (no drawers, no socks, Jack noticed), slopping the green washcloth around until the fire spat.

They had a high-time supper by the fire, a can of beans each, fried potatoes and a quart of whiskey on shares, sat with their backs against a log, boot soles and copper jeans rivets hot, swapping the bottle while the lavender sky emptied of color and the chill air drained down, drinking, smoking cigarettes, getting up every now and then to piss, firelight throwing a sparkle in the arched stream, tossing sticks on the fire to keep the talk going, talking horses and rodeo, roughstock events, wrecks and injuries sustained, the submarine *Thresher* lost two months earlier with all hands and how it must have been in the last doomed minutes, dogs each had owned and known, the draft, Jack's home ranch where his father and mother held on, Ennis's family place folded years ago after his folks died, the older brother in Signal and a married sister in Casper. Jack said his father had been a pretty well-known bullrider years back but kept his secrets to himself, never gave Jack a word of advice, never came once to see Jack ride, though he had put him on the woolies when he was a little kid. Ennis said the kind of riding that interested him lasted longer than eight seconds and had some point to it. Money's a good point, said Jack, and Ennis had to agree. They were respectful of each other's opinions, each glad to have a companion where none had been expected. Ennis, riding against the wind back to the sheep in the treacherous, drunken light, thought he'd never had such a good time, felt he could paw the white out of the moon.

The summer went on and they moved the herd to new pasture, shifted the camp; the distance between the sheep and the new camp was greater and the night ride longer. Ennis rode easy, sleeping with his eyes open, but the hours he was away from the sheep stretched out and out. Jack pulled a squalling burr out of the harmonica, flattened a little from a fall off the skittish bay mare, and Ennis had a good raspy voice; a few nights they mangled their way through some songs. Ennis knew the salty words to "Strawberry Roan." Jack tried a Carl Perkins song, bawling "what I say-ay-ay," but he favored a sad hymn, "Water-Walking Jesus," learned from his mother who believed in the Pentecost, that he sang at dirge slowness, setting off distant coyote yips.

"Too late to go out to them damn sheep," said Ennis, dizzy drunk on all fours one cold hour when the moon had notched past two. The meadow stones glowed white-green and a flinty wind worked over the meadow, scraped the fire low, then ruffled it into yellow silk sashes. "Got you a extra blanket I'll roll up out here and grab forty winks, ride out at first light."

"Freeze your ass off when that fire dies down. Better off sleepin in the tent."

"Doubt I'll feel nothin." But he staggered under canvas, pulled his boots off, snored on the ground cloth for a while, woke Jack with the clacking of his jaw.

"Jesus Christ, quit hammerin and get over here. Bedroll's big enough," said Jack in an irritable sleep-clogged voice. It was big enough, warm enough, and in a little while they deepened their intimacy considerably. Ennis ran full-throttle on all roads whether fence mending or money spending, and he wanted none of it when Jack seized his left hand and brought it to his erect cock. Ennis jerked his hand away as though he'd touched fire, got to his knees, unbuckled his belt, shoved his pants down, hauled Jack onto all fours and, with the help of the clear slick and a little spit, entered him, nothing he'd done before but no instruction manual needed. They went at it in silence except for a few sharp intakes of breath and Jack's choked "gun's goin *off*," then out, down, and asleep.

Ennis woke in red dawn with his pants around his knees, a top-grade headache, and Jack butted against him; without saying anything about it both knew how it would go for the rest of the summer, sheep be damned.

As it did go. They never talked about the sex, let it happen, at first only in the tent at night, then in the full daylight with the hot sun striking down, and at evening in the fire glow, quick, rough, laughing and snorting, no lack of noises, but saying not a goddamn word except once Ennis said, "I'm not no queer," and Jack jumped in with "Me neither. A one-shot thing. Nobody's business but ours." There were only the two of them on the mountain flying in the euphoric, bitter air, looking down on the hawk's back and the crawling lights of vehicles on the plain below, suspended above ordinary affairs and distant from tame ranch dogs barking in the dark hours. They believed themselves invisible, not knowing Joe Aguirre had watched them through his 10x42 binoculars for ten minutes one day, waiting until they'd buttoned up their jeans, waiting until Ennis rode back to the sheep, before bringing up the message that Jack's people had sent word that his uncle Harold was in the hospital with pneumonia and expected not to make it. Though he did, and Aguirre came up again to say so, fixing Jack with his bold stare, not bothering to dismount.

In August Ennis spent the whole night with Jack in the main camp and in a blowy hailstorm the sheep took off west and got among a herd in another allotment. There was a damn miserable time for five days, Ennis and a

291

Chilean herder with no English trying to sort them out, the task almost impossible as the paint brands were worn and faint at this late season. Even when the numbers were right Ennis knew the sheep were mixed. In a disquieting way everything seemed mixed.

The first snow came early, on August thirteenth, piling up a foot, but was followed by a quick melt. The next week Joe Aguirre sent word to bring them down— another, bigger storm was moving in from the Pacific— and they packed in the game and moved off the mountain with the sheep, stones rolling at their heels, purple cloud crowding in from the west and the metal smell of coming snow pressing them on. The mountain boiled with demonic energy, glazed with flickering broken-cloud light, the wind combed the grass and drew from the dam-aged krummholz and slit rock a bestial drone. As they descended the slope Ennis felt he was in a slow-motion, but headlong, irreversible fall.

Joe Aguirre paid them, said little. He had looked at the milling sheep with a sour expression, said, "Some a these never went up there with you." The count was not what he'd hoped for either. Ranch stiffs never did much of a job.

"You goin a do this next summer?" said Jack to Ennis in the street, one leg already up in his green pickup. The wind was gusting hard and cold.

"Maybe not." A dust plume rose and hazed the air with fine grit and he squinted against it. "Like I said, Alma and me's gettin married in December. Try to get somethin on a ranch. You?" He looked away from Jack's jaw, bruised blue from the hard punch Ennis had thrown him on the last day.

"If nothin better comes along. Thought some about going back up to my daddy's place, give him a hand over the winter, then maybe head out for Texas in the spring. If the draft don't get me."

"Well, see you around, I guess." The wind tumbled an empty feed bag down the street until it fetched up under his truck.

"Right," said Jack, and they shook hands, hit each other on the shoulder, then there was forty feet of distance between them and nothing to do but drive away in opposite directions. Within a mile Ennis felt like someone was pulling his guts out hand over hand a yard at a time. He stopped at the side of the road and, in the whirling new snow, tried to puke but nothing came up. He felt about as bad as he ever had and it took a long time for the feeling to wear off.

In December Ennis married Alma Beers and had her pregnant by mid-January. He picked up a few short-lived ranch jobs, then settled in as a wrangler on the old Elwood Hi-Top place north of Lost Cabin in Washakie County. He was still working there in September when Alma Jr., as he called his daughter, was born and their bedroom was full of the smell of old blood and milk and baby shit, and the sounds were of squalling and sucking and Alma's sleepy groans, all reassuring of fecundity and life's continuance to one who worked with livestock.

When the Hi-Top folded they moved to a small apartment in Riverton up over a laundry. Ennis got on the highway crew, tolerating it but working weekends at the Rafter B in exchange for keeping his horses out there. The second girl was born and Alma wanted to stay in town near the clinic because the child had an asthmatic wheeze.

"Ennis, please, no more damn lonesome ranches for us," she said, sitting on his lap, wrapping her thin, freckled arms around him. "Let's get a place here in town?"

"I guess," said Ennis, slipping his hand up her blouse sleeve and stirring the silky armpit hair, then easing her down, fingers moving up her ribs to the jelly breast, over the round belly and knee and up into the wet gap all the way to the north pole or the equator depending which way you thought you were sailing, working at it until she shuddered and bucked against his hand and he rolled her over, did quickly what she hated. They stayed in the little apartment which he favored because it could be left at any time.

The fourth summer since Brokeback Mountain came on and in June Ennis had a general delivery letter from Jack Twist, the first sign of life in all that time.

Friend this letter is a long time over due. Hope you get it. Heard you was in Riverton. Im coming thru on the 24th, thought Id stop and buy you a beer. Drop me a line if you can, say if your there.

The return address was Childress, Texas. Ennis wrote back, *you bet,* gave the Riverton address.

The day was hot and clear in the morning, but by noon the clouds had pushed up out of the west rolling a little sultry air before them. Ennis, wearing his best shirt, white with wide black stripes, didn't know what time Jack would get there and so had taken the day off, paced back and forth, looking down into a street pale with dust. Alma was saying something about taking his friend to the Knife & Fork for supper instead of cooking it was so hot, if they could get a baby-sitter, but Ennis said more likely he'd just go out with Jack and get drunk. Jack was not a restaurant type, he said, thinking of the dirty spoons sticking out of the cans of cold beans balanced on the log.

Late in the afternoon, thunder growling, that same old green pickup rolled in and he saw Jack get out of the truck, beat-up Resistol tilted back. A hot jolt scalded Ennis and he was out on the landing pulling the door closed behind him. Jack took the stairs two and two. They seized each other by the shoulders, hugged mightily, squeezing the breath out of each other, saying, son of a bitch, son of a bitch, then, and easily as the right key turns the lock tumblers, their mouths came together, and hard, Jack's big teeth bringing blood, his hat falling to the floor, stubble rasping, wet saliva welling, and the door opening and Alma looking out for a few seconds at Ennis's straining shoulders and shutting the door again and still they clinched, pressing chest and groin and thigh and leg together, treading on each other's toes until they pulled apart to breathe and Ennis, not big on endearments, said what he said to his horses and daughters, little darlin.

The door opened again a few inches and Alma stood in the narrow light.

What could he say? "Alma, this is Jack Twist, Jack, my wife Alma." His chest was heaving. He could smell Jack—the intensely familiar odor of cigarettes, musky sweat and a faint sweetness like grass, and with it the rushing cold of the mountain. "Alma," he said, "Jack and me ain't seen each other in four years." As if it were a reason. He was glad the light was dim on the landing but did not turn away from her.

"Sure enough," said Alma in a low voice. She had seen what she had seen. Behind her in the room lightning lit the window like a white sheet waving and the baby cried.

"You got a kid?" said Jack. His shaking hand grazed Ennis's hand, electrical current snapped between them.

"Two little girls," Ennis said. "Alma Jr. and Francine. Love them to pieces." Alma's mouth twitched.

"I got a boy," said Jack. "Eight months old. Tell you what, I married a cute little old Texas girl down in Childress—Lureen." From the vibration of the floorboard on which they both stood Ennis could feel how hard Jack was shaking.

"Alma," he said. "Jack and me is goin out and get a drink. Might not get back tonight, we get drinkin and talkin."

"Sure enough," Alma said, taking a dollar bill from her pocket. Ennis guessed she was going to ask him to get her a pack of cigarettes, bring him back sooner.

"Please to meet you," said Jack, trembling like a run-out horse.

"Ennis—" said Alma in her misery voice, but that didn't slow him down on the stairs and he called back, "Alma, you want smokes there's some in the pocket a my blue shirt in the bedroom."

They went off in Jack's truck, bought a bottle of whiskey and within twenty minutes were in the Motel Siesta jouncing a bed. A few handfuls of hail rattled against the window followed by rain and slippery wind banging the unsecured door of the next room then and through the night.

The room stank of semen and smoke and sweat and whiskey, of old carpet and sour hay, saddle leather, shit and cheap soap. Ennis lay spread-eagled, spent and wet, breathing deep, still half tumescent, Jack blowing forceful cigarette clouds like whale spouts, and Jack said, "Christ, it got a be all that time a yours ahorseback makes it so goddamn good. We got to talk about this. Swear to god I didn't know we was goin a get into this again—yeah, I did. Why I'm here. I fuckin knew it. Redlined all the way, couldn't get here fast enough."

"I didn't know where in the *hell* you was," said Ennis. "Four years. I about give up on you. I figured you was sore about that punch."

"Friend," said Jack, "I was in Texas rodeoin. How I met Lureen. Look over on that chair."

On the back of the soiled orange chair he saw the shine of a buckle. "Bullridin?"

"Yeah. I made three fuckin thousand dollars that year. Fuckin starved. Had to borrow everthing but a toothbrush from other guys. Drove grooves across Texas. Half the time under that cunt truck fixin it. Anyway, I didn't never think about losin. Lureen? There's some serious money there. Her old man's got it. Got this farm machinery business. Course he don't let her have none a the money, and he hates my fuckin guts, so it's a hard go now but one a these days—"

"Well, you're goin a go where you look. Army didn't

get you?" The thunder sounded far to the east, moving from them in its red wreaths of light.

"They can't get no use out a me. Got some crushed vertebrates. And a stress fracture, the arm bone here, you know how bullridin you're always leverin it off your thigh?—she gives a little ever time you do it. Even if you tape it good you break it a little goddamn bit at a time. Tell you what, hurts like a bitch afterwards. Had a busted leg. Busted in three places. Come off the bull and it was a big bull with a lot a drop, he got rid a me in about three flat and he come after me and he was sure faster. Lucky enough. Friend a mine got his oil checked with a horn dipstick and that was all she wrote. Bunch a other things, fuckin busted ribs, sprains and pains, torn ligaments. See, it ain't like it was in my daddy's time. It's guys with money go to college, trained athaletes. You got a have some money to rodeo now. Lureen's old man wouldn't give me a dime if I dropped it, except one way. And I know enough about the game now so I see that I ain't never goin a be on the bubble. Other reasons. I'm gettin out while I still can walk."

Ennis pulled Jack's hand to his mouth, took a hit from the cigarette, exhaled. "Sure as hell seem in one piece to me. You know, I was sittin up here all that time tryin to figure out if I was—? I know I ain't. I mean here we both got wives and kids, right? I like doin it with women, yeah, but Jesus H., ain't nothin like this. I never had no thoughts a doin it with another guy except I sure wrang it out a hunderd times thinkin about you. You do it with other guys? Jack?"

"Shit no," said Jack, who had been riding more than bulls, not rolling his own. "You know that. Old

Brokeback got us good and it sure ain't over. We got a work out what the fuck we're goin a do now."

"That summer," said Ennis. "When we split up after we got paid out I had gut cramps so bad I pulled over and tried to puke, thought I ate somethin bad at that place in Dubois. Took me about a year a figure out it was that I shouldn't a let you out a my sights. Too late then by a long, long while."

"Friend," said Jack. "We got us a fuckin situation here. Got a figure out what to do."

"I doubt there's nothin now we can do," said Ennis. "What I'm sayin, Jack, I built a life up in them years. Love my little girls. Alma? It ain't her fault. You got your baby and wife, that place in Texas. You and me can't hardly be decent together if what happened back there"—he jerked his head in the direction of the apartment—"grabs on us like that. We do that in the wrong place we'll be dead. There's no reins on this one. It scares the piss out a me."

"Got to tell you, friend, maybe somebody seen us that summer. I was back there the next June, thinkin about goin back—I didn't, lit out for Texas instead—and Joe Aguirre's in the office and he says to me, he says, 'You boys found a way to make the time pass up there, didn't you,' and I give him a look but when I went out I seen he had a big-ass pair a binoculars hangin off his rearview." He neglected to add that the foreman had leaned back in his squeaky wooden tilt chair, said, Twist, you guys wasn't gettin paid to leave the dogs baby-sit the sheep while you stemmed the rose, and declined to rehire him. He went on, "Yeah, that little punch a yours surprised me. I never figured you to throw a dirty punch."

"I come up under my brother K.E., three years older'n

me, slugged me silly ever day. Dad got tired a me come bawlin in the house and when I was about six he set me down and says, Ennis, you got a problem and you got a fix it or it's gonna be with you until you're ninety and K.E.'s ninety-three. Well, I says, he's bigger'n me. Dad says, you got a take him unawares, don't say nothin to him, make him feel some pain, get out fast and keep doin it until he takes the message. Nothin like hurtin somebody to make him hear good. So I did. I got him in the outhouse, jumped him on the stairs, come over to his pillow in the night while he was sleepin and pasted him damn good. Took about two days. Never had trouble with K.E. since. The lesson was, don't say nothin and get it over with quick." A telephone rang in the next room, rang on and on, stopped abruptly in mid-peal.

"You won't catch me again," said Jack. "Listen. I'm thinkin, tell you what, if you and me had a little ranch together, little cow and calf operation, your horses, it'd be some sweet life. Like I said, I'm gettin out a rodeo. I ain't no broke-dick rider but I don't got the bucks a ride out this slump I'm in and I don't got the bones a keep gettin wrecked. I got it figured, got this plan, Ennis, how we can do it, you and me. Lureen's old man, you bet he'd give me a bunch if I'd get lost. Already more or less said it—"

"Whoa, whoa, whoa. It ain't goin a be that way. We can't. I'm stuck with what I got, caught in my own loop. Can't get out of it. Jack, I don't want a be like them guys you see around sometimes. And I don't want a be dead. There was these two old guys ranched together down home, Earl and Rich—Dad would pass a remark when he seen them. They was a joke even though they was pretty tough old birds. I was what, nine years old and they found

Earl dead in a irrigation ditch. They'd took a tire iron to him, spurred him up, drug him around by his dick until it pulled off, just bloody pulp. What the tire iron done looked like pieces a burned tomatoes all over him, nose tore down from skiddin on gravel."

"You seen that?"

"Dad made sure I seen it. Took me to see it. Me and K.E. Dad laughed about it. Hell, for all I know he done the job. If he was alive and was to put his head in that door right now you bet he'd go get his tire iron. Two guys livin together? No. All I can see is we get together once in a while way the hell out in the back a nowhere—"

"How much is once in a while?" said Jack. "Once in a while ever four fuckin years?"

"No," said Ennis, forbearing to ask whose fault that was. "I goddamn hate it that you're goin a drive away in the mornin and I'm goin back to work. But if you can't fix it you got a stand it," he said. "Shit. I been lookin at people on the street. This happen a other people? What the hell do they do?"

"It don't happen in Wyomin and if it does I don't know what they do, maybe go to Denver," said Jack, sitting up, turning away from him, "and I don't give a flyin fuck. Son of a bitch, Ennis, take a couple days off. Right now. Get us out a here. Throw your stuff in the back a my truck and let's get up in the mountains. Couple a days. Call Alma up and tell her you're goin. Come on, Ennis, you just shot my airplane out a the sky—give me somethin a go on. This ain't no little thing that's happenin here."

The hollow ringing began again in the next room, and

as if he were answering it, Ennis picked up the phone on the bedside table, dialed his own number.

A slow corrosion worked between Ennis and Alma, no real trouble, just widening water. She was working at a grocery store clerk job, saw she'd always have to work to keep ahead of the bills on what Ennis made. Alma asked Ennis to use rubbers because she dreaded another pregnancy. He said no to that, said he would be happy to leave her alone if she didn't want any more of his kids. Under her breath she said, "I'd have em if you'd support em." And under that, thought, anyway, what you like to do don't make too many babies.

Her resentment opened out a little every year: the embrace she had glimpsed, Ennis's fishing trips once or twice a year with Jack Twist and never a vacation with her and the girls, his disinclination to step out and have any fun, his yearning for low-paid, long-houred ranch work, his propensity to roll to the wall and sleep as soon as he hit the bed, his failure to look for a decent permanent job with the county or the power company, put her in a long, slow dive and when Alma Jr. was nine and Francine seven she said, what am I doin hangin around with him, divorced Ennis and married the Riverton grocer.

Ennis went back to ranch work, hired on here and there, not getting much ahead but glad enough to be around stock again, free to drop things, quit if he had to, and go into the mountains at short notice. He had no serious hard feelings, just a vague sense of getting short-changed, and showed it was all right by taking Thanksgiving dinner with Alma and her grocer and the kids, sitting between his girls and talking horses to them, telling jokes, trying not to be a sad daddy. After the pie Alma got him off in the kitchen, scraped the plates and said she worried about him and he ought to get married again. He saw she was pregnant, about four, five months, he guessed.

"Once burned," he said, leaning against the counter, feeling too big for the room.

"You still go fishin with that Jack Twist?"

"Some." He thought she'd take the pattern off the plate with the scraping.

"You know," she said, and from her tone he knew something was coming, "I used to wonder how come you never brought any trouts home. Always said you caught plenty. So one time I got your creel case open the night before you went on one a your little trips—price tag still on it after five years—and I tied a note on the end of the line. It said, hello Ennis, bring some fish home, love, Alma. And then you come back and said you'd caught a bunch a browns and ate them up. Remember? I looked in the case when I got a chance and there was my note still tied there and that line hadn't touched water in its life." As though the word "water" had called out its domestic cousin she twisted the faucet, sluiced the plates.

"That don't mean nothin."

"Don't lie, don't try to fool me, Ennis. I know what it means. Jack Twist? Jack Nasty. You and him—"

She'd overstepped his line. He seized her wrist; tears sprang and rolled, a dish clattered.

"Shut up," he said. "Mind your own business. You don't know nothin about it."

"I'm goin a yell for Bill."

"You fuckin go right ahead. Go on and fuckin yell. I'll make him eat the fuckin floor and you too." He gave another wrench that left her with a burning bracelet, shoved his hat on backwards and slammed out. He went to the Black and Blue Eagle bar that night, got drunk, had a short dirty fight and left. He didn't try to see his girls for a long time, figuring they would look him up when they got the sense and years to move out from Alma.

They were no longer young men with all of it before them. Jack had filled out through the shoulders and hams, Ennis stayed as lean as a clothes-pole, stepped around in worn boots, jeans and shirts summer and winter, added a canvas coat in cold weather. A benign growth appeared on his eyelid and gave it a drooping appearance, a broken nose healed crooked.

Years on years they worked their way through the high meadows and mountain drainages, horse-packing into the Big Horns, Medicine Bows, south end of the Gallatins, Absarokas, Granites, Owl Creeks, the Bridger-Teton Range, the Freezeouts and the Shirleys, Ferrises and the Rattlesnakes, Salt River Range, into the Wind Rivers over and again, the Sierra Madres, Gros Ventres, the Washakies, Laramies, but never returning to Brokeback.

Down in Texas Jack's father-in-law died and Lureen, who inherited the farm equipment business, showed a skill for management and hard deals. Jack found himself with a vague managerial title, traveling to stock and agricultural machinery shows. He had some money now and found ways to spend it on his buying trips. A little Texas accent flavored his sentences, "cow" twisted into "kyow" and "wife" coming out as "waf." He'd had his front teeth filed down and capped, said he'd felt no pain, and to finish the job grew a heavy mustache.

In May of 1983 they spent a few cold days at a series of little icebound, no-name high lakes, then worked across into the Hail Strew River drainage.

Going up, the day was fine but the trail deep-drifted and slopping wet at the margins. They left it to wind through a slashy cut, leading the horses through brittle branchwood, Jack, the same eagle feather in his old hat, lifting his head in the heated noon to take the air scented with resinous lodgepole, the dry needle duff and hot rock, bitter juniper crushed beneath the horses' hooves. Ennis, weather-eyed, looked west for the heated cumulus that might come up on such a day but the boneless blue was so deep, said Jack, that he might drown looking up.

Around three they swung through a narrow pass to a southeast slope where the strong spring sun had had a chance to work, dropped down to the trail again which lay snowless below them. They could hear the river muttering and making a distant train sound a long way off. Twenty minutes on they surprised a black bear on the bank above them rolling a log over for grubs and Jack's horse shied and reared, Jack saying "Wo! Wo!" and Ennis's bay dancing and snorting but holding. Jack reached for the .30-.06 but there was no need; the startled bear galloped into the trees with the lumpish gait that made it seem it was falling apart.

The tea-colored river ran fast with snowmelt, a scarf of bubbles at every high rock, pools and setbacks streaming.

The ochre-branched willows swayed stiffly, pollened catkins like yellow thumbprints. The horses drank and Jack dismounted, scooped icy water up in his hand, crystalline drops falling from his fingers, his mouth and chin glistening with wet.

"Get beaver fever doin that," said Ennis, then, "Good enough place," looking at the level bench above the river, two or three fire-rings from old hunting camps. A sloping meadow rose behind the bench, protected by a stand of lodgepole. There was plenty of dry wood. They set up camp without saying much, picketed the horses in the meadow. Jack broke the seal on a bottle of whiskey, took a long, hot swallow, exhaled forcefully, said, "That's one a the two things I need right now," capped and tossed it to Ennis.

On the third morning there were the clouds Ennis had expected, a grey racer out of the west, a bar of darkness driving wind before it and small flakes. It faded after an hour into tender spring snow that heaped wet and heavy. By nightfall it turned colder. Jack and Ennis passed a joint back and forth, the fire burning late, Jack restless and bitching about the cold, poking the flames with a stick, twisting the dial of the transistor radio until the batteries died.

Ennis said he'd been putting the blocks to a woman who worked part-time at the Wolf Ears bar in Signal where he was working now for Stoutamire's cow and calf outfit, but it wasn't going anywhere and she had some problems he didn't want. Jack said he'd had a thing going with the wife of a rancher down the road in Childress and for the last few months he'd slank around expecting to get shot by Lureen or the husband, one. Ennis laughed a little and said he probably deserved it. Jack said he was doing all right but he missed Ennis bad enough sometimes to make him whip babies.

The horses nickered in the darkness beyond the fire's circle of light. Ennis put his arm around Jack, pulled him close, said he saw his girls about once a month, Alma Jr. a shy seventeen-year-old with his beanpole length, Francine a little live wire. Jack slid his cold hand between Ennis's legs, said he was worried about his boy who was, no doubt about it, dyslexic or something, couldn't get anything right, fifteen years old and couldn't hardly read, *he* could see it though goddamn Lureen wouldn't admit to it and pretended the kid was o.k., refused to get any bitchin kind a help about it. He didn't know what the fuck the answer was. Lureen had the money and called the shots.

"I used a want a boy for a kid," said Ennis, undoing buttons, "but just got little girls."

"I didn't want none a either kind," said Jack. "But fuck-all has worked the way I wanted. Nothin never come to my hand the right way." Without getting up he threw deadwood on the fire, the sparks flying up with their truths and lies, a few hot points of fire landing on their hands and faces, not for the first time, and they rolled down into the dirt. One thing never changed: the brilliant charge of their infrequent couplings was darkened by the sense of time flying, never enough time, never enough.

A day or two later in the trailhead parking lot, horses loaded into the trailer, Ennis was ready to head back to Signal, Jack up to Lightning Flat to see the old man. Ennis leaned into Jack's window, said what he'd been putting off the whole week, that likely he couldn't get away again until November after they'd shipped stock and before winter feeding started.

"November. What in hell happened a August? Tell you what, we said August, nine, ten days. Christ, Ennis! Whyn't you tell me this before? You had a fuckin week to say some little word about it. And why's it we're always in the friggin cold weather? We ought a do somethin. We ought a go south. We ought a go to Mexico one day."

"Mexico? Jack, you know me. All the travelin I ever done is goin around the coffeepot lookin for the handle. And I'll be runnin the baler all August, that's what's the matter with August. Lighten up, Jack. We can hunt in November, kill a nice elk. Try if I can get Don Wroe's cabin again. We had a good time that year."

"You know, friend, this is a goddamn bitch of a unsatisfactory situation. You used a come away easy. It's like seein the pope now."

"Jack, I got a work. Them earlier days I used a quit the jobs. You got a wife with money, a good job. You forget how it is bein broke all the time. You ever hear a child support? I been payin out for years and got more to go. Let me tell you, I can't quit this one. And I can't get the time off. It was tough gettin this time—some a them late heifers is still calvin. You don't leave then. You don't. Stoutamire is a hell-raiser and he raised hell about me takin the week. I don't blame him. He probly ain't got a night's sleep since I left. The trade-off was August. You got a better idea?"

"I did once." The tone was bitter and accusatory.

Ennis said nothing, straightened up slowly, rubbed at his forehead; a horse stamped inside the trailer. He walked to his truck, put his hand on the trailer, said something that only the horses could hear, turned and walked back at a deliberate pace.

"You been a Mexico, Jack?" Mexico was the place. He'd heard. He was cutting fence now, trespassing in the shoot-em zone.

"Hell yes, I been. Where's the fuckin problem?" Braced for it all these years and here it came, late and unexpected.

"I got a say this to you one time, Jack, and I ain't foolin. What I don't know," said Ennis, "all them things I don't know could get you killed if I should come to know them."

"Try this one," said Jack, "and *I'll* say it just one time. Tell you what, we could a had a good life together, a fuckin real good life. You wouldn't do it, Ennis, so what we got now is Brokeback Mountain. Everthing built on that. It's all we got, boy, fuckin all, so I hope you know that if you don't never know the rest. Count the damn few times we been together in twenty years. Measure the fuckin short leash you keep me on, then ask me about Mexico and then tell me you'll kill me for needin it and not hardly never gettin it. You got no fuckin idea how bad it gets. I'm not you. I can't make it on a couple a high-altitude fucks once or twice a year. You're too much for me, Ennis, you son of a whoreson bitch. I wish I knew how to quit you."

Like vast clouds of steam from thermal springs in winter the years of things unsaid and now unsayable—admissions, declarations, shames, guilts, fears—rose around them. Ennis stood as if heart-shot, face grey and deep-lined, grimacing, eyes screwed shut, fists clenched, legs caving, hit the ground on his knees.

"Jesus," said Jack. "Ennis?" But before he was out of the truck, trying to guess if it was heart attack or the over-flow of an incendiary rage, Ennis was back on his feet and somehow, as a coat hanger is straightened to open a locked car and then bent again to its original shape, they torqued things almost to where they had been, for what they'd said was no news. Nothing ended, nothing begun, nothing resolved.

What Jack remembered and craved in a way he could neither help nor understand was the time that distant summer on Brokeback when Ennis had come up behind him and pulled him close, the silent embrace satisfying some shared and sexless hunger.

They had stood that way for a long time in front of the fire, its burning tossing ruddy chunks of light, the shadow of their bodies a single column against the rock. The minutes ticked by from the round watch in Ennis's pocket, from the sticks in the fire settling into coals. Stars bit through the wavy heat layers above the fire. Ennis's breath came slow and quiet, he hummed, rocked a little in the sparklight and Jack leaned against the steady heartbeat, the vibrations of the humming like faint electricity and, standing, he fell into sleep that was not sleep but something else drowsy and tranced until Ennis, dredging up a rusty but still useable phrase from the childhood time before his mother died, said, "Time to hit the hay, cowboy. I got a go. Come on, you're sleepin on your feet like a horse," and gave Jack a shake, a push, and went off in the darkness. Jack heard his spurs tremble as he mounted, the words "see you tomorrow," and the horse's shuddering snort, grind of hoof on stone.

Later, that dozy embrace solidified in his memory as the single moment of artless, charmed happiness in their separate and difficult lives. Nothing marred it, even the knowledge that Ennis would not then embrace him face to face because he did not want to see nor feel that it was Jack he held. And maybe, he thought, they'd never got much farther than that. Let be, let be.

Ennis didn't know about the accident for months until his postcard to Jack saying that November still looked like the first chance came back stamped DECEASED. He called Jack's number in Childress, something he had done only once before when Alma divorced him and Jack had misunderstood the reason for the call, had driven twelve hundred miles north for nothing. This would be all right, Jack would answer, had to answer. But he did not. It was Lureen and she said who? who is this? and when he told her again she said in a level voice yes, Jack was pumping up a flat on the truck out on a back road when the tire blew up. The bead was damaged somehow and the force of the explosion slammed the rim into his face, broke his nose and jaw and knocked him unconscious on his back. By the time someone came along he had drowned in his own blood.

No, he thought, they got him with the tire iron.

"Jack used to mention you," she said. "You're the fishing buddy or the hunting buddy, I know that. Would have let you know," she said, "but I wasn't sure about your name and address. Jack kept most a his friends' addresses in his head. It was a terrible thing. He was only thirty-nine years old."

The huge sadness of the northern plains rolled down on him. He didn't know which way it was, the tire iron or a real accident, blood choking down Jack's throat and nobody to turn him over. Under the wind drone he heard steel slamming off bone, the hollow chatter of a settling tire rim.

"He buried down there?" He wanted to curse her for letting Jack die on the dirt road.

The little Texas voice came slip-sliding down the wire. "We put a stone up. He use to say he wanted to be cremated, ashes scattered on Brokeback Mountain. I didn't know where that was. So he was cremated, like he wanted, and like I say, half his ashes was interred here, and the rest I sent up to his folks. I thought Brokeback Mountain was around where he grew up. But knowing Jack, it might be some pretend place where the bluebirds sing and there's a whiskey spring."

"We herded sheep on Brokeback one summer," said Ennis. He could hardly speak.

"Well, he said it was his place. I thought he meant to get drunk. Drink whiskey up there. He drank a lot."

"His folks still up in Lightnin Flat?"

"Oh yeah. They'll be there until they die. I never met them. They didn't come down for the funeral. You get in touch with them. I suppose they'd appreciate it if his wishes was carried out."

No doubt about it, she was polite but the little voice was cold as snow.

★

The road to Lightning Flat went through desolate country past a dozen abandoned ranches distributed over the plain at eight- and ten-mile intervals, houses sitting blank-eyed in the weeds, corral fences down. The mailbox read John C. Twist. The ranch was a meagre little place, leafy spurge taking over. The stock was too far distant for him to see their condition, only that they were black baldies. A porch stretched across the front of the tiny brown stucco house, four rooms, two down, two up.

Ennis sat at the kitchen table with Jack's father. Jack's mother, stout and careful in her movements as though recovering from an operation, said, "Want some coffee, don't you? Piece a cherry cake?"

"Thank you, ma'am, I'll take a cup a coffee but I can't eat no cake just now."

The old man sat silent, his hands folded on the plastic tablecloth, staring at Ennis with an angry, knowing expression. Ennis recognized in him a not uncommon type with the hard need to be the stud duck in the pond. He couldn't see much of Jack in either one of them, took a breath.

"I feel awful bad about Jack. Can't begin to say how bad I feel. I knew him a long time. I come by to tell you that if you want me to take his ashes up there on Brokeback like his wife says he wanted I'd be proud to."

There was a silence. Ennis cleared his throat but said nothing more.

The old man said, "Tell you what, I know where Brokeback Mountain is. He thought he was too goddamn special to be buried in the family plot."

Jack's mother ignored this, said, "He used a come home every year, even after he was married and down in

313

Texas, and help his daddy on the ranch for a week, fix the gates and mow and all. I kept his room like it was when he was a boy and I think he appreciated that. You are welcome to go up in his room if you want."

The old man spoke angrily. "I can't get no help out here. Jack used a say, 'Ennis del Mar,' he used a say, 'I'm goin a bring him up here one a these days and we'll lick this damn ranch into shape.' He had some half-baked idea the two a you was goin a move up here, build a log cabin and help me run this ranch and bring it up. Then, this spring he's got another one's goin a come up here with him and build a place and help run the ranch, some ranch neighbor a his from down in Texas. He's goin a split up with his wife and come back here. So he says. But like most a Jack's ideas it never come to pass."

So now he knew it had been the tire iron. He stood up, said, you bet he'd like to see Jack's room, recalled one of Jack's stories about this old man. Jack was dick-clipped and the old man was not; it bothered the son who had discovered the anatomical disconformity during a hard scene. He had been about three or four, he said, always late getting to the toilet, struggling with buttons, the seat, the height of the thing and often as not left the surroundings sprinkled down. The old man blew up about it and this one time worked into a crazy rage. "Christ, he licked the stuffin out a me, knocked me down on the bathroom floor, whipped me with his belt. I thought he was killin me. Then he says, 'You want a know what it's like with piss all over the place? I'll learn you,' and he pulls it out and lets go all over me, soaked me, then he throws a towel at me and makes me mop up the floor, take my clothes off and warsh them in the bathtub, warsh out the towel, I'm bawlin and blubberin. But while he was hosin me down I seen he had some extra material that I was missin. I seen they'd cut me different like you'd crop a ear or scorch a brand. No way to get it right with him after that."

The bedroom, at the top of a steep stair that had its own climbing rhythm, was tiny and hot, afternoon sun pounding through the west window, hitting the narrow boy's bed against the wall, an ink-stained desk and wooden chair, a b.b. gun in a hand-whittled rack over the bed. The window looked down on the gravel road stretching south and it occurred to him that for his growing-up years that was the only road Jack knew. An ancient magazine photograph of some dark-haired movie star was taped to the wall beside the bed, the skin tone gone magenta. He could hear Jack's mother downstairs running water, filling the kettle and setting it back on the stove, asking the old man a muffled question.

The closet was a shallow cavity with a wooden rod braced across, a faded cretonne curtain on a string closing it off from the rest of the room. In the closet hung two pairs of jeans crease-ironed and folded neatly over wire hangers, on the floor a pair of worn packer boots he thought he remembered. At the north end of the closet a tiny jog in the wall made a slight hiding place and here, stiff with long suspension from a nail, hung a shirt. He lifted it off the nail. Jack's old shirt from Brokeback days. The dried blood on the sleeve was his own blood, a gushing nosebleed on the last afternoon on the mountain when Jack, in their contortionistic grappling and wrestling, had slammed Ennis's nose hard with his knee. He had staunched the blood which was everywhere, all over both of them, with his shirtsleeve, but the staunching hadn't held because Ennis had suddenly swung from the deck and laid the ministering angel out in the wild columbine, wings folded.

The shirt seemed heavy until he saw there was another shirt inside it, the sleeves carefully worked down inside Jack's sleeves. It was his own plaid shirt, lost, he'd thought, long ago in some damn laundry, his dirty shirt, the pocket ripped, buttons missing, stolen by Jack and hidden here inside Jack's own shirt, the pair like two skins, one inside the other, two in one. He pressed his face into the fabric and breathed in slowly through his mouth and nose, hoping for the faintest smoke and mountain sage and salty sweet stink of Jack but there was no real scent, only the memory of it, the imagined power of Brokeback Mountain of which nothing was left but what he held in his hands.

In the end the stud duck refused to let Jack's ashes go. "Tell you what, we got a family plot and he's goin in it." Jack's mother stood at the table coring apples with a sharp, serrated instrument. "You come again," she said.

Bumping down the washboard road Ennis passed the country cemetery fenced with sagging sheep wire, a tiny fenced square on the welling prairie, a few graves bright with plastic flowers, and didn't want to know Jack was going in there, to be buried on the grieving plain.

A few weeks later on the Saturday he threw all Stoutamire's dirty horse blankets into the back of his pickup and took them down to the Quik Stop Car Wash to turn the high-pressure spray on them. When the wet clean blankets were stowed in the truck bed he stepped into Higgins's gift shop and busied himself with the post-card rack.

"Ennis, what are you lookin for rootin through them postcards?" said Linda Higgins, throwing a sopping brown coffee filter into the garbage can.

"Scene a Brokeback Mountain."

"Over in Fremont County?"

"No, north a here."

"I didn't order none a them. Let me get the order list. They got it I can get you a hunderd. I got a order some more cards anyway."

"One's enough," said Ennis.

When it came—thirty cents—he pinned it up in his trailer, brass-headed tack in each corner. Below it he drove a nail and on the nail he hung the wire hanger and the two old shirts suspended from it. He stepped back and looked at the ensemble through a few stinging tears.

"Jack, I swear—" he said, though Jack had never asked him to swear anything and was himself not the swearing kind.

Around that time Jack began to appear in his dreams, Jack as he had first seen him, curly-headed and smiling and bucktoothed, talking about getting up off his pockets and into the control zone, but the can of beans with the spoon handle jutting out and balanced on the log was there as well, in a cartoon shape and lurid colors that gave the dreams a flavor of comic obscenity. The spoon handle was the kind that could be used as a tire iron. And he would wake sometimes in grief, sometimes with the old sense of joy and release; the pillow sometimes wet, sometimes the sheets.

There was some open space between what he knew and what he tried to believe, but nothing could be done about it, and if you can't fix it you've got to stand it.

THE SHIPPING NEWS

E. Annie Proulx

Winner of the Pulitzer Prize, The National Book Award and Irish Times Award

When his no-good wife is killed in a road accident, New York hack Quoyle heads for the remotest corner of Newfoundland where he finds himself in the middle of an unfolding Atlantic drama. An irresistible comedy of human life and possibility.

'As stark and ruggedly beautiful as the storm-battered coast of Newfoundland.'
Sunday Telegraph

£6.99   1 85702 242 4

ACCORDION CRIMES

E. Annie Proulx

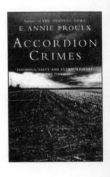

From the author of *The Shipping News*, the intriguing story of a green, two-row button accordion. Its Sicilian maker has a vision of freedom and a future in La Merica. New Orleans brings a violent end to the musician's tale, but the accordion's story is only just beginning.

'This novel confirms Proulx as one of the greatest American writers.' *Independent*

£7.99   1 85702 575 X

All Fourth Estate books are available from your local bookshop, or can be ordered direct from:

Fourth Estate, Book Service By Post, PO Box 29, Douglas, I-O-M, IM99 1BQ   *Credit cards accepted.*

Tel: 01624 836000   Fax: 01624 670923

Or visit the Fourth Estate website at: www.4thestate.co.uk

*Please state when ordering if you do **not** wish to receive further information about Fourth Estate titles.*